'If poetry was the supreme literary form of the First World War then, as if in riposte, in the Second World War, the English novel came of age. This wonderful series is an exemplary reminder of that fact. Great novels were written about the Second World War and we should not forget them.'

WILLIAM BOYD

'It's wonderful to see these four books given a new lease of life because all of them are classic novels from the Second World War written by those who were there, experienced the fear, anguish, pain and excitement first-hand and whose writings really do shine an incredibly vivid light onto what it was like to live and fight through that terrible conflict.'

JAMES HOLLAND, Historian, author and TV presenter

'The Imperial War Museum has performed a valuable public service by reissuing these four absolutely superb novels covering four very different aspects of the Second World War. I defy you to choose which is best: I keep changing my mind!'

ANDREW ROBERTS, author of *Churchill: Walking with Destiny*

'Alexander Baron's *From the City, From the Plough* is undoubtedly one of the very greatest British novels of the Second World War and provides the most honest and authentic account of front line life for an infantryman in North West Europe.'

ANTONY BEEVOR

'A wonderful novel: vivid, rich, profoundly moving and beautifully written by an author who was actually there, it is a novel that takes the reader into the heart of the Normandy campaign. Quite simply, it's one of the finest novels to have been written about the soldier's experience of the Second World War.'

JAMES HOLLAND, Historian, author and TV presenter

FROM THE CITY, FROM THE PLOUGH

Alexander Baron

IMPERIAL WAR MUSEUMS

First published in Great Britain
by Jonathan Cape Ltd 1948

First published in this format in 2019 by
IWM, Lambeth Road, London SE1 6HZ
iwm.org.uk

ISBN 978-1-912423-07-1

A catalogue record for this book is available from the
British Library.

Printed and bound by CPI Group(UK) Ltd, Croydon CR0 4YY

Every effort has been made to contact all copyright holders.
The publishers will be glad to make good in future editions
any error or omissions brought to their attention.

Cover illustration by Bill Bragg
Design and art direction by Clare Skeats

FSC
www.fsc.org
MIX
Paper from
responsible sources
FSC® C020471

About the Author

Alexander Baron (1917–1999)

ALEXANDER BARON was born on 4 December 1917. He grew up in Hackney, East London, and became active in the 1930s in left-wing politics and the anti-fascist movement. During the Second World War he served with the Pioneer Corps in Sicily, Italy and northern France, basing his first novel, *From the City, From the Plough* on his experiences of the D-Day landings and the allied advance into Normandy. The novel was both a critical and popular success, establishing Baron's reputation as a skilled, powerful and authentic writer. It was praised by V.S. Pritchett as 'the only war book that has conveyed any sense of reality to me'. Other reviewers wrote: 'every reader who fought in Europe will acclaim this story as the real thing' and 'we have waited a long time for this war's *All Quiet on the Western Front*. Here it is'.

Baron went on to publish fifteen novels in all, including two more based on his wartime experiences: *There's No Home* (1950), set during the Italian campaign, and *The Human Kind* (1953, later filmed by Carl Foreman as *The Victors*, 1963). Eight of Baron's novels, including the 'War Trilogy', are currently in print. He also wrote numerous film and television screenplays. He died in 1999.

Introduction

War literature is often associated with the First World War, with an explosion of the genre in the late 1920s. Erich Maria Remarque's *All Quiet on the Western Front* was a bestseller and later made into a Hollywood film, while generations of schoolchildren have grown up on a diet of the poetry of Wilfred Owen and the words of Siegfried Sassoon.

Yet the novels of the Second World War – or certainly those written by individuals who had first-hand experience of that war – are often forgotten. Alexander Baron's *From the City, From the Plough* is one of the most impressive from both conflicts and is written from the perspective of the ordinary soldier, rather than the largely officer-penned novels of the earlier war. The book proved popular on publication and has remained admired by commentators and historians ever since. *From the City, From the Plough* depicts a fictional infantry battalion training in England, before going on to fight in the D-Day landings and the ensuing Normandy campaign. The novel's great strength is its unflinching realism; coupled with Baron's skilful economy of language and the unsentimental way such devastating events are portrayed. This lends the work a huge emotional power – less is certainly more in this case.

Alexander Baron joined the Pioneer Corps in 1940, which, according to his unpublished memoir *Chapters of Accidents* was 'because I wore glasses'. To him, this was a disappointment – 'I wanted to be an infantryman' (his first impulse at the start of the war had in fact been to enlist in the RAF, as he had a passion for flying, but he was sent away immediately for the same reason). Baron eventually transferred to the infantry in late 1944, having served in Italy and France. It is this infantry experience on which the novel is based. 'Throughout the book, as the story of the battalion develops, I have tried to keep in the reader's mind the background – the lovely summer of 1944, which made the period of training and waiting seem in some ways so unreal and which in Normandy provided such a contrast to the actual fighting'. The novel's opening chapters focus on this training of an infantry battalion, based on Baron's own experience. The author himself was acutely aware of the importance of this time, writing in his memoir, 'the entire British Army was transforming itself [...] leaders were trained in realistic war conditions [...] By the time we went into training, it seemed as if every division and area Command had its school for the new tough methods'. Such training was vital – training teaches soldiers, in this case citizen soldiers, to kill against the norms of society, and how to react appropriately on the battlefield.

The first half of *From the City, From the Plough*, as the battalion awaits the order to move, beautifully evokes the long periods of boredom inherent in both training and soldiering itself. Baron writes, 'the soldier lives a drama: he never has the time to perceive it. His life, even in battle, is a succession of chores'. He demonstrates the humour and pathos of the soldier, as well as the hierarchy and structure of the battalion – and just how important this is. Baron himself held the non-commissioned officer (NCO) rank of corporal, and in his memoir he comments how 'in a good unit the NCO ought to be able to convince most of his men that they will be safer and more effective if they become a good team'. As well as these official hierarchies, the novel also shows the unofficial hierarchies amongst the men. Very early on, the reader learns that 'Charlie Venable [is] the man who matter[s] in this hut'; while the 'Doggy Boys' of Chapter Six 'lacked nothing. In winter, when the rest of the men had four blankets each, every Doggy Boy had six. While the rest of the battalion supped on bread and cheese and cocoa in a cold, gloomy dining hall, the Doggy Boys resorted every night to the officers' mess kitchen, where they sat at their ease with only a thin partition between them and the colonel and dined, course by course, with the unsuspecting officers'.

Baron's writing lays bare the realities of this group of men, living in such close quarters. Jokes and banter abound – sometimes using language which may not sit entirely comfortably with the modern reader, but which nonetheless gives a veracity to the text. The writing is unflinching in its descriptions of these men – the good and the bad

– and they are by no means shown as angels. Yet perhaps even more important, and touching, are the quiet scenes of almost tenderness which the reader is party to – notable is Charlie Venable's treatment of the young Alfie Bradley, overheard by Lance-Corporal Feather: 'Been awake all the time, Charlie. Charlie, you know what you are? You're a gentleman.' 'Dear, oh dear,' sighed Charlie, 'I do get called some names. Good night, Corp.'

* * *

The D-Day landings of 6 June 1944 play a huge role in the national memory of Britain, Canada and the United States. This was the largest amphibious assault to date, indeed a cross-channel landing was envisaged as early as April 1942, but, due to the complex nature of such operations, the long planning and training was essential. There were five main amphibious landings spanning a distance of almost 55 miles. To the west of Bayeaux were the three beaches of Gold, Juno and Sword where the British and Canadians landed, with the Americans to the east landing at Omaha and Utah. Allied casualties for the D-Day landings were c. 10,000, with 4,500 Allied soldiers confirmed dead. Despite such devastating losses, the landings were successful, and 156,000 allied troops were ashore by the end of the day. Alexander Baron was one of these men. His Pioneer company landed in one of the earliest waves, immediately after the first assault, and Baron witnessed (though didn't participate in) the fiercest fighting first-hand. Later, he wrote, 'in two of my novels there are accounts of the landing in Normandy on D-Day, June 6, 1944. These are based on my memories but I read them today as if they were somebody else's story'.

Contrary to what one might expect, *From the City, From the Plough* depicts the soldiers as surprisingly keen for the action to start. Some are motivated by boredom, while others have more personal reasons. Charlie Venable, having seen the bombing of London and what it has put his beloved mother through, exclaims 'Wouldn'a missed this for a million quid'. After such a long period of training and waiting, the scene just before the men land is short (perhaps surprisingly so) and poignant; 'some of the men were talking, some smoking, some vomiting quietly into brown bags of greaseproof paper'. Then the talking stops as they enter the shallower water, before 'wading with weapons held above their heads towards the wet sand ahead'.

Feature films of D-Day such as *The Longest Day* (1962) and *Saving Private Ryan* (1998) remain popular. Baron himself was critical of war films as he thought they lacked realism. What this novel brings, that perhaps films cannot quite capture, is this realism of the war experience. After all, Baron was there.

A dirty tape wriggled across the beach and the riflemen came stumbling along it, shedding water from their sodden trousers. Mister Paterson flopped beneath a wrecked landing craft that lay broadside on and waited for his platoon to come up. One by one they dropped to the sand behind him. There were German shells falling a little inland, where the first assault troops had already passed, and somewhere among the yellowed, battered houses scattered along the waterfront and the smashed rubble of wrecked pillboxes a machine gun was rapping remotely.

'All right, my lads,' said Paterson breathlessly. He ducked under the bows of the beached craft and ran heavily along the tape. There was a tangle of wire ahead, with German mine warnings poking up everywhere and a few British dead lying with their faces in the sand. They followed the tape along a path torn through the wire and came on to a narrow track running laterally. In front of them now were gentle, dreary dunes rising from pools and runnels of water, with grass growing scantily on their upper flanks. On each side of them sappers were rooting up mines as hastily as potatoes, and a little away to the right a beach dressing station had just been established, with a row of loaded stretchers waiting on one side and a row of corpses laid out on the other, each a still mound under a grey blanket, with big boots protruding at the end. Some pioneers were trying to dig in along the far side of

the road, in the wet sand.

* * *

The author's memoir tells us just how much of *From the City, From the Plough* is taken from Baron's direct experience. Of the men of his own unit, he says 'each was bound in a web of friendships which he did not want to betray [...] Besides, training had conditioned them to war as a natural activity and imbued them with the idea that they knew how to get through it'. Nowhere is this clearer than in in some of the final, deeply moving scenes of the novel, in which Colonel Pothecary leads his men to capture an enemy held bridge:

> *The colonel strode calmly along the road as if he were walking on to a parade ground, looking back sometimes to call encouragement to his men, ignoring the bullets that squealed about him and kicked up little devils of earth at his feet.*
>
> *He was crossing the bridge now, with men streaming after him. It was as if he had, by his own physical strength, lifted the battalion up out of the ground and borne them with him.*

Baron's portrayal of battle is particularly visceral and realistic. Again and again, the importance of comradeship shines through:

> *Battle has its own strange chemistry. The courage and endurance of a group of men is greater than the sum total of the courage and endurance of the individuals in the group; for when most of the group have reached the limits of human endeavour, there is always one among them who can surpass those limits of human endeavour, who will hold the others together and drive them on. It is not the romantic picture of war; but is the truth of war.*

* * *

The final, attritional scenes of *From the City, From the Plough* are based on the attack on Mont Pincon by the 5th Battalion, Wiltshire

Regiment, who were almost wiped out in the action. Baron had heard about the battle and after the war, he wrote:

> It was the climax I needed for my novel. The 5th Wilts became the 5th Wessex. The story leading up to this climax would be a mosaic of my own experiences. Evidently these were typical, for a number of readers who had served with the 5th Wilts wrote to me recalling the events in the novel as real, and characters whom they claimed to recognise. So did many others who had served in other battalions.

From the City, From the Plough was originally called The Fifth Battalion after the fictional 5th Battalion, the Wessex Regiment, then The Englishmen, followed by A Summer's Harvest. The final title was suggested by the publisher Jonathan Cape's wife and evokes the men's origins with their urban and rural backgrounds. Baron started writing the book during the second half of 1946 and finished it the following year. He had a job with a theatre company and therefore worked on the novel every night for three hours after midnight. He put the manuscript away in a drawer, until his friends persuaded him to send it to a publisher. The first print run of 3,000 copies sold out before publication, with From the City, From the Plough achieving both popular success and critical acclaim. Over its lifetime, the book sold in excess of one million copies. With this new edition of such an authentic and moving novel, we can only hope to reach a readership of many, many more.

Alan Jeffreys
2019

PROLOGUE

AT THE END of the first week of August 1944, the Allied armies in Normandy were at last on the move after two months of bloody fighting.

On the right the American armour had broken through and was rumbling southwards across the base of the Breton peninsula towards the Loire. In the centre British troops, massed secretly and striking suddenly, were battering down from Caumont into the switchback of the Bocage, the thickly-wooded hill country. Towards the left of the line, the British divisions which had been fighting for weeks over the same strip of ground, from Tilly down to the Odon, and from the Odon down to the Orne, pushed forward at last, an army of tired, muddy, battle-drunk men leaving behind them Hottot and Hill 112 and a score of other shell-pitted hills and smashed villages. Every night as these men moved forward there was yet another hill or yet another village to take, yet another stream to cross under fire; every night they summoned fresh reserves of strength and will from their exhausted bodies and went forward against the mortars and the Spandaus and the eighty-eights. This time nothing was going to stop them.

Then they came to the last obstacle between their tanks and the flat lands of the French interior, the gateway to the Big Push, the last and highest ridge that forms the southern border of Normandy. For months they had pointed to this ridge on their maps, talked about it, read with foreboding the Intelligence reports of the fortifications that the enemy had installed here. Now it lay before them, twelve hundred feet above sea level; and the battalions of British infantry moved forward once more to the attack.

The Fifth Battalion of the Wessex Regiment had been ordered to deploy along its start line before daylight. Throughout the night the files of riflemen, plodding up and down hill along the narrow, tall-hedged lanes, had looked over their shoulders at the barrage flaring on the horizon, fretting the edges of the night with fire, and had felt its thudding rumble against their eardrums.

Now, towards dawn, the barrage was slackening. The men moved over the last hilltop that faced their objective and walked quietly downhill, their rifles at the trail or slung, hidden from view by the milky, white mist that clung to the hillsides.

Their start line lay along the valley between the two hills, and as they filed down to it, the mist that shrouded their objective began to slowly recede, heaving and billowing, like a glacier in a dream. As the mist crept down towards the valley it revealed the meadows and woods that clothed the hillside, still sombre in the dawn.

The infantrymen filed silently into their positions along the valley, sinking down out of sight against the banks of sunken lanes. The icy dew soaked through their trousers; the chill of the dawn lay like cold steel against their cheeks.

The first light stealing over the ridge, touched the black fringe of treetops up on the hillside, and a multitude of birds awoke to shrill song.

There was no other sound in the morning.

CHAPTER ONE
Reinforcements

THE RAILWAY CARRIAGE was full of men and smoke and the smell of wet uniforms drying. Above each row of seats the space between luggage-rack and ceiling was jammed with packs and equipment. There were more packs piled in the corridor outside, and men squatting on them all along the corridor.

There was the noise of the train and of many men talking and laughing; and in the carriage the noise, wavering and mournful, of a mouthorgan.

'Put that bloody thing away,' said the sergeant who was sitting pressed tight against the window by the crush of bodies. He was watching the rain stream down the windowpane and he did not turn his head as he spoke.

There was a growl of assent from some of the other men, and the private who was playing tapped his mouthorgan on his knee and dropped it in his pocket.

'What's up, Sergeant?' he asked. 'You look pigsick.'

The sergeant turned from the window. 'I'm pigsick all right,' he said bitterly. 'Six years in a regiment, you go abroad with it, you fight with it, you bury your mates, you get stripes in it, you play football for it, you win a bloody boxing championship for it, and what then? One fine morning you wake up, and you find a detail on the board...' he fumbled in his pocket, pulled out a sheet of paper and, unfolding it, began to read: '"Movement order: at oh-eight-thirty hours January fifteenth, nineteen-forty-four, the undermentioned officers and other ranks will parade in Field Service Marching Order, with fifty rounds of ammunition each and the unexpired portion of the day's rations, for transfer to the Fifth Battalion, Wessex Regiment".'

He crumpled the paper and smeared it against the windowpane; he swore, repeating one word furiously, again and again.

The men sat jammed shoulder to shoulder, with their hands between their knees, and watched him, silently. They were all cast in the same mould; all hard, all brown-skinned, all grave and composed of countenance, all with desert ribbons on the left breasts of their tunics.

One of the privates, swaying with the motion of the train, steadied himself for a moment to light a cigarette. He spat out a mouthful of smoke. 'Well, Ah don't mind tellin' yer, Sarge,' he said, "tharrah don't give a boogger what battalion Ah'm in. Ah never asked ter coom in t' first place. If Ah were a Regular it might be different, but Ah'm not, and Green 'Owards don't mean no more t'me than any other regiment.'

'Not even when you've come all the way across the desert with them?' the sergeant asked him. 'And through Sicily?'

'Lewk, Sarge,' answered the private. 'Ah've got one ambition – ter see our lass an' the kid again after t'war, an' what 'appens ter me between now an' then don't mean a thing.'

'Tell 'im, Lanky.' The other men were urging him on now, but he had no more to say. 'Gie us a tab, Lanky.' He passed his cigarettes round the carriage.

'I don't know,' it was a corporal speaking now, 'I reckon I'm sorry to leave the Howards. A good regiment in a good division. An' all our mates there. What they do it for, anyway?'

A half a dozen men started to answer at once. 'Ah, button it up,' said the sergeant, 'all the lot of you. They told us what we'd come back to Blighty for, didn't they?'

'The Second Front,' said the corporal.

'On the nail.' The sergeant was speaking again; the others were all quiet and listening. 'Well, men like us are useful. We've been shot up a bit. We're not apprentices any more. We're tradesmen. We know all about it. So they're sending us to stiffen up some lousy battalion that's never done it before.'

'It's what they call a cay-der,' said the corporal.

'Cah-der,' called a private from the far corner of the carriage.

'Cah-dree.' The sergeant gave the final ruling. 'C-a-d-r-e – cah-dre. That's what we are, a cah-dre. An' I can just imagine what it'll be like there. The colonel'll be about seventy, the sergeants'll all be Chelsea Pensioners and all the other ranks'll have fallen arches or double ruptures. I know these home service battalions.' He turned back to the window. 'Give us a bloody tune,' he said disgustedly.

The mouthorganist took his instrument from his pocket, tapped it elaborately on the palm of his right hand and inflated his cheeks.

There was the noise of the train, and of many men laughing; the noise, mournful and wavering, of a mouthorgan; and the noise of the rain on the carriage windows.

In the next carriage they were talking about leave.

'Reckon we'll get leave again, Corporal Shuttleworth?' asked someone.

Corporal Shuttleworth was taller than the others. He always seemed to be stooping, even when he was sitting down; and there was always something ineffectual, a little bemused, in his face.

'You've had three weeks disembark,' he answered. 'What more d'you want?'

'Well, they'll be running a normal leave rota in this new lot we're going to. Surely we'll be put on that.'

'I reckon we will,' replied the corporal, without enthusiasm.

'He's a glutton for punishment, isn't he, Corp?' said another man.

Another voice. 'So's his missus.' Laughter.

The corporal opened the window, spat and closed the window again. 'He's welcome,' he said. 'He can have mine, too.'

Another corporal, sitting opposite him, leaned forward and touched him on the knee. 'What's up, Charlie? Trouble?'

Shuttleworth pressed his hand against the windowpane, then laid the cold palm against his face.

'The Hero's Homecoming,' he said, 'or Back from the Desert.'

'Gawd,' someone exclaimed, 'another one? There's about fifty divorces laid on in the battalion already. What's your ol' woman do to you, Charlie?'

'Jacked me in for a civvy. I got home; no one there, no furniture, nothing. Chased around. Got a line from the neighbours. In the end I found her in a furnished room in Acton.'

The other corporal let him brood for a moment, then asked,

'What she say, Charlie?'

'Said she was in love; she couldn't help it. I asked her what about trying again with me: I was fond of her, you know. She said no, she couldn't, and she started crying. I was in a terrible state. I could 'a cried myself. I kept on with her, and then she got hysterical. She started shriekin' at me. She said she was glad I'd gone away. If I hadn't she'd 'a been a faithful wife all her life an' never known what a real man'd be like.

'I said: "What d'you mean, Sal?" She stood there shriekin' with laughter at me, and she said this new chap she was with was a man, not half a man.'

'Well, I just clouted her, and left her on the floor crying, and I went off after the other chap. I never even stopped to ask her about the furniture.'

'You should 'a killed the cow,' said someone.

'Shut up,' said the other corporal. 'Go on, Charlie.'

'Gi' me a fag, Len,' said Shuttleworth. 'Thanks.' He lit up.

'Well, I met this other chap comin' out a work. He wasn't a bad-lookin' bloke. Shorter than me, square-cut like. Smooth pink face. Had his hair plastered down. Nice double-breasted blue suit. A clerk he was, a proper toff.

'I pulled him down a side street, an' I said, "Why don't you leave my missus alone?" He said he was sorry, an' they loved each other. He said it was bigger than them. I said, "Don't gi' me that!" I told 'im if he was a man and I was half a man, why wasn't he in uniform? He was unfit. How's that for a laugh? I told 'im to put his fists up, an' he said he was sorry again, he didn't want trouble. He said, "Look here, can't we be sensible about this?" I told him to put 'em up and have a go with half a man.

'Anyway, in the end I started in on 'im. I spoiled his blue serge suit, all right. I give him half a man. I left him on the floor.

'Then I went an' stayed roun' my mother's. I thought they'd have the police on me for bashin' him, but they didn't. Must 'a been my wife. She always was afraid of scandal.

'I never went near them again. I got plastered every night for the rest of my leave. I never worried about the furniture. I haven't even done anything about her allowance yet.

'The cow,' he said. 'Oh, the rotten, bleeding cow.'

'I loved that girl,' he said. 'I loved that bloody girl.'

He watched the rain streaming down the window. 'Half a man,' he said, wonderingly.

On his left breast, among his campaign ribbons, was the red, white and blue strip of the Military Medal.

'Half a bloody man,' he mused.

A whistle shrieked. The men swayed with the speeding train. The carriage was full of smoke and the smell of wet uniforms drying. The rain streamed down the windows.

CHAPTER TWO
The Fifth Battalion

THE FIFTH BATTALION, Wessex Regiment (Lieutenant-Colonel Henry Pothecary, commanding) lived on the bleak flanks of a hill looking down on the English Channel.

Across a waste of sodden turf, wrapped in winter mists, lay Nissen huts like rows of slumbering black beetles. Cinder paths veined the hillside, at the foot of which ran a rutted, muddy lane leading to a sentry post and to the main road.

Beyond the lane was a cinder parade ground from which the battalion, on its morning parades, looked out over the fields and woodlands which fell away, in a pastoral pattern, towards the sea. The battalion commander, facing his men each morning, stood before a backcloth of grey sky and white-combed grey sea.

Away to the west the veils of mist thickened into a darker haze of smoke beneath which a great seaport lay.

Here lived the soldiers of the Fifth Battalion, six hundred men with mud on their boots, their faces whipped red-raw by the stabbing wind and the icy, thousand-needled rain. They listened day and night to the undertones of the wind, to the creak and groan of corrugated iron roofing and the mutter of loose doors. Before their eyes as they stepped shivering from their huts each morning was the Channel, the grey Channel, and beyond it – the grey mist.

The Fifth Battalion of the Wessex Regiment was talking politics.

For four and a half years the battalion had led its own placid life, moving from one village to another, guarding bridges that no one ever crossed and defending dumps which even the War Office appeared to have forgotten; men joined the battalion, went on their leaves, got girls into trouble, punched their sergeants' noses and went to jail, did legendary deeds in public houses and left the battalion. The most memorable events in the battalion's history were a pitched battle with the Irish Guards in the streets of Andover in 1941, the winning of the Divisional football championship in 1942 and an all-night booze-up out of regimental funds in 1943. The battalion trained and route marched and manoeuvred, sent droves of men to battle school, and dozed on NAAFI benches in disciplined silence in front of a succession of Ministry of Information lecturers, in a spirit of cheerful absent-mindedness, of bewildered resignation at the inconsiderateness of their commanders in ordering such things, and in utter disregard of the fact that somewhere ahead of them lay battle, murder and sudden death. The march of great events had left them, on the whole, unmoved. Only from time to time, when fighters thundered overhead, tiny splinters of silver moving in wide-flung patterns out across the Channel; when they heard the guns of Alamein, recorded by the B.B.C., reverberating in their huts; when they waited each morning at the sentry-box by the main road for the newspaper-boy on his bicycle to bring the latest news from Stalingrad, did they stir with excitement.

On Christmas night, when they had crawled into their blankets gorged with pork and belching beerily, all this had ended. Every day since then fresh sheets of orders on the company notice boards had plunged the battalion more deeply into a chaos of activity, rumour and speculation; and politics – the speeches of statesmen, the prophecies of military correspondents, the leading articles and the paragraphs of war news – had become their first concern.

A lorry load of new Bren guns arrived and groups of men gathered in the canteen talking about the Second Front; a score of jeep trailers – little two-wheeled contraptions like boy scouts' trek carts – were delivered, and in dozens of Nissen huts men crowded round the red-hot stoves arguing about the strength and weakness of Fortress Europe.

On New Year's Day the battalion post corporal, a lean and sceptical old sweat with North-West Frontier ribbons on his tunic, leaned back in his chair in his little office behind the armoury, and, carving the air contemptuously with the stem of his pipe, informed a circle of lance-corporals (all waiting for their sections' mail) that there was absolutely nothing to worry about. 'I 'eard the colonel tell the ord'ly room sar'nt we was 'ere for the duration. An' besides, there's me with my varicose veins and 'ow many more like me? They don't send a battalion like that into action.'

They don't.

On January 3rd there was a medical examination for the whole battalion. On January 5th ninety-four men – the sick, the lame and the incurably lazy, the post corporal among them – left the battalion. On January 10th fifty replacements arrived from Infantry Training Centre, beefy, ruddy, awkward lads, none more than twenty years old. On January 15th a training cadre of forty-four battle-hardened desert veterans arrived from the Green Howards.

The Fifth Battalion of the Wessex Regiment was at war strength.

'Good night, sentry.'

The sentry by the road, muffled in scarf and cap-comforter and bowed over his rifle, jolted himself to attention. He recognised the broad, stocky figure of the battalion commander at his side.

'Good night, sir.' He relaxed again over his rifle as he heard the colonel's boots plodding off behind him down the lane. This was routine. Every sentry knew that he had to expect a visit from the Old Man at eight o'clock in the evening, after the officers had dined. It was all right, they would tell a newcomer going on his first spell of guard duty, the Old Man was no snooper, 'not like some'. It was just his way, to walk round the camp every night, in the bitterest winter weather, to say good night to the sentries, to poke his head into the blue fug of the NAAFI for a moment (and only his head, for he scrupulously respected the sanctity of the NAAFI, the only inviolable retreat permitted to the other ranks), to chat in the cookhouse with the night cooks and boilermen before returning, pipe in mouth, greatcoat collar turned up, hands deep in pockets, to his hut. He was a good 'un, was the Old Man. 'Our Dad', they called him.

Colonel Pothecary blinked at the light as he stepped into his hut and banged the door behind him. He was a square man with a square face, with greying hair parted in the middle. In civilian clothes he would have passed as a master builder with a small but prospering business, a plain man, plain speaking, with no nonsense about him; all of which he was.

'Hello, Noel,' he said to his second-in-command, who was sprawling deep in an armchair by the stove. 'Higgs brought in the coffee yet?'

Higgs emerged from the bedroom partitioned off at the end of the hut. 'On the other stove, sir,' he announced ingratiatingly. 'Coming right up.' He was a wizened little runt of a man in canvas slippers; he had been on the list of unfit men to leave the battalion, but he had pleaded himself off it.

'You know,' Major Norman's voice, coming from the depths of the armchair, was the most unmilitary voice in the Fifth Battalion, the bleating, piping, fantastically-affected voice of a musical comedy caricature, 'you know, I can't imagine why you trudge around this camp every night. The men probably loathe you for it.' The slim and beautifully-attired upper half of his body appeared as he sat up and looked at the colonel with large, reproachful eyes. 'Every evening after tea,' he announced, 'I say blast their hides and forget about 'em till the next morning. I am a thoroughly selfish beast; I have no social conscience; I loathe Welfare, and all that is therein; and I thank God for people like you who make it possible for people like me to loaf by the stove and persistently shirk our responsibilities.'

The colonel sipped his coffee appreciatively. 'Damn good stuff this,' he said heavily. 'Lucky we don't remember what real coffee tastes like!'

He blew his nose and began to fiddle with his pipe. 'The Brigadier can never understand how we get on so well together, Noel,' he said. 'I sometimes wonder myself.'

'It's because we both see through each other so easily,' said Norman.

'Perhaps. But it's funny, all the same. Take a chap like me. Plain man, come up through the Terriers. Work for my living. And an educated chap like you. Don't I bore you stiff?'

'On the contrary,' said Norman, 'you fascinate me. It's my own kind that bore me. They're all cut so precisely to pattern. But you plain people are so immeasurably profound and always so capable of the unexpected.'

11

'That's nice to know,' said the colonel. 'I must say I always like to listen to you even when I can't understand a word you're saying.'

He opened his writing case. 'Well,' he said, 'I won't keep you from your book. I've got a couple of letters to write.'

'One to the wife,' said Norman.

'Yes,' said the colonel.

'And one to the boy.'

'Yes,' replied the colonel, a little defiantly, and bent to his writing.

Dear Biddy [his first letter began]: *I received your letter yesterday and the bill from the Bazaar. I shall take it up with them. Yes, Sarah did write to me, but you shouldn't worry, she takes offence at anything. As a matter of fact I always did think that nothing would be better for Sarah than a bit of plain speaking. She thinks that she only has to fly off the handle and everyone will rush about to soothe her. It's like people with hysterics, you have to slap their faces. Be firm, my dear, and you can always count on me to back you up. How is Don liking it at home? Not fed up with himself, I hope, and taking his mother out once in a while. You must not worry about the boy, Biddy, it seemed from your letter as if you were a little. He has to go. He is old enough to, and he is a lad with plenty of spirit. But our boy will be able to look after himself. And now, about me. I am hard at it. We are all very busy here, and it doesn't look as if I'll be able to manage any more of those nice weekends for a while. However, I'm looking for a place where you can stay in town, for a week or two, and I can come over and see a lot of you very often. You know, I still miss my Biddy, when I'm away. (You see, there's no fool like an old fool.) Well, dear, look after yourself and don't worry about the boy. Send me the other vests from the bottom right-hand drawer in the dressing table. Also the studs in the cellophane packet underneath.*

> *Your loving husband,*
> *Harry*

He looked guiltily up at the armchair by the stove. Only a book and a pair of hands were visible. He bent over the letter again and painstakingly added two rows of crosses beneath his signature. He folded the letter, put it in an envelope and took a fresh sheet.

My dear Donald [he wrote]: *Your letter was very guarded, but I'm an old soldier and I can take a hint. So it looks as if you will soon be off to sea to 'bring home the bacon'. Well, that's what you want, I know you're looking forward to it. Glad you had a nice New Year's party with your friends. You must be running through the £ s. d. pretty fast, so I'm sending you a tenner. Use some of it to take your mother out and buy her a present or two, you should do what you can to take her mind off things, poor mother, the house will be empty with both of us away. I wish I could come home again just for a day or two to say cheerioh, but it's impossible. We're doing our little bit too, you know. Still, come down yourself for a day if you can, and if not I know you'll write again before you go. Must close now. England expects, as you sea-dogs say,*
      Your affectionate
      Dad

The colonel finished his business at the table, went to a sideboard, poured two glasses of whisky and took them across to the stove. A hand reached up from the armchair and took one of the glasses. Both men drank.

The colonel leaned over the armchair and looked at the book that Norman was reading. It was Plato's *Republic*. He grunted non-committally, pulled another armchair up to the stove and settled in it, making satisfied noises. He wriggled about for a moment, and produced from beneath himself a book, on whose cover flaunted an insufficiently-dressed lady and the title, in flaring red letters, *But Once a Virgin*.

'Hot stuff this,' chuckled the colonel, and applied himself to his book.

CHAPTER THREE

On the march

'B'TTALION...ATTEN...SHAH!'

There was a single crash of boots on the cinder parade ground, then silence; not a man stirred.

'B'ttalion...slope...HAHP!'

The rifles came up together: smack... two-three; smack... two-three; smack. Not a man stirred.

'Battalion will advance in column of platoons from the right, Number One Platoon leading. Battalion... right... turn!'

From the flank, the high, desperate voice of a platoon officer: 'Number One Platoon, by the right, right wheeyell... quick... MARCH!'

The battalion moved off, platoon after platoon.

Colonel Pothecary studied his men as they marched past him. He was happy. These men are proud, he thought, they march as if they like it. They're beginning to look like a battalion.

They were grinning as they swung by him. That was a good thing, the colonel thought, remembering the weeks of training through which the battalion had passed, the nights spent shivering under frosty hedgerows, the days of crawling in the mud, hacking with pick and shovel at the chalk hillsides, practising on the ranges with rifle and grenade, streaming over assault courses, squatting round maps in the lecture hut. Already the hundred newcomers, veterans and recruits, had found their place in the battalion; men who had frozen and sweated together, ate, slept and grumbled together, boxed and played football together for six weeks were no longer strangers to each other. And here it all was, on this route march, the grinning, the pride, the arms going up together, the boots thudding along the rutted lane. Colonel Pothecary was proud of his battalion.

* * *

There was an old man from Lancashire,
He swallowed a blade of grass,
One grew out of his ear-'ole
And the other grew out of his arse.

The battalion had left the main road and was marching along a grassy ride that followed the ridge of a great, bare backed spur of downland. The salt wind from the Channel battered at the men's faces and as, platoon by platoon, they recovered from the long uphill march, they joined in the singing.

If you don't believe me and you think I'm telling a lie,
Just ask the girls from Manchester, they'll tell you the reason why.

The colonel was marching at the head of the battalion with his second-in-command. The colonel was swinging his walking stick as if he were out for a morning's walk in the country. He was singing lustily.

'Don't be anti-social, Noel,' he shouted above the buffeting wind. 'Let's hear you sing.'

Norman eyed him ferociously. 'You love this, don't you?' he complained. 'You're like those damned open-air enthusiasts I always have the misfortune to meet on holiday, who won't rest until they've dragged me out for nice, healthy walks and nice, healthy games of golf.'

'Cheer up, Noel,' said the colonel, 'this'll put ten years on your life.'

'No thank you,' said Major Norman. 'I'd rather die young.'

'No doubt you will,' said the colonel. They marched on in silence for a while; then he spoke again. 'Had a letter from the wife last night,' he said. 'She hasn't heard from the boy yet. She went down to the shipping office the other day. They told her not to worry, it was quite normal. I shall have to get her down here for a few days. Take her mind off things. Any idea where she could stay?'

They talked hotels. The regimental sergeant-major approached them. It was time for a break, he said.

'We'll get down into the valley out of the wind,' said the colonel, 'then we'll give 'em a rest.'

'Noel,' he said a few moments later, 'I could do with a rest myself. I'm pretty fit, but I'm no chicken.'

There was a village in the valley below them, with the wind snatching at the smoke from its chimneys. Traffic crawled along a ribbon of road.

'You don't have to do all this,' said Norman.

'I have to,' said the colonel. 'I have to lead them, haven't I? I have their lives to look after. My boy's away at sea – his life's in the hands of his captain. I can't be less conscientious than I expect that man to be. Anyway,' he chuckled, 'I shall have my rest after the war.'

'I know,' said Norman. 'I've heard it all before. A couple of years back in the business, then retire at fifty and leave it to the boy. But say the boy doesn't want to. Suppose he likes the sea.'

'Don't worry,' laughed the colonel. 'He doesn't want to remain a sailor any more than I want to remain a soldier when this lot's over. He's a shrewd boy. Got his head screwed on the right way. He'll do well in the business, all right. And I,' he said, 'I shall retire to my potting sheds and cultivate roses.'

She'll be coming round the mountains when she comes,
She'll be coming round the mountains when she comes –

The battalion was marching in the sheltered valley, steel-shod boots crashing on the metalled road. Women were coming to the gates of cottage gardens with buns and apples; there was shouting and jesting all along the ranks. Dogs and children raced and tumbled alongside; small boys on bicycles came swooping past the column ringing their bells madly.

Roll out the barrel,
We'll have a barrel of fun,
Roll out the barrel.
We've got the blues on the run.

The first stragglers had fallen out already, the men who were working their loaves. They sat by the roadside loosening their bootlaces amid a storm of jeers from the passing platoons, or limped exaggeratedly towards the rear under a barrage of ribald comment from the ranks.

Now's the time to roll the barrel,
For the gang's all here.

A halt. Sergeant Ferrissey sat on a milestone with his platoon squatting and sprawling all round him. Sergeant Ferrissey was a handsome, dangerous man, with a lean, wine-dark face, a black moustache and eyes like black berries under their lids. He was going through his letters.

'Ten bob from my woman in Exeter,' he announced, unfolding a postal order.

'Twenty fags from a woman in Andover.' This acknowledging of tributes was a daily ritual of his. He opened a third letter.

'Which of your women is that from?' asked his corporal, a solemn little ex-schoolteacher named Gonigle.

'The wife,' said Sergeant Ferrissey disgustedly. 'Half a bleeding crown.'

Quando nel fango debbo caminar
Sotto il mio bottino mi sento vacillar.
Che cosa mai sara die me?
Ma poi sorrido e penso a te-
A te, Lili Marlene, a te, Lili Marlene.

The battalion was on the march again and a file of veterans, careless of their comrades, were singing softly. They were dreaming, as they dreamed every day, of the blue hills of Sicily, of the blue glare of the sky and the blue Ionian sea, of the blinding white sunlight and the white walls of villas, of the black grapes hanging heavy on the vines and the orange trees in golden groves, of the mules and the great oxen and ancient shepherds with their pipes, of lizards sunning themselves on stones, and of the signorinas, the lovely, kindly signorinas.

The sky darkened and the wind began to drive a fine rain in their faces.

There was a break for lunch. The men relaxed by the roadsides, sitting on groundsheets, glistening gas-capes over their shoulders, eating their haversack rations.

Sergeant Ferrissey stood looking into the wood that bordered the road.

'You look like a bloody poacher,' Gonigle said to him.

'I am a bloody poacher,' said Ferrissey, 'born and bred.' He stood for a moment with his head cocked like an alert dog. 'Who's for some eggs?' he asked.

'What a bloody sergeant,' said Gonigle.

'And what a bloody corporal he's got,' said Ferrissey. 'I'll make a man of you yet, Golly. Comin' for some eggs?'

A couple of the men joined them and they moved warily through the woods. Soon they could hear what Ferrissey had heard from the roadside, the noise of poultry. They came to a chicken-wire fence, with poultry runs a few yards beyond. To their right a path led to a one-storey house. They were hidden – scarcely hidden – from the house by a scanty fringe of trees.

'You first, Golly,' said Ferrissey. 'Let's see if you're a soldier.'

Gonigle lay on his back with his head close to the wire. The others strained and lifted the wire a little. Gonigle pressed himself against the ground and squeezed through underneath the fence. He wriggled across to the poultry runs and disappeared inside. A few seconds later he emerged, still flat on his back, with the breast of his tunic bulging above him. He crawled back to the fence and passed the eggs from his tunic one by one to a private who slipped them into his tunic. Then he squeezed back under the fence.

'You'll do,' said Ferrissey. 'Who's next?'

There were footsteps on the path. One of the privates, who was just getting down, straightened hurriedly up.

A woman was standing among the trees watching them. They stood in awkward silence, uncertain as to how long she had been standing there.

Then Ferrissey stepped quickly forward. 'You'll have to get back to the house, madam,' he said sternly. 'Manoeuvres. It's for your own safety, ma'am.' He took her gently by the shoulder and turned her towards the house. With his hand still on her shoulder he walked her back along the path. She was a tall, not unattractive woman.

'Holy smoke,' grunted Gonigle. 'That's his best yet. Come on.' They hurried back to the road and waited. Minutes went by. Officers hurried along the ranks warning the men to put their mess tins away and get their equipment on. They waited for the whistle signal to fall in, and they watched the woods for Ferrissey.

The whistles were already shrilling when he reappeared. The woman was with him. He stood very close to her for a moment, then hurried back to the road.

The battalion moved off.

'Bit of all right, Sarge, eh?' said one of the men behind him.

'Pick up the step,' growled Sergeant Ferrissey.

There was less singing as the afternoon went by, and although the wind grew colder and attacked the column at hourly intervals with sudden flurries of rain, more and more men were unbuttoning the cuffs and collars of their tunics, tilting their helmets to the backs of their heads to ease the weight, and shifting their rifles from one aching shoulder to another.

They were marching southwards again towards the sea, and they had the long climb to the crest of the downs ahead of them. They trudged grimly upwards, leaning heavily forward, each man's eyes on the pack bobbing in front of him, each man's thumbs hooked in the straps of his equipment to take the strain off his back.

There were no more stragglers. The weak had all been cast off in the morning.

The leading platoons topped the crest and felt with joy the salt Channel gale battering again at their faces. Now there was only the march downhill into camp, with showers and a hot dinner and the red-hot stoves of their huts waiting for them.

'I suppose,' said Corporal Gonigle to Sergeant Ferrissey, 'that after all this you'll go dancing tonight. And find yourself another woman in the bargain.'

'Not tonight, lad,' said Sergeant Ferrissey. 'These village girls are not for me. Snivelling little bitches not hardly out o' school. Tits no bigger than 'alf a crown. And the way they behave!' he exclaimed disgustedly. 'Got no morals at all. Give me,' said Sergeant Ferrissey piously, shifting his rifle to his left shoulder, 'give me a nice, respectable 'ore any day.'

CHAPTER FOUR
Honeymoon Hall

OUTSIDE IT WAS DESOLATE; the clouds hurrying across a green, fantastic sky, the turf soft and sucking underfoot, the huts looming grim and black in the darkness, and the keen wind moaning in from the sea. But when the orderly sergeant stopped, shivering, outside the hut which bore on its door the neatly-painted signboard

HONEYMOON HALL (NUMBER NINE PLATOON)

and opened the door, he stepped into a little world of warmth. He closed the door behind him and shut out the vast and frigid night. Standing in this windowless, tunnel-shaped room, with the high double-decker wooden beds crowding along each side, with the firelight and shadow, the air heavy with heat, was indeed like standing in a tunnel deep underground remote from all the noises and troubles of the living world.

The men were crowded round the stove in the middle of the hut; this was the heart of their community. Some of them were sitting on their beds, others on four benches placed round the stove. Most of them were holding their wet, freshly blancoed packs or webbing equipment straps in front of them to dry in the heat of the stove; for it was Friday night, and this was a weekly duty. More equipment hung drying on lines across the hut.

'Pay attention, lads,' said the orderly sergeant. 'Detail for tomorrow morning.' He caught sight of a can of tea brewing on the stove. 'I'll have a drop of that, if you've got some to spare.'

'Lay orf, blubberguts.'

The orderly sergeant was a big man but not sensitive about his bulk. He walked down to the other end of the hut and stopped in front of the man who had spoken.

'Getting mingy in your old age, Charlie,' he said pleasantly.

Charlie Venable looked up from his cards. Lank, black hair flopped down over his pale, V-shaped face. 'Gawd,' he said, 'ain't you dead yet?'

'Old soldiers never die,' said the orderly sergeant.

'You ain't exactly fadin' away,' said Charlie Venable, prodding the orderly sergeant's sagging belly. 'I should say you got triplets in there. Who done it, Sergeant?'

'You will have your joke,' said the orderly sergeant unperturbed. He badly wanted a drop of tea, and he knew that Charlie Venable was the man who mattered in this hut.

'For Gawd's sake,' said Charlie. 'I'm gambling. Go away. You bring me bad luck. 'Ere,' he said violently, 'give 'im a drop a char an' get rid of 'im.'

'Gambling,' said the orderly sergeant, sipping his tea gratefully, 'is a serious offence. Don't let me catch you doing it.'

Charlie Venable held his hand of cards up in front of the orderly sergeant's face. 'Good enough?' he asked.

'Good enough,' said the orderly sergeant solemnly, and nodded his head approvingly as Charlie raked in his winnings. 'You're a good gambler, Charlie,' he said. This was the highest praise he knew for a soldier.

He called for attention again and announced the next day's orders. It was always the same on Saturday mornings; a nice, easy programme – Regimental Sergeant-Major's Parade – an hour of glittering, crackling drill; then a long break at the canteen, with a lecture and a hut inspection to finish off the morning. After that they were free to leave barracks for the day.

The orderly sergeant backed unwillingly away from the stove and opened the door. 'Good night, lads,' he said, and left the hut.

It was quiet again in the hut, in the flickering red firelight, and very domestic. Most of the men talked quietly round the fire. A couple were squatting on their beds shaving; one or two were writing letters. A man named Bailey, who had gone to bed with a chill, was shivering and sniffling under his blankets. From among the card players on Charlie Venable's bed came the clink of coins.

Alfie Bradley, the baby of the platoon, put his writing case away, slipped his fountain pen in his pocket and went over to watch the card players. He was small and thin, like a little whippet. He was fair-haired, and twenty years old.

'Written to your ma, Alfie boy?' asked Charlie Venable, without looking up from his cards. 'That's a boy. You be a good boy to your ma...' he put his cards down on the blanket and raked in the kitty '...she's the only good woman you'll ever know, Alfie.'

Alfie flushed; he was sensitive about women. He lay in bed every night and listened to his comrades talking about their wives and the women they found; they were so casual, so confident, and it was so hard for him to hide from them the fact that life was still fear and mystery to him.

'I don't know,' said Alfie timidly. 'Some of the married chaps seem to have done all right.'

'Ah,' said Charlie Venable, 'but what goes on when their backs are turned? Answer me that. Look at the married women down in the village. There's not one of 'em straight. Think it's different anywhere else?'

'You don't know my missus,' said one of the men by the fire.

'Maybe I do,' said Charlie. 'I been around.'

'That's not funny,' said the man by the fire.

'No offence,' said Charlie amiably. 'My little joke, mate.'

He shuffled the cards deftly and dealt another hand. 'You're right, though, Alfie boy,' he said, 'you find yourself a nice little girl an' don't take no notice of me. But don't you go with none of them women in the village. You think of your ma, Alfie, an' look for one like 'er.'

'Can I sit-in?' asked Alfie.

'You help me play my hand,' Charlie Venable advised him, 'and keep your money in your pocket.'

* * *

'How's it goin', Baldy?'

At the foot of Charlie Venable's bed a soldier was kneeling on a large sheet of plywood scrubbing a pair of anklets. He looked up and answered Charlie.

'All right, cocker. Nearly done now.'

Baldy was Charlie Venable's batman, his body-servant, his slave, his faithful squire. Baldy was a man with two selves. On parade, wearing beret or steel helmet, he was a soldier, tall and sturdy, his face firm and confident, enduring on the march, quick and ruthless with the bayonet. But with his head bared, and the great, brown-mottled bald patch at the back – the consequence of some childhood illness – revealed, he slackened and became Baldy, unwilling to go into a public house, afraid to go to a dance, refusing to talk to women for fear of their laughter. He was a lonely man, and without confidence. One day Charlie Venable, in a generous moment, had stopped by Baldy's bed and said, 'Comin' down the village for a drink, Baldy boy?' Since then they had 'gone mates' together. It was Charlie's nature to pair off with someone like this, just as in the East End street that was Charlie's home the prettiest girls always went out with the fattest and ugliest. Baldy, on his side, made no secret of his devotion to Charlie. He made Charlie's bed for him, blancoed his equipment, ran errands for him to the canteen and fought at his side whenever there was a rough house.

Charlie, quick and insolent and proud to the point of arrogance, accepted this homage as his due. Whenever he clashed with an officer or insulted a sergeant Baldy was at his shoulder, gulping and apprehensive but loyally heaping insult on his master's insult; so that each time Charlie was led away to the guard-room his baldheaded Sancho Panza went with him.

'Will you do mine, while you're about it?' asked one of the card players.

'Tanner,' said Baldy. 'Tanner a pair.'

He took the sixpence and the anklets and set to work again. For half a crown he would blanco the whole of a man's equipment; for any single item he charged sixpence. He had a thriving business.

Most of the platoon were asleep. At the side of the bed nearest to the door Lance-Corporal Feather knelt briefly and prayed. The men who were still awake watched him curiously but without derision.

As he slid into his blankets Charlie Venable asked him: 'Prayin' for us, Corp?'

Lance-Corporal Feather smiled. 'For all of us, Charlie.'

'Reckon it does any good?'

'Well, it makes you feel better, Charlie.'

'Not me, Corp,' said Charlie. 'Not me it doesn't. People 'ave been prayin' for a million years an' it didn't do 'em no good. It didn't stop the last war an' it didn't stop this one. It didn't stop the bombs comin' down in Bow, neither. No offence to you, Corp. Put your trust in God; an' I don't think! Put your trust in Charlie Venable; that's my motto.'

Men stirred and raised themselves on their elbows under the blankets, listening. They had these discussions every night after lights out, talking softly for hours in the luxurious warmth of the stove about love and God and aircraft and electricity and Communism and Eddie Phillips and the Arsenal.

'I'll tell you when it does you good,' said one of the other men. 'When you're away. I'm not one for religion, but when we were in Africa I used to lay there and think about the wife and kids, and think, well if there is a God then let him look after them. If you think there is someone who can look after them, well, it's a comfort. And I tell you when else. Sometimes you're laying there in a battle and you think you'll never get out of it, and I don't care who you are then, you'll pray to God to get you out alive.'

'Kiddin' yourself,' said Charlie Venable, 'lowerin' yourself. When I'm in a corner I won't say, "Please God get me out of 'ere." I'll say, "Now then, Charlie boy, it's up to you to get yourself out of 'ere, an' no one else." God 'elps those 'oo 'elps themselves.'

'In the last war,' said another voice, 'there was a bloke with a Bible in his pocket, and this Bible stopped a bullet one day. It was right over his heart.'

'Jus' shows yer,' said Charlie Venable, 'Battle order, eh? Small pack, two grenades, fifty rounds an' Bible at the alert.'

'Well,' said someone, 'it's just as well to play safe. You never know.'

'Gaw,' said Charlie disgustedly, 'that's low. That's bloody low.'

He turned over on to his other elbow and spoke to Lance-

Corporal Feather, 'Lot o' bleedin' sinners, ain't we, Corp? Given up hope for us?'

'No, Charlie,' said the lance-corporal sleepily. 'You're a Christian, Charlie, even though you don't know it.' He stretched himself cosily in his bed and felt the warmth of the stove toasting the left side of his blanket. He was happy here. There was warmth and trust and tenderness and loving-kindness in this hut. 'Good night, lads,' he muttered.

Charlie Venable slipped out of bed and padded across the hut to where Bailey was lying. He went back to the stove and poured the last of the tea into his mug.

''Ere, boy,' he said to the sick man, 'drink this up.' He reached for his greatcoat and tucked it across the foot of Bailey's bed. ''Ave a good sweat, Bailey boy. You'll be all right in the morning.'

CHAPTER FIVE
A courtship

A LIEUTENANT-COLONEL rules an infantry battalion: majors and captains sit frowning behind tables, award minor punishments and sign their company orders: but the regimental sergeant-major is the First Soldier of the battalion. His is an authority more sternly defended than any other's; his dignity more jealously guarded. The colonel may unbend, may appear in his shirtsleeves, may ostentatiously fraternise with other ranks; but never the R.S.M.

Every Saturday morning for one hour the Fifth Battalion of the Wessex Regiment acknowledged this fact. The colonel, his company commanders and their subalterns lurked in their offices or retired to the warmth and comfort of the mess; and on the parade ground that looked out over the mist-veiled Channel Regimental Sergeant-Major McBean drilled an officerless battalion.

Six hundred riflemen stood stiffly to attention, silent and alert, the bitter wind stabbing at their faces. A hundred yards away from the nearest rank stood the R.S.M., arms locked at his sides, his body erect and tall as a lance, his chin up, his voice carrying against the sobbing March wind with the harsh, unanswerable authority of a bugle-call. This lean, brown man from the Hebrides with the impassive face and the soft, musical accents of the islands never shouted. When he uttered his commands he did not strain, his cheeks did not grow red, his chest did not swell. He just stood there, his lips rolled back from his teeth, with the harsh, echoing, triumphant commands ripping from him; and ploughmen working behind their steaming horses in the fields far below, looked up as they heard the distant voice echoing faintly but clearly on the wind.

And the men loved it. They prepared for this parade as if for their own weddings, blancoing, and cleaning boots, brasses and weapons with furious zeal. They stood tensely, grinning with their eyes from rigid faces while the R.S.M., who did not spare his n.c.o.s, shouted, 'Come on, you sergeant-majors, get a hold of those slopes!' or 'Set an example, you n.c.o.s! You're leading soldiers on parade, not a rabble of wee weans coming home from school!'

They loved it because, marching in perfect order, in beautifully-spaced ranks, with all the arms coming up together and all the boots crashing down together and the bayonets glinting together away along in front as far as the eye could see, all the slog and mud and freezing rain of the past week came to make sense; Number One Platoon and Number Nine Platoon, 'A' Company and 'B' Company and 'C' Company, desert-ribboned Geordies, quiet country boys and salty Cockneys all became the single entity, The Battalion; and they were full of pride.

They loved it because this man had their confidence. Ever since he had come from the Black Watch with fourteen years' Regular service behind him, he had shown himself to be just and kindly, always ready to intercede for some inarticulate private on trial before the colonel, always willing to listen, his head cocked interrogatively on one side, to an application for a weekend pass. And he played football. How he played football! Streaking down the field in the attack, whipping the ball past half a dozen defenders with some miracle of sleight-of-foot that brought a roar of ecstasy from the touchline, he had become the talk of the battalion, its idol, its White Hope.

His slogan was, 'Off parade, off parade; on parade, on parade.'

This morning Regimental Sergeant-Major McBean was on parade.

He began by marching the battalion round the perimeter of the parade ground for five minutes to warm the men up, standing in the middle like the ringmaster in some gigantic circus, calling the time, noting every arm that did not swing high enough, every rifle that wavered. Then he gave them five minutes of arms drill, making them slope arms, present arms, slope arms, order arms, slope arms, present arms, slope arms, order arms, until every move was perfect and not a man flinched between words of command.

'Goin' into town today?' muttered Charlie Venable between motionless lips.

'Yes,' whispered Alfie Bradley in the rank in front of him, his head scarcely moving.

'STOP THAT TALKING IN YOUR PLATOON, SERGEANT

SHANNON.'

Now the battalion was wheeling and manoeuvring, splitting up into companies and platoons, coalescing again into a single, snaking column, turning and halting to form one rectangular mass and moving off again into new and more intricate patterns, the material of an artist, shaped and moulded at his command.

The battalion was dismissed and the men swarmed off the parade ground.

'There won' 'alf be a queue at the NAAFI,' said Charlie Venable. 'Let's get weaving.' He broke into a trot. 'Come on, you silly sods,' he shouted, 'last man there's a bastard.' Number Nine Platoon streamed after him.

'Man,' said Corporal Meadows, 'look at 'em all. You'd think you were back in Cairo.'

'Or Catania,' said Corporal Warne.

They stood in the crowded High Street with their backs to a shop window, hemmed in by the throng of footloose soldiers and Saturday afternoon shoppers.

'Fifty Div.,' said Corporal Meadows.

'Seventh Armoured,' said Corporal Warne.

'Jocks.'

'Durhams, Howards, Seaforths, Gordons — Man, it won't be long now.'

On the shoulder patches of the soldiers streaming into town, and on the mudguards of the lorries that came charging down the High Street were the old familiar divisional emblems of their Eighth Army days.

'There's somethin' in the air all right,' said Meadows. 'They didn't bring all this lot back for nothing.'

'Tons of time,' said Warne.

'Why tons of time?'

'February. Can't invade now. They've got to wait for the good weather. May the fifteenth,' said Corporal Warne. 'You wait and see. May the fifteenth.'

'Well,' said Corporal Meadows. 'Sooner done, sooner finished. Roll on the peace.'

'Amen,' said Corporal Warne. 'Let's eat.'

They picked their way through the crowds, enjoying the festive air of the streets. It was just like home, all this; the hubbub of voices, the hawkers in the gutter, the young couples with their shopping bags, so happy to be walking together arm-in-arm after the lonely week, the gay colours of carrots and cabbages and beetroots heaped in the greengrocers', the neat pyramids of brightly-labelled tins in the windows of the provision shops.

It was early in the afternoon but there were queues outside the cinemas already. The concrete paths that intersected the broad lawns around the Town Hall were lined with girls waiting for soldiers and soldiers waiting for girls, and blocked every few yards by groups of soldiers and girls crowding noisily together. Soldiers were waiting in line outside overcrowded restaurants and overflowing canteens, and leaning patiently against the doors of public houses. The great Army lorries came snorting into town, each with another cargo of soldiers; and in every street pedestrians scurried and scuttled out of the path of hurtling jeeps piloted by somnolent Americans.

The two corporals made their way down a quiet side turning near the waterfront and entered a small, shabby restaurant.

The place was almost full but one glass-topped table in the warm corner of the room near the kitchen was unoccupied, the chairs tipped forward against it.

The corporals made themselves comfortable at the table.

A waitress appeared, a thin pleasant girl in her late twenties.

'They're here, Phyl,' she called into the kitchen, and came to the table. 'We kept your table for you.'

'Hello, Dinah,' said Corporal Meadows. 'Hello, Phyl.' The second waitress appeared, plump and thirty, gleaming black eyelashes, cheeks raddled with powder, strong legs in shabby stockings.

'Any ham left?' asked Corporal Meadows. 'You kept some for us, didn't you?'

Phyllis ran for the ham, while Dinah set out plates and bread and tea things. The corporals began to eat concentratedly while the girls stood doting over them. At other tables people rapped with spoons and grumbled and waited and went unserved.

'I bet you had a terrible week,' said Phyl, 'with all that weather.'

'Ah,' said Corporal Warne, his mouth full. 'Where's the sugar, lass?' She ran for the sugar.

'What about some pastries?' said Corporal Meadows. Dinah vanished and returned with some pastries.

'Are you going back tonight?' asked Phyl. 'Or are you in town for the weekend?'

'Going back tonight,' said Corporal Meadows, lifting the last shreds of ham on his knife. 'More tea?'

She poured the tea.

'We'll meet you when you've finished,' said Corporal Warne. 'Six o'clock?'

'Six o'clock.'

The corporals rose and pulled their berets from under their shoulder straps. 'What's the damage?' said Corporal Warne.

'Two cups of tea,' said Dinah. 'Let's say fourpence and forget the rest. Where you off to now?'

'Canteen,' said Corporal Warne. 'They serve you a good meal there. See you at six.'

* * *

It was hot in the Town Hall. Alfie Bradley, standing against the wall watching the dancing couples drift by, his tunic unbuttoned halfway to the waist, was scarlet and sweating and lonely.

On the dais at the end of the ballroom a six-piece band thumped and brayed epileptically, its noise mingling dizzily with the babble of conversation and the clatter of crockery in the refreshment bar. Hundreds of little Lana Turners smiled up at the faces of their soldier partners; dozens of Betty Grables leaned languidly on the chests of lank Americans. There was a waltz, the lights dimmed, the couples moved dreaming in the darkness, treading on clouds, their faces turning bright yellow, wine-red, bilious green under the revolving limelight. There was a quick-step. Charlie Venable came whirling by like a Dervish in battledress.

'Come on, Alfie boy,' he yelled, 'let's have some action.'

Alfie grinned feebly, afraid to look down at the girls who sat primly and expectantly against the wall.

He had to dance; he knew he had to dance, with Charlie here watching him and half the platoon in the hall. That girl there, he thought; no, she's too old. That one, then? No, don't be silly. She dances too well. What about that one? He moved towards her, then relaxed – vastly relieved – against the wall as she was whisked from her chair by a sailor.

But this one, Alfie, this one, this one. She was sitting just across the hall, her hands on her lap, watching the dancers with a fixed smile of misery on her face. She looked young, terribly young, even younger than Alfie; she had a plain blue dress on, an unremarkable dress, and unremarkable brown hair. She was thin and pale and badly made up. She leaned forward a little on her chair, her shoulders rigid. She did not dare to look about her. She was waiting for someone to ask her to dance. She must have been waiting a long time.

Alfie charged clumsily across the hall. He was standing before her now, bold with fright.

'Dance?' he asked huskily. He waggled his thumb stupidly at the crowd of dancers.

'I don't mind,' she whispered.

He took her and held her loosely, a foot from him, and steered her into the press of dancers.

'What's your name?'

'Floss,' she whispered.

He took her round in an awkward turn.

'My big feet,' he said. 'Did I hurt you?'

'Oh, no,' she whispered. 'You dance lovely. What's yours?'

'Alfred.'

'You in that lot up the camp?'

'Yes.'

'The Wessex, aren't you?'

'Yes. Whoops.' They collided with another couple, lost the step and stood hesitantly for a moment before they moved off again.

Alfie was counting the step silently to himself: one-two-three, one-two-three, one-two-three.

'I know,' she whispered. 'My sister goes with a boy in the Wessex. He's a cook. His name is Matthew. Do you know him?'

'Matthew what?' asked Alfie.

'Matthew Southcott. He's a tall boy. He's here with her now. I came with them.'

'I know him,' said Alfie. Poor Floss, he thought, they brought you along like they brought me along.

The dance ended and he asked her eagerly if she would like some lemonade. He led her to the bar and fought his way through to the counter. It took him a long time to get served. The harassed woman behind the counter took little notice of him when he spoke up amid the clatter or tapped nervously with a shilling. He felt silly and apprehensive, jammed there in the crush, and he kept looking over his shoulder to see if Floss was still there. Each time he looked she smiled at him, nervously, over-brightly. She pushed through to him. 'It doesn't matter,' she said, 'really it doesn't. I'm not all that thirsty.'

'Yes you are,' said Alfie, 'you wait over there.' He brought her the lemonade at last and stood over her proudly.

They went in to dance again. He looked out for Charlie Venable and steered Floss ostentatiously past him.

'Hi-yer, Charlie,' he called.

Charlie held a thumb up in greeting over his partner's shoulder.

'Do you come here often?' asked Alfie. He felt more confident now. Each time they bumped into someone Floss was thrown against him and after a while she did not move away, but kept close to him. Is this how they tell you, Alfie wondered, is this how they tell you it's all right?

'Every week,' she said. 'I don't go out otherwise. Except to pictures. Do you come here every week?' she asked. 'I haven't seen you here before.'

Her hand was holding his more tightly. It was damp. Alfie streamed with sweat, and drew away for a moment to mop his face apologetically as they danced. He wondered what was going to happen next; what he ought to do. He was terrified.

'Oh,' he said gruffly, 'I drop in sometimes, with the boys.'

There was a pause, and they stood in the centre of the hall waiting for the next dance.

'Not fed up with me yet?' asked Alfie.

'Ooh, no.'

Somewhere amid the din and chatter the band began to throb again. 'I like this one,' she whispered. She began to sing, 'When the Blue of the Night' over his shoulder. Alfie whistled the tune softly with her. They were very close together now, and her dry hair was tickling his mouth.

There were more dances and more intervals. Alfie sweated, trembled inside his battledress, lost track of time.

'I'm not much of a one for dancing,' said Alfie, dancing, 'it doesn't mix with football.'

'You're doing very well,' she said solemnly, not whispering now.

'You been to pictures this week?' she asked, following him to the bar again.

'Went today,' said Alfie. 'Up the Regal. Saw Rita Hayworth.'

'Do you like Rita Hayworth?'

'Mmm. Smashing. Smashin' dancer. Not as good as you, though.'

'Go on, pull the other one.'

'I will if you'll let me.'

'That's enough from you.'

More dancing. More searching frantically for something to say. More long pauses when they both sang with the band to cover their shyness. Then Alfie managed to say it. He had been trying for an hour to say it.

'Comin' outside?'

Outside meant the dark gardens around the Town Hall, the dark lawns and shrubberies, where the soldiers went with their girls. Outside was what Floss had been dreading; Alfie, too, had been dreading it, but something was driving him forward, Charlie Venable whirling past and half the platoon in the hall watching him; oh, to walk out through that door with a girl on his arm and half the platoon there to see.

'Comin' outside?' His throat was parched and painful.

'Yes.' She was whispering again.

They were walking, now, in the cool darkness, watching the cigarettes glowing like fireflies in the shadows, and away through the distant trees, the yellow-lit trams go clanging by. They were listening to the sound of their shoes on the concrete path, pretending not to see the couples huddled on the benches or to hear the whispering and scuffling and giggling in the night. Neither of them could think of a thing to say.

'Floss.' He halted her and thrust her to the side of the path. He spoke in a rasping whisper. The back of his mouth seemed to be all stuck together. 'Floss, do you like me?'

Floss whispered something; he could not hear it. He pushed his face against hers suddenly and kissed her. She did not put her face up, and he kissed her on the side of her nose; he could taste the powder.

He found her mouth and kissed her again, pressing her soft and unresponsive lips back hard against the gums. It wasn't very thrilling. He grew angry and pulled her hard against him, groping with his hands. Her body was rigid and resistant. She began to tremble violently and wept quietly. The quick anger faded suddenly and he was terrified again; he, too, began to tremble.

'Don't cry.' He could think of nothing less awkward to say. She still wept. He wiped her eyes clumsily with his handkerchief. 'Don't cry, Floss. It's all right. I didn't mean anything, Floss.'

She snuffled once or twice more, then blew her nose and was quiet again.

'What did you come out here for, Floss?' He was full of bewilderment, and despairing. He would never understand them, he would never know what they wanted, he would never know when, he thought with anguish.

'I didn't know,' she whispered. She wiped her lips with her handkerchief. 'All the other girls do,' she said brokenly. 'I thought... I thought... ' She began to snuffle again.

'I was frightened,' she said. She looked up at him suddenly. 'You

35

were frightened, too,' she said accusingly, 'you were shivering like anything.'

'I wasn't,' said Alfie stoutly.

'Oh yes you were.'

'Oh no I wasn't.'

'You've never done it before?' she said. 'Have you?'

'Who?' said Alfie. 'Me? That's what you think.'

'Go on,' she said derisively, but sure of herself at last, and with affection, 'you can't kid me.' She squeezed his arm.

Alfie laughed, relieved and at ease for the first time. 'Oh, Floss,' he said. 'Oh, Floss...' He put his arm round her and they walked back to the hall together.

* * *

It was very late, and it was growing cold on Floss's doorstep.

'How old are you, Floss?' asked Alfie.

'Nineteen.'

'Honest? You really are?'

'Yes.' Indignantly. 'Why shouldn't I be? Don't I look it?'

Hastily. 'Oh, yes, Floss. Yes, honest, Floss.'

'How old are you, Alfie?'

'Twenty. Nearly twenty-one.'

'Have you got many other girls, Alfie?'

'Well,' he weighed his words importantly. 'None really serious. What about you?'

'Mmm,' she pouted, 'if I told you, you'd be as wise as I was.'

'Come on, Floss,' said Alfie, 'I want to know.'

'Why do you want to know?'

'Why d'you think I want to know?'

'Well,' she said solemnly, 'if there was, there won't be now!'

There were footsteps on the stairs inside the house and, through the blackout, the glow of a light switched on.

'It's mum,' she whispered, 'she's waiting up.'

Alfie was terrified. 'Next week,' he said, 'at the dance?'

She nodded, and let him kiss her. Alfie could hear footsteps in the hall now. 'Look,' he whispered urgently, 'not at the dance. In the afternoon. Two o'clock outside the Town Hall. All right?'

She said, yes. They kissed again and Alfie fled.

He hurried through the empty streets, walking faster and faster until he was running, still hoping to catch the last truck back to camp. Inside he was glowing, he was radiant. A girl of my own, my Floss, a girl all of my own; and half the platoon there to see.

The last trucks had rolled back into camp. The crunch of feet on the cinder paths and the banging of doors had ceased. Under the black-bellied clouds split by canyons of green moonlight the camp lay silent again.

Corporal Shuttleworth stood sagging against the door of his hut, drunk, vomiting, ashen of face. He entered the hut, closed the door uncertainly behind him and stood swaying in the flickering firelight.

He reeled about the still hut, bumping into beds, collapsing once on to all fours and rising drunkenly to his feet. He was mumbling softly to himself and singing unintelligibly.

Two men slipped out of bed and padded barefoot across to him. They took him by the arms and led him gently to his bed. They pulled his boots off, lifted him and slipped his tunic off, unbuttoned his shirt and trousers and spread his blanket over him.

'You bitch,' they heard him mumbling, 'you rotten, lousy bitch.'

They went back to their beds and slipped into the warm blankets, luxurious with the heat of the stove against their feet.

'Oh, Sal,' moaned Corporal Shuttleworth; and the men lay under their blankets listening. 'Oh, Sal, Sal, Sal,' he wept himself softly to sleep.

CHAPTER SIX
The Doggy Boys

MEN LOOKED UP SUDDENLY under the rims of their steel helmets as the stillness of the morning was broken by the rush and rustle of shells overhead; they cowered against the sodden turf as the first shells exploded a few hundred yards in front of them, then rose and moved forward behind the barrage as the whistles shrilled. Everywhere they were rising up from the tall grass, from folds in the ground, from sunken roadways, until the hillside, empty of life a few minutes before, was alive with the khaki figures that swarmed forward behind the thudding barrage.

Cast up high on the desolate beach behind them lay the empty landing craft; more craft were lurching forward in the shallows, their ramps crashing down into the water, their loads of riflemen streaming ashore; and more were bobbing in on the white-capped waves that came racing endlessly out of the Channel mists.

The morning was cold; the men shivered in their wet clothes. But the knife-edge of winter was gone from the wind; the sun shone in a pale sky. At the end of March there was already a breath of spring in the air; and the naval guns were booming somewhere over the skyline, the shells were rushing and rustling overhead, the thudding barrage was flinging up billowing domes of earth and smoke in front of the Fifth Battalion.

'Get on there, lads, get on there.'

Colonel Pothecary strode uphill, swishing at the grass with his cane, driving the leading sections closer to the barrage.

'Come on, my lads, up on your feet; you won't get hurt.'

The colonel plodded on past a group of men who had flung themselves to the ground. He went on for twenty yards, not looking round, drawing dangerously close to the leaping barrage, until he heard the men on the move again and slackened his pace to let them come up with him.

They were moving parallel to a road which ran on lower ground; the roar of armour came to them from the road and they saw tanks scuttling inland like a procession of beetles. Aircraft muttered high above their heads in the pale sky.

'Never seen nothing like this before,' panted Charlie Venable, as he squirmed under a fence and scrambled to his feet behind Mister Paterson, the platoon officer.

'This scheme's a kind of dress rehearsal,' said Mister Paterson, not turning his head as he talked. 'I heard that Monty was around somewhere watching it.'

'Reckon they mean business at last?' Baldy had come scrambling up alongside Charlie Venable.

'Well, if they don't,' said Charlie,' after all this, they won't see me much longer.'

He leaped across a ditch, landed on all fours in the mud and rose painfully to his feet: 'I'll resign,' he said, 'I'll bleeding resign.'

Night had fallen, and the men of the Fifth Battalion were lying under the hedgerows, trying to sleep, with only groundsheets and greatcoats to keep them warm.

The colonel came down the road, pipe in mouth, greatcoat collar turned up, listening as he walked to the mutter of voices in the darkness.

Some of the men were asleep, the desert veterans, the men who could sleep anywhere; but most of them were talking in the darkness, some complaining of the unaccustomed hardships to which they were being exposed, some speculating and exchanging gossip about the coming invasion. One group huddled together at the crossroads singing sentimental songs; their soft, sweet, adolescent voices left the colonel with a bewildering sense of pain. Long after he had passed them by he remembered the round, red faces, framed by the upturned collars, illuminated for a moment in the darkness by the glow of cigarettes. Quiet, uncomplicated farmers' boys from the west, the kind who formed a sort of passive mass in the battalion, the kind who – unlike the Jocks and the Cockneys and the Geordies in their midst – never gave him any trouble. My bumpkins, he thought, my poor little bumpkin boys, what is there in store for you, do you ever dream what there is in store?

39

Two days later they were back in camp. The manoeuvres were over, but the feeling of tension which they had brought to the battalion remained. The unreality which had always overhung their training, the sense of playing some game without purpose, was gone. At last they felt that they were at war; they began to think in terms of a living enemy. Excitement and impatience began to stir among them. The newspapers were full of the battles in Italy and of the Soviet breakthrough in the Ukraine. Men of the Fifth Battalion, thinking back later to those days, remembered the hush that fell in the crowded canteen at nine o'clock every evening as the wireless news bulletin began, the way the clatter of cups suddenly ceased, the groups of men waiting, all their heads turned towards the loudspeaker up on the wall, and the quick stirring of triumph among them as they heard the latest Soviet Order of the Day, the new lists of towns liberated. Every day's newspapers brought fresh news to provoke rumours and debates in the huts. The King had been visiting Army units, Montgomery was touring the war factories, a Cabinet Minister announced in Parliament staggering production figures of what he called, amid cheers, 'Weapons for the invasion'. And – for the first time in three years – there were air raids again; the German bombers were over London and the south coast towns every night, with quick, savage attacks. The men of the Fifth Battalion, lying in their warm blankets every night, heard the beat of engines as the bombers crossed the coast, and the distant answering of the guns; and they were glad that the battle was near.

* * *

'Higgsy.'

Sergeant Bender put his cards down and looked round. 'Higgsy,' he shouted again, 'come here, you dozy bugger.'

Higgs came padding across the hut.

'Higgsy,' said the sergeant, 'they think I'm taking the mickey. Tell 'em.'

'Tell 'em what?' fenced Higgs.

'—', said the sergeant, 'tell 'em what you told me.'

'Oh,' said Higgs; 'about leave, you mean?'

He waited for a moment while an engine under test roared and screamed. His questioners were sitting round a coke brazier in a corner of the long, gloomy workshop of the carrier platoon, to which Sergeant Bender belonged.

'Well,' he said with relish, 'it's going to be cancelled.'

He waited again to measure the effect of his announcement on the men round the brazier; Sergeant Bender; Jock MacGuinness, a chunky little miner from Fife; Charlie Venable; Dickie Crawford, a scowling fair-haired boy from the London markets; Rabinowitz, the big, black-haired Jew; and Baldy. They all looked sceptical.

'Cancelled, he says,' jeered Rabinowitz, 'so they should ring up Hitler on the telephone and tell him in advance to get ready. Higgsy,' he said, 'you're *meshuggah*.'

'*Meshuggah*, am I?' Higgs was indignant. 'Want to bet? Here...' he pulled out his wallet and banged a handful of notes down on the table. 'Come on,' he said, 'come on, you big, black bastard. Let's see yours. Come on. Let's see your money talk.'

'Quiet,' said Dickie Crawford. 'You're like a couple of old cows at closin' time. Is that the griff, Higgsy?'

'May God strike me dead if it ain't,' said Higgsy fervently. 'Have I ever given you a wrong tip? The Old Man was talkin' about it breakfast-time. You know he was at Brigade last night.'

'The sods,' Charlie Venable was on his feet, the angry blood flushing up into his cheeks. 'My leaf comes up next week. My bleed'n' leaf I been sweatin' my guts out for this last three months.'

'It's just your bad luck,' said Sergeant Bender. 'It had to come some time. You know what Churchill said in Parliament about the invasion.'

'That strikebreaker!' said Charlie bitterly. 'I'm 'aving my leaf. — Churchill. — Monty. — the Old Man. And — the lot of you,' he said violently. 'I'm 'aving my —ing leaf.'

'All right,' said Sergeant Bender amiably, 'have your leave. We ain't stopping you. What's so wonderful about leave all of a sudden?

There's women there. There's women here. There's beer up there. There's beer down here. You can go to the dogs up there. I take your bets down here. What you worrying about?'

'You,' said Charlie bitterly. 'You don't want to go home, you don't. You're afraid of your bleedin' missus. Me, I'm thinking of the ol' lady. She's been up there for three months in them new raids. I want my bleedin' leaf.'

'Big mouth,' grunted Rabinowitz, 'you'll stop here and like it. Your deal.'

Charlie took the cards and shuffled. 'They've 'ad it,' he said as he dealt the hand. 'From me they've —in' 'ad it. No leaf, no soldierin'. That's Charlie Venable.'

The little community that had its meeting place in the carrier workshop was known throughout the battalion as the Doggy Boys, because its members were linked by their common passion for greyhound racing. The dogs were their hobby and their livelihood. They were scientists of form; not gamblers but shrewd and cautious financial speculators who invariably prospered. They had their friends on every track; they collected and pooled and sifted every day a mass of information, scandal, gossip and rumour; they knew when a dog was doped and when a dog was going to win. They shared their knowledge but they rarely let it leak out. To them the rest of the battalion were the mugs, the poor, benighted cash customers who enabled bookies and Doggy Boys alike to live in comfort.

Within the battalion they were an aristocracy. Members of the blessed freemasonry of the tracks, confident that wherever they went they would meet 'one of the boys' from Clapton, from White City or from Harringay, they were the wonder of the country boys who formed the bulk of the Fifth Battalion.

They lacked nothing. In winter, when the rest of the men had four blankets each, every Doggy Boy had six. While the rest of the battalion supped on bread and cheese and cocoa in a cold, gloomy dining hall, the Doggy Boys resorted every night to the officers' mess kitchen, where they sat at their ease with only a thin partition between them and the colonel and dined, course by course, with the unsuspecting officers. They were in possession of books of weekend-pass forms and of railway warrants which they had removed from the orderly room; they had hirelings in the office who obediently brought them the battalion's rubber stamp on request. They were as dandified as they had been in civilian life, and had the run of the stores. They ran a thriving black market in boots, socks and underclothes which they sold to the rest of the battalion and to the villagers. When they wanted to get a load of stolen goods out of camp Sergeant Bender would take it out in one of his carriers. Higgs, the colonel's batman, was their servant and spy. The little man had big ears that protruded like butterflies' wings; thanks to him, the Doggy Boys missed nothing. They were Londoners, but they had attracted to themselves the most desperate spirits in the battalion – little MacGuinness, who was gambling mad and who, in a fight, would kick his opponent's face in when he had him down; Sergeant Ferrissey, the lean, dark poacher; Scannock the Scouse, the battalion's most dangerous drunkard, from the slums of Liverpool; and more like them. Yet the Doggy Boys themselves were not desperate characters. They were highly skilled at staying on the right side of the law. They were all masters of insolence and could drive a sergeant crazy and get away with it. None of them was ever drunk; and though they whored with gusto when they were in London, they disdained to pursue the village women to whom their comrades were attracted. Living amongst men who were poor for half the week and penniless for the other half, they all had bulging wallets; and all of them were wildly generous. It was a commonplace in the battalion that you could always cadge a quid off one of the Doggy Boys and no questions asked.

'I knew a geezer once,' said Rabinowitz, 'never knew a blind thing about the dogs. He went down Clapton one night and put a quid on the first race, come away with three. He put it on the second race and took eight. He went on doin' that all the evening, and finished up with three hundred. Never knew a —ing thing about the dogs. Not a thing. I knew the geezer.'

'Jus' shows yer,' said Dickie Crawford.

'If that had ae happened in Glasga,' said Jock MacGuinness, 'the bookies would ae put the boys on him. They'd ae half-kilt the —er and got the money back off him.'

'Bleedin' savages you are up there,' said Bender.

'Ay,' said MacGuinness pleasantly, 'wi' hairy ears. Stand up an' I'll tear yez apart.'

'Just tear these apart,' said Sergeant Bender, spreading his cards on the table.

'Leaf,' said Charlie Venable viciously. 'I'll give 'em leaf. I'll give the bleeders leaf.'

Higgs's prophecy was soon fulfilled. The last days of March brought a series of measures that convinced even the most sceptical of the coming storm. There was a ban on travel to Ireland. The whole of the east and south coasts were closed to travellers from other parts of the country. And leave was cancelled.

On the night of March 31st Charlie Venable put on his overcoat, stuffed his razor and spare socks into the pockets and walked out of the camp. The next morning he was marked absent. A month later he was declared a deserter. Charlie Venable had resigned.

CHAPTER SEVEN
Sergeant Shannon

'HOW DO I LOOK, BOYS?'

Dickie Crawford tightened the buckle of his best battle blouse and, turning slowly, displayed himself to the rest of the Doggy Boys.

From the group sprawled round the table in the corner of the carrier shed came all the noises of a barnyard.

'What you doin' tonight, ducks?' yelled Rabinowitz.

'Come to pappa,' said Sergeant Bender, slapping his knee invitingly.

'Ye're all right, Dickie,' grunted Jock MacGuinness. 'Ol' Nancy Norman'll never be able to resist yez.'

'Think so?' said Dickie contentedly, stopping in front of a fragment of mirror and setting his beret at the correct angle. 'I'll tell 'im a tale,' he said. 'I'll make the cowson cry 'is eyes out.'

He walked towards the door.

'Hook your collar up,' Sergeant Bender said. 'If McBean sees you, you'll be the one to cry your bleedin' eyes out.'

'Who?' answered Dickie, fastening his collar. 'Mac? 'E's all right. I'll drop him a tosheroon.'

More barnyard noises. Even the Doggy Boys could not take seriously the idea of offering a half-crown bribe to the R.S.M.

Dickie paused for a moment in the doorway and faced the April morning.

'Get a basinful o' this,' he said appreciatively, thumping his chest with both fists as he noisily inhaled the cool, salt-laden air. 'It don't arf smell good. Why don't yer go out an' get some exercise, you lazy rotten sods. Up the village an' back free times. Do you more good than playin' brag it will.'

'Exercise,' jeered Sergeant Bender. 'You'd take a bleedin' taxi from King's Cross to Saint Pancras. — off, you, before I do somethin' I'll be sorry for.'

'Wish me luck,' said Dickie, walking away down the cinder path.

'Luck!' Sergeant Bender shouted after him, 'I seen you at the dogs. You got the luck of the Nine Blind Bastards. You don't need no more.'

Dickie Crawford whistled as he walked across the camp, well pleased with himself. The breeze from the sea was keen and exciting against his face; sky and sea and countryside, extending immeasurably about him, made a pattern of pale blue and vernal green. There were white, fast-moving wisps of cloud that challenged him to quicken his pace and, somewhere, a hint of sunshine, a faint, melting warmth against the skin.

Dickie Crawford was a son of the London markets. Shop windows were more beautiful to him than a seascape, sodden black warehouse walls more exciting than a wide horizon, mounds of decaying vegetables in a gutter more sweet than a breeze laden with the scent of wild violets. But this morning the breeze aroused him, the skyline beckoned. He felt strong and exultant – and imprisoned.

The spring was in his blood; Easter was near; and there was no leave. A battle lay somewhere ahead; and there was no leave. Below him in the valley railway lines gleamed. Eighty miles away at the end of those lines was London; the little house leaning forward across a pavement in Camden Town; the markets thronged on Saturday afternoon; the people hurrying to the dogs, tense and absorbed; the girls, gay and challenging in the brassy, brightly-lit saloon bars; and there was no leave.

He stopped whistling; he stiffened his shoulders back and began to swing his arms self-consciously. He was in the administrative section of the camp now, where officers prowled and sergeant-majors lurked.

He came to a hut with the sign ORDERLY SERGEANT over the door. He knocked.

'Come in,' a voice rumbled.

Dickie opened the door and poked his head in. 'Ord'ly Sarnt?' he said. 'Take us up to Nancy Norman, will yer?'

'What for?' mumbled the orderly sergeant, his mouth full of bread and cheese. 'Sarnt-major's job. Go to the office.'

'Nah,' said Dickie, 't'ain't Orders. Pers'nal interview. Private talk. Me an' old Nancy. I booked it yesterday.'

'What you after?' asked the orderly sergeant, buckling on his belt and coming to the door. 'Leave?'

'Compassionate,' said Dickie mournfully. 'I'm in trouble. Dead in trouble. 'E'll 'ave ter let me go.'

'My arse he will,' answered the orderly sergeant. 'Come with me.' Major Norman's office was at one end of a Nissen hut that stood amid a riot of bushes on the edge of a wood. The door of the office stood open when Dickie Crawford and the orderly sergeant reached it, and the office was empty.

''s funny,' mused the orderly sergeant. 'He was here a minute ago.' He looked at Dickie in sudden surprise. 'What you gogglin' at like that?'

Dickie pointed in silence at the thickets.

' — me drunk!' whispered the orderly sergeant in wonderment.

Between the faintly stirring leaves of the bushes they could discern the outline of a man on all fours, his khaki-clothed backside towards them. He raised his head a little, very cautiously, and they could see the gleaming, sleekly-brushed hair.

'Strewth!' exclaimed Dickie. 'It's 'im.'

The man in the bushes jerked round at the sound of Dickie's voice. A bird flew whirring away.

Major Norman climbed to his feet and emerged from the thicket.

'Bird-watching,' he said without embarrassment. 'A civilised occupation. I recommend it, Crawford.'

'Yessir,' said Dickie stiffly.

'Beautiful creatures, birds,' Major Norman went on pleasantly, 'and quite free from human vices. For instance,' he said mildly, 'they don't walk about the camp with fountain pens poking out of their pockets.'

'Yessir,' said Dickie, thrusting the offending pen out of sight.

'Well,' said Major Norman, 'don't let my little sallies upset you. Just relax and come inside.'

Dickie, who had been standing rigidly at attention, followed him into the hut. The major seated himself behind a small wooden table and leaned forward on his elbows, toying with the sweatband of his cap. 'Now,' he said, 'how can we help you?'

'Well, sir,' said Dickie Crawford, 'I'm in trouble. I wondered if I couldn't 'ave a few days compassionate leave.'

'What's happened?' asked the major gently. He picked up a pencil and began poking his pursed lips with it.

'My girl's gorn orf wiv anuvver geezer.'

'H'm.' The major nibbled the pencil thoughtfully. 'I'm sorry, Crawford. But that's hardly a reason for giving a compassionate leave at a time like this, you know. Unfortunately it's not the kind of thing the Army considers to be a disaster.'

'We was engaged,' volunteered Dickie. He had selected this story from among many others that had come to mind because it had seemed to him the one which could the least easily be disproved. Now he began to realise its limitations.

'You haven't been in before to ask for a marriage leave,' the major pointed out.

'No, sir,' answered Dickie, 'I was just goin' to when I got 'er letter.'

'Where is it?'

'Where's what?'

'Her letter,' said Major Norman patiently.

Dickie groped for an answer. 'Oh,' he said. 'I never fought you'd want ter see it.' He picked up his tale triumphantly. 'I posted it straight back to 'er married sister. Asked 'er to talk to 'er, I did.' His eyes shone happily. He felt like a boxer who had fought his way out of a corner in which he was being pummelled; he was beginning to enjoy this.

There was a hint of admiration in Major Norman's gaze now. He, too, was a man able to enjoy the battle for its own sake.

Major Norman clasped his hands in front of his mouth and gnawed both thumbnails at once. 'It's rather a coincidence, isn't it,' he remarked, 'that this tragedy should occur on the eve of Easter?' He awaited Dickie's reply with the sympathetic interest of a man watching a star batsman performing.

Dickie was in his stride now. He came back without a second's hesitation. 'I give 'er all me money ter look after,' he said solemnly.

'She'll go an' do it all in over the 'olidays if I don't get up there.'

Major Norman throttled an impulse to shout, 'Bravo!' Instead he commented sadly, 'You know, Crawford, I'm very sorry for you. Very sorry indeed. But I can only grant compassionate leave if it's a matter of life and death affecting some close relative. That hardly applies in this case, does it?'

'Oh yes, sir. It does, sir.' In for a penny, in for a pound, thought Dickie. 'Me muvver. She's got a weak 'eart. It'll be the death of 'er if she 'ears about this.' A note of emotion crept into his voice. 'You jus' think of it, sir. Me waitin' ter go over the water an' fight, maybe never come back. An' 'er dyin' of worry.'

This time he grinned shamelessly at the major. Somehow an understanding had been established between them. Dickie knew that the major knew he was lying; he also knew that the major did not care; and the major knew that Dickie knew he knew; and he did not care.

As two gladiators might once have fought to the death without reason and without rancour, so Dickie Crawford and Major Norman returned to the fray.

'We'll have to verify your story,' said the Major. 'Of course,' he added, with the gentlest touch of malice, 'that's easily done. I'll wire your local police station. They'll send a man round to check up on the facts. It's the usual thing, you know.'

'D'yer want ter frighten my muvver ter deaf?' exclaimed Dickie Crawford indignantly. 'Sendin' the p'lice round the 'ouse. We've never 'ad no coppers in our 'ouse an' we don't want 'em now. And,' he added, 'it's no use sending 'em round the girl's place. She'd say anything ter stop me getting a leave, wouldn't she? It's only natural.'

The major stared at the wooden table-top in silence for a few seconds, chewing at his nails. He looked up at Dickie and spoke.

'Crawford,' he said reflectively, 'get me the orderly sergeant.'

'Yessir.' Dickie went to the door and called the orderly sergeant in.

'Orderly Sergeant,' said Major Norman, 'take this man down to the cookhouse and find him a job. One that'll last him the rest of the day.'

The orderly sergeant grinned gloatingly at Dickie. 'I got just the job, sir,' he said. The cookhouse drains are blocked up.'

'Oh,' said Dickie bitterly, 'so that's where the smell comes from. I fought it was the sergeants' mess.'

'Quiet,' said the orderly sergeant. 'Salute the officer an' fall out prop'ly.'

'And Crawford.' Major Norman was speaking again, and Dickie halted by the door. 'You're damn lucky it's me you came to see with a story like that. The colonel would probably have had you in the guard-room by now.'

'Yessir.' Dickie made to move off again.

'Crawford.'

Half-in, half-out of the hut, Dickie stopped again and turned wearily.

'Yessir.'

'There'll be a pass waiting for you at the guard-room Thursday night. See you're back in camp by next Tuesday morning. Don't let me down, mind.'

Dickie gaped.

'Mad,' he said wonderingly to the orderly sergeant as they walked off together, 'stone mad.'

A platoon of riflemen in battle order came crashing along the cinder path at the double. Dickie Crawford and the orderly sergeant drew back to let them go by.

'Hep right, hep right, hep right, hep right.' Shannon, a stocky little sergeant, burdened like the rest of his men with steel helmet, rifle and pack, was gasping the step at the head of the platoon. Mister Paterson, Number Nine Platoon's officer, was bounding easily alongside.

There was Easter in the air, with the sun coming up among the veils of high cloud and the cool, damp breeze stirring the hedgerows. The men gulped the sweet breeze as they ran; it stirred their blood as it stirred the leaves in the treetops. They were excited and eager; they ran confidently and unflaggingly.

They left the camp behind them, crossed the main road, stumbled

– cursing and laughing – for half a mile across a field of clogging stubble. In a meadow beyond they slowed down to quick time at the sergeant's word of command and thudded across the turf, slack and breathless now, until there came the merciful halt.

The sergeant gave the order to fall out for a five minutes' break. He drew aside with the officer as the men broke ranks and settled themselves in sprawling groups on the grass. He took a cigarette from the case which the officer proffered him, fished in his pockets for matches and struck a light. Sergeant and officer smoked in silence for a few moments.

Mister Paterson spoke. 'Satisfied with them, Sergeant?'

'Aye,' answered Sergeant Shannon, 'they're game enough. An' they're learnin'.'

'We've been driving them pretty hard these last few days,' said Mister Paterson, 'we'll give 'em something easy this morning for a half-hour or so and then double them back to camp.'

'I'll take 'em on a bit of revision wi' the Bren,' suggested Sergeant Shannon. 'That'll do 'em no 'arm.'

'O.K.,' agreed the officer. 'I'll leave them to you. Fall them in again whenever you want to.'

They stood for a few moments, smoking, looking over the men.

'Know anything about the new chap you brought me this morning?' Sergeant Shannon asked suddenly. 'The Paddy.'

'Mulrooney.'

'Aye, that's him.'

'No. He came in yesterday with the reinforcement detail. We've got him to fill Charlie Venable's place. What makes you ask?'

The sergeant dropped his cigarette end and ground it into the turf. He shrugged his shoulders. 'Nothin',' he said. 'I've got a feeling, that's all. Old soldier, isn't he?'

'By his ribbons. I haven't looked at his documents yet,' said Mister Paterson. 'Think you'll have trouble?'

'I'm not worryin'.'

The sergeant turned to the platoon and shouted. 'All right, my lads, put them tabs out now and get fell in.'

As the platoon jostled into ragged ranks Sergeant Shannon

watched the man he had been discussing. Mulrooney was a great, broad shouldered Irishman, lumbering and clumsy, towering angrily above the heads of the rest of the platoon. His face, red and rugged with muscle, was stamped with sullen lines that never left it; his eyes were small and glittering and suspicious, flickering and never still, the only thing quick about the man. He moved into the front rank and stood with his rifle at ease. Men spoke to him, keen to make a newcomer welcome. He never answered.

'Right now, my lads,' said the sergeant sharply, 'you're like a lot of Old Age Pensioners queuein' up in t' post office. Get fell in properly an' pick up your dressing.'

When the platoon stood in orderly ranks the sergeant turned the front rank to the right and the rear rank to the left, and marched them round so that they formed, with the remaining rank, three sides of a square. He moved into the centre of the square, spread his groundsheet on the grass and told two of the men to do the same. Then he had the platoon's three light machine guns placed on the sheets.

He called three men out. Each lay behind a gun. At his word of command they stripped the weapons down until, twenty seconds later, the parts of each gun lay neatly spread on its groundsheet. Three more men came forward. They dropped to the ground, and as deftly and skilfully reassembled the guns.

Sergeant Shannon looked around him. Most of the platoon were watching intently. One or two seemed bored. The big Irishman stood slackly, looking away over their heads towards the sea. He caught the sergeant's eye and for a moment returned his stare. Then he turned his head and looked out to sea again.

The move was deliberate, studied. Sergeant Shannon knew about men, and he knew that there was a challenge to him here. But he was determined not to pick on the man; he ignored him, and moved over again towards the men at the guns.

Three more men came out. They were just beginning to dismantle the guns when the sergeant heard a rumbling whisper behind him. He knew before he turned that it was the Irishman.

'That'll do, Mulrooney,' he said quietly, 'pay attention now, like the rest.'

'Private Mulrooney,' rumbled the Irishman.

'What's that?' The sergeant straightened up sharply towards him.

'Address me by me rank, Sergeant,' said the Irishman, 'same as I do you. I'm a soldier wid service, Sergeant. I know me rights."

The sergeant sucked at his lower lip for a second. 'You may be with us quite a bit,' he said quietly. 'Why look for trouble? You'd do best to learn to get on wi' the lads an' wi' me. This lawyer stuff'll do you no good 'ere. I know your rights as well as you do, an' I'll not try an' deny 'em to you. Now stand up straight an' pay attention.'

The Irishman straightened up. The other men were watching him now; he did it exaggeratedly, derisively. His face was impassive but his eyes were grinning.

The sergeant ignored him and called the attention of the platoon back to the guns. As he directed the next three men he fought with a little core of worry within. Was he being too easy? he wondered. Was he giving this man the idea that he was frightened of an encounter? Maybe, he thought, I should have acted on my hunch and ridden him from the start. Give this kind an inch and they take a yard an' a half. The Irishman would be clever; he knew that; damned clever, able to goad and ridicule an n.c.o. without saying anything punishable, able to call to his aid every rule in the King's Regulations.

The sergeant looked up to call the next three men. He found half the platoon ignoring the guns, looking instead at the Irishman. Mulrooney stood, turned half-away, leaning on his rifle.

'Mulrooney,' said the sergeant, 'I'll not tell you again. Face your front.'

Mulrooney faced front.

'What's the first thing you do,' snapped the sergeant, 'when you strip a Bren?… Private Mulrooney?'

'No offence, Sergeant,' answered Mulrooney. His voice was unexpectedly soft, and deadly. 'But I was strippin' them guns before you was out o' school. Do you not wonder I don't interest myself in it no more? Look…' He held up his arm with the service stripes on the sleeve. 'Seven years, Sergeant,' he said. 'You'll not be ignorin' them now, will youse?'

Here was the challenge direct. Sergeant Shannon knew that his platoon liked him; but they had not yet been into battle with him; some of them had only known him for this short period of training; he knew how uneasy was the relationship, how easily it could be upset, how quickly he could be discredited. He knew that this man, sullen and alone though he was, had the fire in him and the brute power that would make him contend for the leadership of any group in which he found himself, regardless of rank. Threats or punishment would not stop this man; Shannon knew that. The Irishman had the resource and the prestige of an old soldier; and above all, he would be among the men, day and night, living with them in their hut, while Shannon only saw them on parade; intriguing, provoking, telling his tale with the sly skill of an old soldier. Shannon knew his man; and he knew that the only way to avoid being made a fool of by this towering Irishman was to make a fool of him, to win the rest of the platoon against him, to isolate him. There would be no absorbing of this man into the group; to try would be foolish.

'Out here,' barked Sergeant Shannon, 'at the double.'

The Irishman came out into the centre of the square.

'Smarter than that,' said the sergeant. 'You'll have to learn to move smarter than that wi' us. Get back in t' ranks, an' when I shout "Move!" – let's see you move.'

The Irishman went back.

'Move!'

The Irishman came out – fast. He flopped behind a gun and expertly dismantled it. He climbed to his feet, grinning.

'Are ye happy, Sergeant?' he asked. He knew that he had disappointed Shannon.

'Fall in,' snapped the sergeant, 'an' none of your sauce.' He watched the Irishman's awkward bulk thoughtfully. He had done wrong, he knew, to tackle Mulrooney on his own ground. Weapon drill, everything that was of the parade ground, would be second nature to this man. But there were other things, new things, that were strange to an old soldier. And the man was clumsy.

'Right, my lads,' said the sergeant a few minutes later, 'we'll finish off wi' five minutes of all-in, then we'll have a double back to camp.'

The platoon spread to form a circle. 'All-in' was a battalion custom, a favourite with the men. It consisted of five minutes of close combat. Every platoon had it once a day. The colonel insisted on it as the ideal adjuster of relationships between junior leaders and men. They played it as a game. The officer or n.c.o. stood in the middle of the ring. He would point at one of the men, who would rush him and try to throw him, using one of a hundred tricks the whole battalion had been taught in its close combat training. Whichever of the two men was thrown would remain in the centre of the ring and would, in turn, beckon another man to come forward and give combat. No weapons were permitted; nothing else was barred. The only way out of the ring was to throw an opponent.

Now Sergeant Shannon was in the centre of the ring. He knew who he was going to call out; the whole platoon knew. He beckoned to Mulrooney and the Irishman moved forward, his head down. The sergeant was gambling his leadership now on one throw. If this man were able to fling him to the ground, he would be finished as a leader; Mulrooney would always be his master.

Mulrooney was circling him cautiously, keeping well away. The sergeant moved to keep him face-to-face. Brains, he wondered, or brawn? Was this just an old soldier circling him or had he learned new tricks? How much had this man picked up in seven years of brawls in streets and pubs and Indian brothels?

Now! Oh, by Jesus, it was so simple, and the answer came in a second as the Irishman came rushing in towards him with his arms outspread. The sergeant ducked in, seized Mulrooney's arm, and flung the whole weight of the man – without even feeling it – over his shoulder. So simple, and in a second, and as pat as the gym instructor ever did it.

Mulrooney scrambled to his feet.

'Had enough?' mocked the sergeant. Mulrooney rushed again and Sergeant Shannon threw him again. Mulrooney lay on his back, scarlet and panting.

'On your feet, Mulrooney,' said the sergeant. 'Try one of the lads. They can all throw you,' he taunted, 'every one of 'em.' He knew now what he had to do. A primeval wrestle in front of the platoon wasn't enough. He had to let the men come forward now, every one of them if necessary, and one by one get the better of the Irishman. Every man in the platoon must leave this meadow feeling a better man than Mulrooney, despising him.

'Well, Mulrooney,' said the sergeant, 'who's it to be?'

Mulrooney looked around him. His eyes were glowing with hatred. He stabbed with his finger at the biggest man in the platoon, Baldy.

Baldy came in and they grappled. For a moment the Irishman got his arms round Baldy and the sergeant leaned forward anxiously. Then Baldy's smooth, gleaming skull came up and cracked sickeningly against the Irishman's chin. Mulrooney lurched like a swaying tree. Baldy ducked in at him and Mulrooney crashed to the ground.

The sergeant stood over him without pity. 'Try again,' he said coldly, 'you can't quit till you've thrown someone.'

'Is it me that's said I was wantin' to quit?' roared Mulrooney. His angry eyes grinned again as he beckoned to little Alfie Bradley.

At once there was absolute silence. The man next to Alfie tried to pull him back, but little Alfie, eager, blond, light and lithe as a whippet, was in the ring.

'I'll kill youse,' Mulrooney snarled, and rushed at the boy. All the choking hatred for these men banded against him exploded, in a mad, blind blood-lust. He was going to obliterate this boy, to trample him into the grass. There was a sudden shout of anger from the watching men and the whole platoon surged forward as Mulrooney swung a great, steel-shod boot in a murderous kick at the boy's stomach. But Alfie whirled aside like a flicker of light, and raised his own boot; and Mulrooney's shin, with all the mighty force of Mulrooney's own kick, met the edge of Alfie's boot. The Irishman screamed shrilly and toppled, writhing to the ground.

Again there was silence. Then a hubbub of excited talk. The sergeant's voice slashed through the noise. The platoon quietened and re-formed its ranks.

Mister Paterson, who for the last half-hour had been sitting on a stile watching the platoon, was back at Sergeant Shannon's side. He looked down at the sprawling, gasping Mulrooney without making any comment.

'Are you comin', Mulrooney?' asked the sergeant pitilessly. Mulrooney struggled to his feet, picked up his rifle and limped into the ranks.

'Sling your rifles, lads,' called the sergeant. 'Left turn. By the right – double march!'

The platoon moved off at a smart double. Mulrooney, in agony, struggled along with them, bobbing up and down with his damaged leg. No one tried to ease the pace for him; there was no mercy. The sergeant, knowing that this was the time to complete his victory, increased the pace. The men, eager to identify themselves with the sergeant, to match him in strength and endurance, followed his lead.

Mulrooney dropped back, yard by yard, through the ranks. His face was streaming with sweat, convulsed with pain and rage. He tried bitterly to keep up, but fell behind the last file. No one even looked round. The platoon drew away and left him pounding agonisedly across the ploughed field. At last, at the limit of endurance, he admitted defeat and slowed down to a walking pace.

The Irishman was tiny and alone now, and limping far behind. The platoon came out on to the main road and slowed down to quick time.

Mister Paterson took his place at their head and gave them the command to march to attention. 'Come on, my lads,' urged Sergeant Shannon, 'never mind those aching legs. This is where you show what you're made of.'

With their rifles smartly at the slope they marched into camp with pride and precision, in perfect ranks, in perfect step, arms swinging waistbelt-high like linked shafts in a single machine.

'Platoon…' they knew they were being watched from a score of huts… 'halt!'

The platoon cracked to a halt and held it. Not a man wavered. With the same precision they turned to their front, picked up the dressing, ordered arms and stood at ease. They waited; in silence they waited for Mulrooney. Minutes later he reached the parade ground and limped to his place in the ranks. He was finished, beaten; this moment of silence was as decisive, as ceremonial as a drumming-out.

'Platoon… officer on parade… dis-MISS!'

They broke ranks and rushed for their hut. Mulrooney limped after them, alone.

They were finished training, now, until after Easter. They had four days of leisure which they might spend in camp or in the neighbouring town.

Alfie Bradley changed hurriedly into his best battledress and packed his valise. He was blindly happy, intoxicated with triumph, enraptured, exalted. In front of the platoon, in front of the whole platoon, he – Little Alfie, the baby, the pet to be patted on the head, had brought a giant crashing to the ground. In front of the whole platoon. And now he was going to his girl, to stay for a weekend at the home of his own girl, his Floss.

The whole platoon was busy, noisy, happy.

Only Mulrooney lay face downwards on his bed, silent and immobile.

And, across the hut, Baldy sat gloomily on the edge of his bed, and wondered when he would hear from Charlie Venable.

CHAPTER EIGHT
The Mad Major

AT TWENTY-SIX MINUTES past three on the morning of Friday, April 28th, the sergeant commanding the guard of the Fifth Battalion was sitting huddled over the stove-in the long, gloomy guard-hut. The off-duty men lay sleeping in a row along one side of the hut, sprawled snoring or muttering on their palliasses with blankets heaped over them. There was a little pool of dim light in the centre of the hut, cast by the glowing stove and the flickering hurricane lamp at the sergeant's feet. The rest of the hut was in darkness. A bucket of cocoa stood on the stove. The sergeant had a Woodbine between his lips; his eyes smarted with fatigue and there was a fog of sleep inside his head. He wore his greatcoat like a cloak over his drooping shoulders. A clock on the bench beside him ticked thunderously in the silence; thirty-four minutes before the next change of sentries. He settled forward somnolently.

Away in the darkness at the end of the hut the door creaked. The sound crept into the guard commander's reeling consciousness; he was fingering the upturned collar of his coat and beginning to turn on the bench when the explosion split the silence into a million ringing fragments and the violet, blinding flash lifted him to his feet and flung him forward against the stove. In the next seconds, as the roar of the explosion lingered in the men's ears, echoing as if contained in the gloom and smoke of the guard-hut, it filled with fresh noises; the crash and clatter of the falling cocoa bucket, the moaning of the sergeant lying scorched and writhing by the red-hot stove, the clatter of boots and the confused hubbub of the off-duty men lurching, dishevelled, to their feet; violent voices outside the hut; and in the air, the sharp and heavy stink of high explosives.

Hubbub and confusion; men bending over the sergeant, dragging him out of the pool of cocoa that spread slowly on the dusty concrete; men ramming home the bolts of their rifles and staggering towards the door of the hut; and a voice, high and sharp as a whiplash:

'Turn out, the guard!'

The voice rallied the guard; each man stopped for a moment in his tracks; a startled tableau in the gloom.

'Outside, the guard! Come on, come on!'

They knew the voice. Savage understanding seeped into them. They clattered out of the hut and formed up in two lines in the darkness outside. The sergeant raised himself painfully on to all fours, then heaved himself up on to his feet. His left cheek was a great grey blister. He followed the men out.

The voice was lashing at them again in the darkness.

'Three minutes to turn out the guard. What do you think this is, a war or a Sunday afternoon picnic?'

The men, plunged suddenly into the chill of the night, stood shivering over their rifles, peering sullenly at the slim, straight officer who stood before them; Major Maddison, commander of 'B' Company, the orderly officer for the night. He turned on the guard commander who stood, swaying slightly, beside him.

'I'll have you stripped for this, Sergeant,' he said. The words, flat, hard, even, whined past the men's ears like bullets. 'Sleeping over the stove on guard. If we'd been overseas you'd have all been dead men by now. I came past your sentry without being challenged. I opened the door of your guardroom. I threw a sixty-nine grenade in among you. If I'd been a German I'd have tossed something a little more deadly at you, you know. You'd have all been in little pieces now. And I could have taken a raiding party into the camp and shot the whole battalion to ribbons.'

The sergeant licked his dry lips and pressed his clenched fists into his sides. He could not speak.

'Get the men into open order.' The voice was lashing at his blistered face again. 'I'll inspect them.'

The sergeant croaked a command and the ranks parted. Major Maddison moved from man to man, flashing the light of his electric torch on each man's equipment to see that it was correctly worn, groping over their bodies with his hands to see that their water-bottles were full and their pouches packed with ammunition. Within the rough, enveloping clothes lean bodies cringed and stomach muscles contracted with shame and anger under the insulting hands.

The officer was away from them again, and the voice came at them once more from the dawn darkness.

'Change your sentries, Sergeant. Put the sentry on Number Three post under open arrest. And consider yourself under open arrest.'

The sergeant brought his rifle up on to his left shoulder and slapped the butt in salute. He spoke a final command and the men broke ranks and returned to the hut. He stood watching as the officer walked briskly away. Pain stabbed at his face and humiliation choked like a fist in his throat; his eyes were hot and he wished he were able to cry.

The men were waiting for him inside the hut.

'That mad bastard,' one of them growled, as the sergeant closed the door behind him and leaned wearily back against it, 'you can get him court martialled for that.'

'Them sixty-nine grenades,' said another, 'they're dangerous things. Mister Paterson told us. They can blow your foot off if they drop near enough. And that little lead pellet in them can kill someone.'

The 'sixty-nine' was a training grenade, made of bakelite, dangerous only for its noise and its blast; its use in confined spaces was forbidden.

The sergeant was standing with his hands over his face. One of the men came close and pulled the hands away. 'Christ,' he said, 'the sergeant's hurt. Look here.' The others crowded round.

'I fell with my face against the stove,' mumbled the sergeant. He was very weary now, and beginning to feel sick. 'I'm going down to the sick bay, get it dressed. Take over, Bill.'

'Don't worry, Sergeant,' his corporal said. 'Go down with him, Quinan.'

Quinan put his arm round the sergeant's shoulder and turned him to the door. They went out together.

'That Maddison,' said the corporal when they had gone. 'He'll get a bullet in the back one of these dark nights. He's mad. He's raving mad. That's all he lives for, war. War, war. He's not human.'

'D'ye mind, Corporal,' said one of the men, 'on that scheme last February?... would nae let his company have any rations for two days. The rest o' the battalion was feedin' a' the time. He said ye had tae lairn tae go hungry in war.'

'I know,' said the corporal,' he was instructing up at the div. battle school when I was there. A platoon was coming off the assault course and he heard 'em grumbling. He took 'em back round the course twice, without stopping. Half of' em dropped in their tracks. He went round with 'em. You know,' he said, 'he's a tough bugger. He trains like a bloody greyhound. He don't smoke. He don't drink. They say he can't stand the sight of women.'

'What the —ing hell does he live for, then?' asked one of the men.

'I told you,' answered the corporal, 'war. He thinks there's nothing like it. He thinks doin' all this kind of thing's for our own good. At the battle school he used to come on parade and point his stick at you and shout, "What's your job, soldier?" And you had to come up to attention and shout back at him, "Kill."'

The corporal walked back to the centre of the hut, settled himself on the bench by the stove and pulled his greatcoat across his shoulders like a cloak.

'Kill,' he said gloomily, 'God knows what they'll do with men like that when all this is over. Shut 'em up like mad dogs, I reckon.'

'They'll send the likes of him out to India,' said one of the men, 'to keep the blacks in their places.'

'Ye mean they'll send 'em tae the Clyde,' said the Scot who had spoken before, 'tae keep us in our places.'

'Maybe,' said the corporal. 'Go up to the cookhouse, Scotty, and ask the night cook for some more cocoa. Get into kip, the rest of you.'

The men settled down on their palliasses, some to sleep, some to talk softly. The corporal leaned forward, relaxed, towards the heat of the stove. Around him there was a splash, flickering and undefined, of dim light, from the hurricane lamp and the glowing stove. The rest of the hut was in darkness.

There still hung faintly in the air the acrid smell of high explosive.

'Who's the last one?' asked Colonel Pothecary.

'Scannock, sir,' said the R.S.M. stiffly, 'he's up again – drunk, fighting, fouling the billet, insubordination. And Major Maddison's waiting to see you after that.'

'Scannock,' said the colonel wrathfully. 'I'm sick of seeing that man. Last time he was in here I talked to him like a Dutch uncle. It doesn't seem to have done him any good.'

'It's only the drink he lives for, sir,' said the R.S.M. 'He's Irish from Liverpool – as low as they come – live like a pig, work like a horse, drink like a fish.'

'Bring him in,' said the colonel.

Low as they come, thought the colonel, as the prisoner and his escort marched in, their boots crashing in quick time on the concrete floor. He looked up at the man in front of him. Scannock the Scouse, the terror of the battalion; Scannock who, drunk, would knock a man down and trample his face with steel-shod boots; Scannock, a queer, sagging shape of a man, a paradox of muscle and fat; Scannock, who could stand to attention with his back rigid but his shoulders hunched hopelessly forward; Scannock, an uncomprehending face of seamed brown leather, a wide low forehead overhung with untamed black hair, a flat nose with broad nostrils that would twitch in anger, a glimpse and a stench of yellow teeth between slack and drunken lips.

The sergeant-major was intoning the charges, the row of men in front of the colonel's table stood rigidly, each swaying ever so slightly on boots that might have been cemented into the floor.

The colonel scratched with the third finger of his right hand at the green baize tablecloth, counted the holes and the inkstains, plucked at a loose end of green cotton. Like another race of beings, he thought, remembering the grey Liverpool streets, the shrieking tenements, the smell of cabbage-water and dust and babies. He thought of his own home, the rooms sweet and full of sunlight, and the homes of his workpeople. He knew them well, for he lived on good terms with his people; their world was the same as his and the little front parlours in the little Lancashire streets were all neat and clean, with shining brass and gleaming blackleaded grates, the curtains fresh, the windows fanatically cleaned, the mirrors, the crockery, the souvenirs from Blackpool all spotless. He knew these people and liked them, but...

'Sir, at twenty-three forty-one hours on Saturday, April 29th...' The corporal was staring over the colonel's shoulder at the wall and reciting his evidence with the toneless regularity of a machine gun.

...but, thought the colonel, hearing the evidence remotely as a noise, without taking it in... but deep down at the bottom of society, far below workpeople like his own, feared and hated and despised, indeed, by them, was a submerged multitude of Scannocks; in every port, in every great city there was a slumful of them; the ones who worked the longest for the lowest wages; who were little trouble to their employers because they were like beasts of burden and because they rarely came together, like other working men, to fight, but fought each man for himself, more often than not with each other, wild, anarchic beasts.

The corporal was still giving evidence. The colonel half-heard him, each phrase registering as a confirmation of his own thoughts. 'Entered the camp drunk and singing... urinated in the doorway of his hut... fell asleep across his bed fully clothed... spewed and urinated in his bed... refused to clean his own bed area in the morning... said it was the billet orderly's job... swore at his section corporal, was insubordinate, was placed under close arrest... '

The colonel knew Liverpool. When he was a young man, before he had set up on his own, he had worked in Liverpool as a foreman, with a dozen Scannocks under him. He could see Scannock's home now, while the corporal was talking; the room on the stone landing, the man and his wife hiccuping drunk and wrestling across the stale bed, with bugs dropping on to the pillow from the wet, peeling wall and the children huddled staring in the other bed across the room; the wife, ancient at thirty, with puffy red face, wispy hair and flaccid, pendant breasts, squatting over the stinking bucket in the corner; the husband washing in the bowl of scummy grey water that had been standing three days on the table.

Scannock was speaking now, defending himself lamely, gutturally. The man did not understand, he did not know, he must be wondering what these people were so upset about. We took him, thought the colonel, for the first time in his life since he escaped from school at fourteen; we took him and we made him wash every day and take a bath every week; we made him cut his hair and shave and even, occasionally, clean his teeth; we put him in a clean uniform and made him change his underclothes every week; we made him eat with a knife and fork and leave the table clean; we made him use the lavatory; we made him do these things, but he can't for the life of him, see why; to him these things are not yet the normal processes of life; they are silly, irksome, unnecessary things the Army is forcing him to do. And when he's drunk, when he wets his bed, when he swears at another man who happens to wear two stripes on his sleeve, there's nothing, in the foggy hinterland of that brain of his, to tell him he is doing wrong. When I sentence him it won't be a punishment to him, but a blow struck at him by his enemy, the world. Justice has as little logic for him as a lorry charging down upon him from a Merseyside fog.

'Twenty-eight days field punishment,' said the colonel. 'Ask Major Maddison to come in, please.'

He told Maddison to sit down, and watched him pull a chair up to the table.

'Smoke?'

'No thank you.'

The colonel decided to be firm with the man, but his resolution melted now that they were face to face. After all, he was a damn good soldier; the brigadier thought the world of him and even the divisional commander remembered his brilliant record as an instructor at the battle school.

'There may be trouble about that grenade in the guard-room, Maddison,' he said at last.

'Why?' Maddison asked coolly. He was short, alert and tensed as a terrier, hard and slim.

'There'll be an Accident Report Form going through.'

'Did the sergeant make any trouble?' asked Maddison.

'No,' said the colonel, 'he came and asked my advice.'

'What did you tell him?'

'I asked him to forget the matter.'

'For my sake,' the colonel had said to the sergeant. Ill at ease with his officers, whom he regarded as gentry; as people a cut above himself, the colonel was on the most intimate of terms with many of his n.c.o.s. Alone, once in a while, with a sergeant or a sergeant-major, he would speak as frankly, confide as gratefully as a brother.

'You asked him?' echoed Maddison bitterly. 'God, this British Army is a pantomime. You asked him? I catch the man out, I teach him and a dozen other soldiers a lesson they'll never forget – a lesson that may save their lives one day – and because he gets a burn and a bit of a fright I'm supposed to tremble in my shoes. Do you know,' he said, 'what they do in the German Army? They strap officer candidates in an electric chair and put shocks through them to see how they endure. That's soldierliness. That's manhood.'

'That's the German army,' said the colonel, 'this isn't.'

Major Maddison had spent a holiday in Germany before the war. He still remembered with a glow the green-clad giants goose-stepping in ranks of sixty-four past the saluting base with burnished spades at the slope; the young men playing volleyball, naked and sunburned, their blond hair all tousled; the avenues of white masts with their flags streaming and crackling in the wind.

'More's the pity,' said Major Maddison. 'Every time I look at my men I wonder what'll happen to them when they meet the enemy. Do you know what we've got to beat?' he asked. 'Soldiers, Spartans, trained and hardened from boyhood, as men should be trained, ruthless and fearless and in love with death, as men should be. Not dragged to war but going gladly. Bound by the mystic communion of soldiers.'

The colonel, like everyone in the officers' mess, had often heard Maddison talking about the mystic communion of soldiers. Neither the colonel nor the most be-ribboned of his officers had any idea what this was.

'And then,' said Maddison disgustedly, 'I look at this rabble of mongrels we're trying to turn into soldiers. Slack and spineless in their clothes. Hands in their pockets and cigarettes in the corners of their mouths as soon as your back's turned. Their only pleasures are to sit with their women gaping at a cinema screen...' Maddison hated the women whom he saw clinging to the arms of his men; shrill and white-skinned creatures, soft as slugs, stinking of scent; they turned his stomach '...or drooping about in a dance hall listening to some Jewboy crooning through a microphone. Not a warrior among them.'

'Thank God for that,' said the colonel heartily. 'Warriors, indeed!'

'My job,' said Maddison obstinately, 'is to train men for battle. The divisional commander approves of my methods. We had casualties every day at the div. battle school. There were no complaints. I was told it showed that I was doing my job. What I want to know now is, are you going to back me up or aren't you?'

'What I want to know;' said the colonel, 'is... are you going to stick to safety regulations or aren't you?'

'Sweat saves blood,' said Maddison. 'The men must learn to suffer.'

'Brains save sweat,' said the colonel. 'Teach the men to think.'

'I'll teach them to fight,' said Maddison. Sometimes he had hope for his men; sometimes he felt kinship with them. When a man came crashing through a barbed-wire obstacle, the pencil-lines of blood seeping up from the scratches on his face; when a platoon came streaming over a wall like a pack of hounds, Major Maddison would feel excited and close to them; and when, especially, he went down as he often did to see them going through the showers he would stand in the doorway of the long, noisy hut, watching the fine slender young men padding about, naked and gleaming wet behind veils of steam; he would grow exultant with emotions which he could not fathom and would walk away flushed with love for these men of his – until, looking down into the lane below the camp, he would see a soldier strolling with his girl and would feel sick and contemptuous once more.

The colonel stood up behind his table. 'You'll teach them to fight,' he said curtly, 'and I'll tell you how. No more sixty-nine grenades in huts. No more of your little pranks with guncotton. Keep out of trouble, Maddison. There's going to be enough trouble for us all in a very little while.'

Maddison smiled grimly. 'Trouble you call it? I say speed the day.'

The colonel could stand the other man's presence no more. 'That's all,' he said. 'I shall treat it as a disciplinary matter next time.' He looked at his wristwatch. 'I think I'll get a wash before dinner,' he said. 'I'll see you in the mess.'

'I wish I could make up my mind about that man.' The colonel, back in his own hut, was drying his hands on a towel and speaking to Noel Norman.

'Maddison?' said Norman languidly. 'The men call him the Mad Major. He's a horrid little tick. He gives me the creeps. He was a superintendent, or something, before the war, in the police force.'

'Yes,' said the colonel. 'When he sits there hammergagging about the mystic communion of soldiers I don't feel it's safe to trust my men with him. Yet he's a brave man – a good soldier – I'm tempted to say the best officer in my battalion. Better than you, Noel.'

'That isn't much of a recommendation.'

'Yes,' said the colonel. 'I can't help respecting him for that.'

There was an uneasy silence for a moment.

'Heard from the boy yet?' asked Norman.

'No,' said Colonel Pothecary. 'There's no news yet. But the shipping office says it's quite normal. They're away at sea for weeks at a time.' His voice was obstinately cheerful. 'Can't post letters at sea, you know.'

'Of course,' said Major Norman. 'Let's go down to dinner.'

'I reckon we'll be away before he's back from this voyage,' the colonel went on. 'Did I tell you what they were saying up at Brigade this morning? There's a regular sweepstake on up there. I even heard the date named.'

'May the fifteenth?' laughed Norman.

'Yes,' said the colonel. 'How did you know?'

'My batman told me,' answered Major Norman. 'He heard it in the Horse and Hounds.'

The door banged behind them.

'May the fifteenth, I tell you.' There was a crush of men arguing round the wall map in the battalion canteen. At the green, beer-stained tables there were as many men discussing, disputing, crowding over newspapers, as there were playing cards. Every night there was news to make them more excited, more argumentative. The air offensive over France and Germany was reaching proportions that had never before been known. A security ban had been applied to prevent foreign diplomats from entering or leaving the country and from sending any communication out of the country. A Defence Regulation had been introduced to permit the control of roads in southern England for military traffic. All overseas travel had been cancelled. England was being sealed off from the outside world. German E-boats were prowling the Channel in search for the massing of an invasion fleet; the newspapers reported clashes at sea, and the men of the Fifth Battalion themselves sometimes heard, in the silent night, the distant thudding of guns from across the dark waters.

'May the fifteenth.' Alfie Bradley sat in a corner of the canteen, insulated from the noise around him, his heart thumping with excitement, penning the ninth page of a letter to his Floss – whom he would be seeing again in five days' time.

'May the fifteenth.' In the corporals' clubroom at the end of the canteen hut Corporal Gonigle sat at the piano, lackadaisically playing 'Some of These Days' in a broken, discordant rhythm. Meadows and Warne, two corporals who had come back from the desert, lounged against the piano and talked in turn at him through the blue cigarette smoke.

'Ay,' said Meadows, 'another couple of weeks, man, an' we'll be duckin' mortars again.'

'Blood an' shite,' said Warne gloomily, 'more blood an' shite.'

Gonigle had not yet been in battle. He had spent a lot of time, mostly at nights, wondering what it would feel like ducking mortars.

'May the fifteenth, is it?' he said. 'I must say it's the openest secret I ever heard.' He went on thumping the piano doggedly.

May the fifteenth, thought Major Maddison standing in front of the mirror on the wall of his hut, Lord God of battles, let it be so. May the fifteenth. He saw himself, bleeding and smoke-blackened, lurching forward through a rain of down-pattering earth with the explosions reverberating in his ears; he saw himself snatching up a rifle and wielding a reddened bayonet; he could feel it meeting the coy resistance of flesh; there was a tickle of delight in his biceps as he thought of it.

He fumbled in the drawer of his bedside table and took out a little box. There was a strip of ribbon in the box. He stood close to the mirror and held the piece of ribbon against his left breast. With the first finger of his right hand he stroked the right side of his moustache. Something moved in the corner of the mirror. He turned angrily – still holding the ribbon to his breast – and saw his batman standing in the doorway of the hut.

'Get out,' he snarled. 'And knock before you come in next time.'

The batman, panic-stricken, bobbed an unnecessary salute, slammed the door behind him, and scuttled away to the officers' mess kitchen to tell how he had seen Major Maddison trying on the ribbon of the D.S.O. in front of his mirror.

CHAPTER NINE
Before the harvest

TO THE MEN of the Fifth Battalion there had never been a summer in their lives like the one through which, as in a dream, they were now living. The sun was rich and radiant upon the land and the trees burgeoned into great rustling clouds of glinting green; the shoots of young corn sprang from the furrows, taller and thicker each week until the brown ploughland was hidden from view. Blue-shadowed clouds piled, snowy and serene, along the skyline, towering into an immensity of sky in which the day long drone of aircraft echoed and lost itself, robbed of its menace.

Strange, dreamy days of false tranquillity; a group of men sitting cross-legged on the grass, sleepy and sodden with sunshine, while an n.c.o. stood among them explaining the mechanism of the little wooden mines that were waiting, on the beaches across the water, to blow their feet off; a soldier and his girl lying behind a hedge, drunk with the scent of the hot grass, while on the road a few yards away the endless convoys rumbled down towards the coast; men marching or huddled over their rifles in lorries, the significance of what they were doing lost in the fascination of watching a rabbit scampering across the road, a lark tumbling from the blue vault of the sky, a child waving from a window.

The mysterious processes of war were carrying the Fifth Battalion, as if on a conveyor belt, towards its destiny. Somewhere in an office a folder was being taken from a steel cabinet, a great mechanical card-index was whirring, teletypers were clacking their frantic messages; harassed, middle-aged brigadiers were sitting round long, oak tables adding up battalions and divisions, fumbling with slide-rules, running nicotine-stained fingers down the columns of ammunition tables. A thousand clerks and typists were working overtime, irritably and impersonally as if it were an income tax collection that employed them, instead of the destiny of six hundred sunburned men idling in their shirtsleeves on a hillside above the sparkling Channel. In Whitehall, in requisitioned country mansions, in hidden headquarters burrowed deep underground, the lights burned day and night, girls scurried about corridors clutching big, buff envelopes. Somewhere there were these thousands of people planning a war, people with a strange fever stirring among them, the same fever that sweeps the floor of a Stock Exchange; people whose typewriters, sealing-wax rubber-stamps, filing systems were the instruments that shaped the dark tomorrow of the Fifth Battalion; and it was as if by some strange chemistry that, as the fever of suspense mounted among these pallid legions, it drained from the men of the Fifth Battalion. Like the spring of an over-wound watch, the tension which had been five months growing in the camp on the hillside broke in the sweet, May sunlight.

Perhaps it was because certainty had come to them at last. For months they had wondered: will it be? Now they were sure. Living in their own land, among their own people, they were as isolated from their homes as if they were abroad; sealed off in a coastal area that was forbidden to travellers; without leave; their mail censored by their officers as if they were abroad; the convoys crowding the roads day and night; the landing craft bobbing in rows in the harbours. In the first days of May every man in the battalion had to reduce his kit to assault scale. All spare clothing was collected by the quartermasters. Personal belongings were stowed in the men's kitbags which were labelled and sent to their homes at the Army's expense. Now they were stripped for action, and suddenly sure of what was to come.

The men were fit; their strength surged exulting in their veins. They were trained, they were armed and equipped as they had never been before. They were confident, and all their excitement vanished. They were calm now, and outwardly indifferent, waiting without impatience or foreboding. They gave themselves up to the summer, and passed their days in a stupor of content, drugged with sunshine, anaesthetised by the scent of blossoming flowers, lazy and languid and enchanted by the richness that was coming to life all round them. The dizzy hours and days reeled past them as they slept in the sun, lulled by the drone of bombers and of bumble-bees.

Private Oh-Three-Seven Smith was a little anxious.

'I reckon we'll be away before the harvest, Corporal,' he said.

'I reckon we will.' Corporal Shuttleworth was not very interested.

'Going to be a good harvest this year, Mister Hodge is thinking.'

'Is he?' said Shuttleworth. 'Leave me alone. I'm writing.' He was huddled on his bed with a writing pad on his knees. The blanket was littered with crumpled sheets of paper.

Oh-Three-Seven Smith pulled his beret on to the back of his head. 'I'll be off down there,' he said.

Shuttleworth looked up. 'Down where? Hodge's Farm again?'

'I promised Mister Hodge I would. It's been hard going getting the barley in in time.'

'Christ Almighty!' Shuttleworth exploded. 'It's been the hottest day in weeks, we've been marching our feet off all day. Look at the others... look at 'em...'

Most of the platoon were sprawling on their beds, with their boots off, smoking.

'And you go off,' he went on, 'to break your back working. It's knockin' off time now, Smithy. Lay down an' give your feet a rest.'

'They'll be working for three hours yet in Ten-Acre Field,' said Oh-Three-Seven Smith, 'till its gets dark. There's a lot to do down there.'

'He's a mean bugger,' said one of the men as Private Smith went out, 'he kills himself workin' every night for a couple of bob.'

'It's not the money,' said Shuttleworth, 'he likes it. There's a lot o' these swedebashers go down the farms every night to put some work in.'

There were, in fact, many men in the Fifth Battalion whose greatest pleasure was to work on the land whenever they could get out of the camp. They came from the farmlands of the western counties in which the battalion had originally been raised. Successive dilutions had flooded the battalion with men from all parts of the British Isles but there was still this core of countrymen, a kind of passive mass within the battalion of big, beefy, awkward lads with shy, red faces, whose names rarely made news or even figured on the charge sheets, who spent their evenings (when they were not out working) sitting quietly on their beds talking to each other, writing long letters or grubbing in the enormous parcels of food they were always receiving from home. They had the reputation of being miserly with money and generous with food. They were poor hands at gambling and past masters at rabbiting. They were easy to pick out in the dining hall, where they clenched their knives and forks in their fists and, bending low over their plates, shovelled vast quantities of food into their mouths humbly and absorbedly. They were good soldiers, enduring, uncomplaining, not without initiative but rarely inspired. Their speech was a delight to hear, broad-vowelled and leisurely, full of rich, rolling r's.

Oh-Three-Seven Smith made his way down the lane and along the main road past the village with the relaxed, unhurried gait of the countryman who saves his energy for the work to come.

He had been enjoying himself these last three weeks. It had been a race, down on Hodge's Farm, to get the last crops sown by the beginning of May, to get the barley in and drill the swedes and mangolds, to broadcast the grass and clover seeds for next year's hay and get it harrowed in.

They would be just about finishing the job off tonight; it gave him a pleasant feeling inside to think of a job like that accomplished. After that the evenings would be more leisurely; there would be a lull, during which tractors and equipment would get fresh coats of paint to protect them from the weather, the beams of the barns would be creosoted again, the mangolds ground for the bullocks and fresh stocks laid in of fertiliser and cattle feed.

And there would be time for talks with Mister Hodge. What a man that Mister Hodge was! Private Smith had never known a farmer like him; young, and full of science – he had been to one of those agricultural colleges – and always ready to teach. He could tell you all about the soil, chemistry, not the old stuff that the old men mumbled about in the corner chair down the pub, and all about every disease that every animal in the farmyard might ever get, and how to feed them, and how to look after the poultry, and all about drainage – he would bend over a map and mark out lines on it just like an officer, and in a few weeks that field would be as dry and firm as you could want.

'Evenin', Mister Hodge.' He was taken by surprise. He had not expected to see Hodge coming down the road towards him, at this time of evening, when the sky was still pearly with sunlight. And Charlie Benbow with him, too.

'Hello, Tom. It's saved you a walk, meeting us. We've finished up in Ten Acre; we're just going down to the Ploughman to celebrate. You'll come, won't you?'

Tom. He was a nice man, Mister Hodge, and his wife a nice woman; she laid a lovely supper in front of you. For the last five years Private Smith had grown unaccustomed to being called Tom. He only heard the name from his mother when he was home on leave. In the battalion, he was one of a tribe of Smiths, each of whom bore some distinguishing title. There was Sanitary Smith, the chief latrine-wallah (sometimes known by a more pungent and equally alliterative nickname), and Smith-In-The-Signals, and a score of other Smiths each of whom had been trained to accompany his surname with the last three digits of his Army number. So that when Tom Smith saw a finger jabbed at him and heard a voice bark, 'What's your name, you?' it had become a reflex for him to jerk to attention and answer, 'Oh-Three-Seven Smith, sir.'

It was nice, in the evening, to come out of camp and leave the saluting and the sentries behind you, and to sit in the kitchen at Hodge's place or in the public bar at the Ploughman among kindly farming folk who called you Tom. It was the next best thing to being home with mother.

They were turning in through the door of the Ploughman, and settling themselves in their accustomed places at the plain wooden table. Private Smith preferred this dark, dingy, low-beamed little four-ale bar, with its sawdust-covered floor and the same dozen and a half farmhands gathered every night, to the gaudy, rowdy Horse and Hounds at the other end of the village, where most of the battalion flocked to crowd bawling around the strident piano and to woo the fancy women of the district. At the Horse and Hounds you poured beer down you till you had to spew it up; at the Ploughman you sat with friends and made your pint last.

Oh-Three-Seven Smith sipped his ale appreciatively and listened respectfully to the conversation of his seniors. Under their elbows on the table there were newspapers, with stories of thousands of bombers roaring over Europe, with headlines: KING'S MESSAGE TO HOME FLEET – GOD SPEED BEFORE THE BATTLE. But tonight, among his friends, Private Smith spoke not a word about bombers or battles, but talked happily of pigmeal and ribrollers, seed-harrows and granular fertiliser.

'You're getting busy up at the camp again, Tom,' remarked Mister Hodge. 'We could hear the rifles going all day on the range.'

'Ah,' said Tom, 'we're never finished training.'

'Balloon'll be goin' up soon, by the look of things,' said Charlie Benbow.

'Before the harvest,' said Tom. That was the only thing that worried him. He paid little heed to the battalion's warlike preparations; he never wondered what might be in store across the water; certainly he had never known the breath of fear. But sometimes he felt a little anxious because he would be taken away before the summer was at its height, and just when Mister Hodge, who had so much to teach him, was getting interested in him. 'I don't think I'll be with you for the harvest, Mister Hodge.'

Mister Hodge laughed heartily. 'Never you worry about that, Tom, lad,' he said. 'You'll have your own harvest to get in by then. Eh, lad? You deserve another pint for that. Drink up, Tom, boy, and I'll get you one.'

'I'll be sorry for all that, Mister Hodge,' said Tom solemnly. 'I've never been on a farm like yours before. All this science. It's a good thing for a farmer, knowledge.'

'There's always after the war,' said Mister Hodge. 'If your mother'll let you stay away for a year or two more, I'll be pleased to have you with me. Anyway, we shall be friends, shan't we, and write to each other? You're going to write when you're away, aren't you, Tom?'

Tom blushed. 'If it's all right with you, Mister Hodge. Oh,' he said, as Charlie Benbow brought another pint along, 'I haven't finished the other one yet.'

They fell to talking about the war again. The newspapers told of fresh victories in Italy and of a great Russian offensive in the Crimea.

'Old Staylin,' chortled Charlie Benbow, wiping a spot of froth from his straggling moustache, 'he's the boy. He knows what he's doin' of all right. More than some of them over 'ere.'

'They say,' Tom butted in, eager to repeat a joke that was going the rounds of the Fifth Battalion and which represented almost the sum total of Tom's political knowledge, 'they say old Stalin's sent a telegram to Churchill, askin' if he sh'd stop at Calais or come on over here.'

They all laughed. Old Charlie thumped the table with his huge fist. 'Ah,' he said, 'he's the boy all right. Told 'em to burn the crops, 'e did. Burn the crops, 'e told 'em. An' they did.'

Tom laughed again, immoderately. He was light-headed with happiness. The talk flowed on around him, but he did not hear it. He was thinking only on Mister Hodge's words. 'There's always after the war… I'll be pleased to have you with me.' To be a free man, and to work here, with Mister Hodge and Old Charlie and the others. There was no war for Tom Smith, and no thought of tomorrow's battle in his mind; only after the war, and the job at Hodge's Farm.

He became attentive again. Mister Hodge was speaking to him about poultry. Tom's mother kept hens. Mister Hodge knew all about hens, and gave Tom regular advice about them, which was faithfully passed on to Mrs Smith in a series of long letters.

'Send your mother this, Tom,' said Mister Hodge, putting a pamphlet on the table. 'If she hasn't got it already it'll be of interest to her.'

'I'll copy it out, Mister Hodge,' said Tom sturdily, 'and keep this one for myself to learn from.'

He was light-footed with joy as he walked back to camp, later, in the cool dusk. A job with Mister Hodge. Science. Knowledge. It was a proud thing, knowledge.

He swung into camp.

'Good night, mate,' said the sentry.

'Night.'

Tom Smith was Oh-Three-Seven Smith once more.

It was close to midnight and in the stuffy hut with its end windows blacked-out, most of the men were asleep. Only round two beds, on each of which a man crouched writing, was there a flicker of candle-light.

Corporal Shuttleworth crumpled a sheet of paper and threw it savagely away. He paused for a moment and cocked his head, listening. Far off, in the night, he heard the distant mutter of aero-engines. Another raid. They came over every night, now, to bomb the port a few miles away. There was little danger here in the camp; but every night there was the noise of the bombs and the guns to remind the Fifth Battalion of another reality beyond the summer's heat.

He began to write again: My Dearest Sal — . He stopped. His lips shaped the words. 'My dearest Sal — .' What would she say when she read that? Would she laugh? Or cry? Or tear it up? Or show it to the other chap? That was the worst thought of all, the thought of Sal showing it to the other chap. He had been trying to write for weeks, as the prospect of going away drew nearer. Sometimes he prayed, in an anguish of impatience, for the day to come and with it the end of this misery; then, thinking of the day, and of going away without even seeing her again, the pain would come back, more heartbreaking than ever, almost more than he could bear. Love – love on the pictures was one thing; but Corporal Shuttleworth's love was a rat gnawing at his heart, a physical burden that drained him of bodily strength and left him ill and absent-minded, unable to eat for days, sleepless, dazed, always close to retching. There was only drink to help him sometimes, and then only for a little while, to forget the wife who had left him, the strapping, blonde girl who had scarred him with her contempt.

The roar of engines was loud overhead now, and higher by an octave than before. The first guns began to slam and the bursting shells coughed in the sky.

He bent to his letter again. My Dearest Sal — . How to write

78

this time? He had begun a hundred letters and posted none. How to write? – to appeal to her pity? – to recall the happiness of their first months of marriage? – to play on her desire for security? – to try and turn her against the other man? – to let her know that he would soon be going into battle? (But she might be glad, he thought with terror, she might be glad, she might wish me dead.) More than once he had written to hurt her, to rouse her anger, had filled pages with foul words and bitter accusations. He had torn these letters up like the rest. My Dearest Sal — .

The hut shook and the doors rattled with the banging of the guns. In the night sky the din of engines was deafening as the German bombers-turned overhead to make their run in towards the port.

My Dearest Sal — . Corporal Shuttleworth stuffed the writing pad under his pillow, blew the candle out and crawled underneath his blankets. The pain was like a cord tightening round his throat. 'Soon, soon, soon,' he prayed under the blanket, 'dear God, put an end to this soon.'

The other candle-light burned on. Private Oh-Three-Seven Smith was writing to his mother. He peered at the pamphlet by his side and copied a phase painstakingly; then turned back to the pamphlet.

Cod liver oil as a two per cent addition to any mash is worthwhile. It helps health, growth and fertility. Calcium in some form, as oyster or cockle shell, limestone grit or dust, or even as crushed chalk, is necessary for bone and shell.

There was the dull, spreading broo-oom of bombs exploding, and the hut quaked. Private Smith hardly noticed it.

Although animal protein in the mash is required, experiments have shown that ten per cent is the maximum, and this may be reduced to five per cent by using fishmeal with five per cent of soya-bean meal.

Every battery in the area was firing now. The anti-aircraft barrage was a wall of sound through which the noise of the bombers' engines penetrated fitfully. Private Smith finished his letter and licked the envelope thoughtfully as shrapnel clattered on the corrugated iron roof of the hut.

He blew out his candle. 'Good night, Corporal,' he whispered across to Shuttleworth's bed. There was no reply. He pulled his blanket up over him. Outside, the raid was at its height. Private Oh-Three-Seven Smith rolled over, grunted, pushed his face against the straw-filled bolster, and fell fast asleep.

CHAPTER TEN
Days of waiting

AT CLOSING TIME on a Saturday night towards the end of May, Privates Blair and Richardson, riflemen of the Fifth Battalion, came reeling out of a public house to find themselves lost in a stifling white fog of smoke. They only came into town once a week and this was their first intimation that this seaport town, which each day became more crowded with troops and transport waiting for the invasion, was being hidden every night under a vast smokescreen.

They lurched along the pavement, supporting each other, laughing and spluttering inconsequentially at each other; two stocky little Yorkshire tykes with Africa ribbons on their tunics and too much beer inside them.

It was funny and mysterious and bewildering, this pungent, blank whiteness in which they wandered, alone amongst crowds, the pavement heaving under them and their heads a whirl. They suddenly heard voices harsh and loud in their ears and turned truculently, looking for trouble, to hear the voices fading eerily away in the smoke. They could hear footsteps, snatches of song, girls laughing and squealing in mock protest. Faces appeared briefly and vanished past them; and every ten paces or so one of them would step off the kerb with a jolt and sit in the gutter, quaking with laughter, until his comrade hauled him up on to his feet again.

They lurched on, zigzagging across the pavement to collapse in the gutter or stumble into a shop doorway, with no idea where they were going; and both of them were as lost and lonely inside as their bodies were in this ghostly street. Way-aye, man, make way for a soldier. And, wrapped inside that, the chill human core of terror at a new departure, the gnawing, desperate impatience at the waiting for an unknown day.

Somewhere, beyond the woolly, white smoke, a clock struck eleven. They heard buses go by every few minutes, the last buses. As they heard each bus pass they waved their arms wildly and yelled and screeched; dimly they were aware that they had to get back to camp. The buses grumbled away into the smoke. The streets had emptied; there were few voices now.

'Hey, Geordie,' sniggered Private Blair, who had staggered away to his left, 'look here.' He was leaning against the bonnet of a jeep.

Private Richardson toppled forward into the jeep and crawled into the front seat. 'Aye, aye, man,' he said, 'three cheers for the ol' battle buggy.' Private Blair was still clambering in as the jeep jerked away from the pavement.

'Sort 'em out, Geordie lad,' he shouted as Richardson fumbled with the controls, 'they're all there.' He was standing, swaying, in the back of the jeep, holding on to Richardson's shoulders. 'Put your foot down, Geordie!'

Geordie put his foot down; the smoke, the glimpses of shopwindows, the gleams of light through the blackouts, went streaming away past them, and the night wind battered at their faces.

'Yahoo-oo.'

'Yahoo-oo.'

'Ya-hippee-ee.'

Darkness had seeped into the smoke and they flung their Redskin yells into a frightening gloom as the jeep swerved to and fro across the deserted tramlines.

The smoke thinned; they could see the stars above them and the trees flashing past. They were heading out of town, but in which direction they did not know.

They were travelling on a main road, bordered by dense, dark woods. Along the roadside, for mile after mile, were parked convoys of great, silent trucks waiting their turn to move down to the docks, to the waiting ships.

The jeep was hurtling along the white line now, at its maximum speed. Blair and Richardson were singing at the tops of their voices, intoxicated anew by the roaring wind. The grey ribbon of road came flying towards their headlamps. They had a second's glimpse of a road junction ahead of them. On a sudden impulse Private Richardson jammed the steering wheel over to the right.

'Rommel,' he screamed into the darkness, 'here we come!' The jeep turned the corner at seventy miles an hour and exploded into the back of a ten-ton lorry.

The Fifth Battalion had suffered its first casualties.

'It's the waiting,' said Colonel Pothecary, 'it's getting on their nerves.'

'It's getting on mine,' said Noel Norman, sipping his whisky. 'What price May the fifteenth now?'

'The Brigadier says it can't be before June the fifteenth now.'

'What's so sacred about the fifteenth of every month?' asked Norman. He squirted more soda-water into his glass. 'First it was March the fifteenth, then April, then May, now June. I suppose it's one of those things like having an "r" in the month.'

'It's the tides,' explained the colonel, 'the Brigadier was telling us. It's something to do with the tides; I can't remember exactly what.'

He reached for the decanter and refilled his glass.

'You know,' he said, 'there's such a thing as over-training a battalion. That's what I'm afraid of now. I told the Brigadier it was hard to keep a training programme going in these circumstances. D'you know what he said?'

'What?'

'"Give 'em drill, Pothecary, give 'em drill."'

'It's strange,' Norman held his glass up to the light and frowned at the grains of cork floating in his whisky. 'Higgs opened this bottle with a penknife, the little beast. I was saying, it's strange how you can get a sort of change of mood almost overnight. All of-a sudden you feel it, one morning. Nothing happens, not a word is spoken, yet you can feel it right there on parade.'

'Feel what?' The colonel could not understand. 'I don't follow. D'you think I'm letting them get too slack? Surely it's better to let them rest than to drive them too hard? They'd only get stale that way. There's nothing more for us to do now but wait. Or do you think we should have more games? Pendleton's driving his crowd mad with football and paper-chases, say it's good for their morale. Should we be doing that?'

'I don't think it's that exactly,' said Norman. 'Tell me, how do you feel?'

'How do I feel? Well, I feel pretty confident.'

'Yes?'

'I feel prepared. We've got everything we need. We've – well, we've sort of cut the painter. Here we are living with our kits packed to assault scale, our equipment all buckled together ready to slip on, our pouches full of ammunition. Our mail is censored and we can't go home. Damn it, Noel, we're ready to go. That's how I feel. Ready to go.'

'Precisely. Now imagine how one of your own riflemen must feel. He's just as ready, just as impatient. He's confined to camp far more than you are and he knows much less about what's going on. He's living just now in a fever of impatience. In a little while he'll start getting desperate. That keen edge that we've spent all this time sharpening will get blunted. That's what's wrong.'

'Yes,' said the colonel. 'Do you know what they've started chalking on the transport?'

'"No leave, no babies"? I saw it on a wall in town last weekend.'

'A slightly different version. "No leave, no Second Front." '

'I shouldn't take that too seriously.'

'Of course not, but it's a sign, Noel, isn't it?'

'So was what happened to Blair and Richardson. And so are the charge sheets; men punching each others' noses and slanging their n.c.o.s all over the shop.'

The colonel stroked his nose.

'I suppose,' he said, 'it's these flaps we've been having that have unsettled them. A couple of weeks ago this place was like a holiday camp. Nobody gave a damn.'

'These flaps' were a series of test embarkations that had taken place during the previous fortnight. Startled villagers and citizens of the seaport town had seen columns of infantrymen trudging, on four different occasions, down to the docks and filing aboard landing craft. Each time the rumour had spread in the town that 'it' had started. Each time the troops had returned and the civilians, arguing in groups at their front doors, declared that it had been called off again, or that it had all been done to fool Jerry's spies, or that it was only a practice. In fact these embarkations had been carried out to enable the Movement Control organisation to time them and ensure the accuracy of its schedules.

Norman nodded. 'The embarkations shook them up a bit. I think the first time they all imagined it was the real thing. Since then, they've really started feeling the suspense. Oh, to hell,' he said suddenly, 'this is my fourth. Neither of us has drunk like this before.'

'I'll give you a game of rummy.' This was an innocent occupation to which the colonel was much addicted.

'You're an old robber, aren't you? I lost ninepence to you last night. You must be out to ruin me.'

'Lock, stock and barrel,' chuckled the colonel, shuffling the cards.

'Have you heard the story about the fifteen Poles and the girl in the railway carriage?'

He dealt the cards deftly.

The events of the past week had indeed aroused the men of the battalion from their summer torpor; not only the test embarkations, but the sight of fresh units arriving day after day, dispersing to encampments among the woods where they waited, together with the Fifth Battalion, for the order to embark; the roads choked with tanks and artillery moving down towards the sea, the women running out of the houses to offer apples and jugs of tea to the festive crews. The battalion's drivers, returning from their errands, told of huge parks of transport and equipment stretching for ten miles and more at a time along the fields on both sides of the main London road. Others, who had been down to the port, described how the streets near the waterfront were cordoned off by military police and barred to the public, with more troops piling in every hour to squat on the pavements and await their turn to embark. Rumours thrived, mad and fantastic rumours; and the days, which a week or two before had gone spinning lazily by, became a torment.

NO BEER – Private Scannock spelled out the sign painfully. He stood in doubt for a few moments, looking at the card nailed to the door of The Ploughman. It took time for the meaning of things to register in Private Scannock's mind. No beer; and they were dry at the Horse and Hounds as well.

'It's a sad thing, Scouse, when there's no beer for the likes of us.'

He recognised the Irish accent, the ingratiating voice.

'Reckon there's any up Wintersley?' he asked, turning towards Mulrooney, who was standing across the road in the dusk.

'There'll not be any left there by now,' said Mulrooney, 'with the rest of the brigade quartered up there. No, Scouse, it's cocoa and bed for you and poor old me tonight.'

Scannock swore. There was a well of savagery in his breast, thrusting up in him to find an outlet. Drink and battle were the only ways he knew to give vent to it. Both were denied him, and he was desperate.

'Come for a walk, Scouse,' said the Irishman, 'it'll do ye good.'

Scannock was not used to having friends. There were few men in the battalion who cared to go drinking with a dirty, inarticulate Liverpool bruiser. Mulrooney, himself alone and at bay, had found him sitting by himself in the canteen one evening and had bought him a couple of pints. Since then they had gone out drinking together several times. There was no liking between them; neither was capable of this. But Scannock, with his dim and groping brain, found in the other a quick cunning on which he could lean. Mulrooney, in turn, had his own reasons for cultivating this dumb and desperate man.

'It's a cryin' shame,' he said, as they left the village behind them, 'the way they treat us boys at a time like this.'

Scannock did not answer.

'Don't ye think so, Scouse?' the Irishman urged.

'How d'you mean?' Scannock grunted.

'Why,' said Mulrooney, 'it's like kings they should be treating us now, should they not! What do they pay us? Not enough to buy a good night's drinking. What can we do, now, with the few pieces of silver they fling at us every week?'

Scannock stopped and looked at him suspiciously.

'Out with it, Paddy,' he said.

Mulrooney chuckled. 'Ah, Scouse,' he said admiringly, 'ye're sharper than they think, aren't youse?' He took Scannock by the arm and drew him towards the hedge.

'Are you game for a bit of fun?' he said softly.

'Fun?'

'For a man with guts, that's what it will be. Listen, have ye ever done a night's work at Hodge's Farm? No? Well, I have. Hodge, the farmer, he pays ye when ye've done, in the kitchen. He has his money in a cash box, a black tin box. And when he's paid youse he puts it away in the kitchen-cupboard.'

Scannock looked at him sceptically.

'Yes, man,' Mulrooney went on, 'in the cupboard. They trust everyone, these people. In notes and silver there must be ten pounds in that box. And there's only a window with an ordinary catch, to open, and ye're in.'

Scannock hesitated.

'Mother of God, man,' whispered the Irishman, 'is it yellow ye are? Ye'll have money in yer pocket – an' it's small money they'll niver be able ter trace. Think of it … ' his fingers dug into Scannock's arm, 'there's always drink for the man who can put the money down. Ye'll be after knowin' that already. An' the women, them lovely fat whoors at the Horse an' Hounds. They'll niver look at the likes o' you an' me until we're flush, but then they'll be after us, boyo, they'll be after us an' cryin' out for a kip when we can jingle the money in our pockets. Come on, Scouse, the divil himself'll spit in yer eye if ye turn this chance down.'

Scannock spoke at last.

'Them women wouldn't come with us.'

'Sure, an' they will too,' said Mulrooney fiercely. 'If it's shy of 'em ye are I'll fix one up for ye.' Scannock's glittering eyes told him that he was near to prevailing. He put his face close to Scannock's and spoke thickly, rapidly. 'I'll spread one out on the bed for youse, with a fat, white belly ready an' waitin' for youse. It's a quare man ye are if ye won't know how to paddle yer own boat then.'

It was months since Scannock had flung his wife across the bed. He had not had a drink for forty-eight hours. His pockets were empty. And the savage, frustrated energy that the days of waiting had stored up in him was driving him crazy. He would go anywhere, follow anyone, to burst the bonds of inaction.

'I'm on,' he grunted.

The plan was Mulrooney's. Scannock was to creep up to the farmhouse, force the kitchen window and get the cash box from the cupboard. Mulrooney had explained carefully to him where it was. Mulrooney would wait along the path. The dog, he explained, was the danger. He had a piece of meat, drugged meat wrapped up in his handkerchief, he said. He was going to feed that to the dog. This was the worst job and he wanted to do it himself. Scannock thought about the scheme; he was incapable of considering it critically – it was a struggle simply to absorb it. When he had done so, he had no questions. He followed Mulrooney.

They crossed the empty paddock, and came to the path leading to the farmhouse.

'I'll wait here,' whispered Mulrooney, 'if there's any danger I'll whistle youse ter clear out.'

'This as far as you're comin'?'

'Sure, an' it's me that has the dangerous job,' whispered the Irishman, 'out here in the white moonlight, like a flea on a bald head. Gwan along with youse, now.'

Scannock clambered over the gate; he had sufficient sense not to try to unfasten the rusty catch. He walked slowly, on toes and heels, along the path. He felt the moonlight on him like a searchlight; the crunch of gravel underfoot sounded thunderous to him. In a panic he moved to the side of the path and walked on the turf. Even then he could hear the thud of his own feet. He came to the house and skirted it slowly. He counted: one window, two, the green side door; here was the kitchen window.

He fumbled with the spike of his jack-knife, and began to wrench at the woodwork above the catch. Force it, Mulrooney had told him, force it quickly, no one will hear. Scannock thought he had a better idea. He scraped and poked for a while to no purpose. He put the knife away and picked up a stone. He wrapped this in his dirty handkerchief and drew back to swing it at the window.

'HEY.' A voice, and boots crashing on the gravel. It was a strange voice.

He ran along the side of the house. The boots were crashing after him; the voice was shouting. There were voices inside the house, and doors thudding. The hedge was ahead of him, thick and impenetrable.

He turned to his left and ran along the hedge, back towards the road. He tried to keep his head down as he ran. The moonlight was pitiless. He could hear his pursuer cutting back diagonally across the turf, thus gaining on him. There were other people coming from the house now, and running up the path, parallel with the hedge he was following.

He was out of breath; the drink had ruined his wind; a stitch made running an agony.

He was back at the paddock fence, and scrambling over it. Leaning against the fence was a bicycle. The angry voice and the footsteps were very close behind. He jumped on to the bicycle and lurched across the paddock; slow going, and the man behind running almost as fast as he was pedalling. Through the gate now and on to the road; the wheels gripped the metalled surface and the bicycle swooped away. Scannock glanced over his shoulder and glimpsed a police uniform. He pedalled harder; the voices faded behind him.

A mile along the road he dismounted and flung the bicycle into the hedge. He left the road and cut across the fields. They had seen the uniform; perhaps they had seen his face. He had to get back into camp without passing the sentry. They would telephone and there would be a roll-call. He had to get back to his hut before them.

As he ran, he tried to collect his thoughts, to work out what had happened. The policeman – he must have been cycling home down the road past the paddock; he must have seen Scannock from there prowling round the house. Mulrooney, then? Where had he been? Scannock slowed down involuntarily as he tried to marshal the suspicions that were jostling confusedly in his mind. Mulrooney – he must have seen the policeman coming; he must have hidden and then run for it. Why didn't he whistle? – the lousy, rotten, filthy traitor, why didn't he whistle? He wanted to get away, did he, without drawing attention to himself? Not a thought for his mate, eh?

When Scannock crawled under the barbed-wire fence at the back of the Fifth Battalion's camp, he was close to doing murder. Betrayal; that to him was the vilest of crimes; betrayal; that and cowardice were things he could neither understand nor forgive.

He entered his hut quietly, without being intercepted. Everyone was asleep. He moved quietly across to his bed, undressed and slipped into his blankets. He lay for a while staring up at the ceiling. He felt shame, now that he was safe, at the useless and stupid way in which the affair had ended; no drink, no fight, no woman – and betrayal. He burned, frustrated, explosive. His thoughts, inchoate in the darkness, were a procession of obscenities. He lay awake for hours, staring at the door with glittering eyes. No one came.

No one came that night, nor was there much trouble the next day. The village policeman and Hodge, the farmer, came to the battalion's first parade the next morning and walked along the ranks, helpless in front of the six hundred staring faces. They were both anxious to get it over. After all no harm had been done. The colonel said a few words to the battalion afterwards. The battalion had a good record, he said, and he asked them not to spoil it now. They had all got a bit keyed up in the last few days, he said, but this wasn't the way to work it off. Save it for Jerry, he said. Some of the men laughed.

Private Scannock did not laugh. Nor did he save it for Jerry.

Two nights later the Fifth Battalion had its third casualty. Private Mulrooney was found in a ditch on the Wintersley road with his skull cracked and three ribs fractured. His face had been trampled until it was scarcely recognisable; his mouth was full of smashed teeth.

When he recovered consciousness in hospital he found a policeman waiting by his bedside with notebook and pencil. Private Mulrooney shook his head and closed his eyes again. A little while later he asked the doctor feebly, 'Will I be goin' back there?'

'It'll be a month or two before you're fit, soldier,' the doctor answered. 'Lie back, now, and take it easy.'

Private Mulrooney relaxed, gratefully. After three weeks he would, by Army regulations, be struck off the strength of the Fifth Battalion.

No, he said, when the policeman leaned over him again, he had no statement to make. No statement at all.

CHAPTER ELEVEN
Ready to move

ON SUNDAY, MAY 28TH, Private Charlie Venable came back to the Fifth Battalion.

It was just after six o'clock in the evening when he walked past the astounded sentry at the main gate, strolled into the guard-room, flipped his beret on to the table and greeted the guard commander.

'Wotcher, my old tosh. 'Ow's the ol' battalion gettin' on?'

The sergeant put down the pen with which he had been scratching at his guard report, and stared at Charlie.

'You wanner poke your eyes back in, tosh,' said Charlie pleasantly, 'before they come poppin' out. Any char left in the ol' bucket, Sarge? I'm entitled to me supper, you know.'

'Strewth!' said the sergeant at last. 'I'd better let the orderly room know you're back.'

Charlie hung his greatcoat on a nail and settled himself comfortably on a rolled-up palliasse. 'Not 'alf,' he said, 'give 'em a chance to put the flags out. I should 'a let you know I was comin', shouldn't I? Then you would 'a turned out the guard to welcome me.'

'We'll welcome you, all right,' said the sergeant. 'It'll be close arrest for you, and a court martial.'

'Nah,' scoffed Charlie, 'not now. We'll be away in a few days. You know what Dad's like. 'E'll keep me under escort till we're on the ship, then 'e'll turn me loose.'

The off-duty men of the guard had all come crowding round. They had rather the air of courtiers doing homage.

'Do you mean to say you knew what you was comin' back to?' one of them asked in awe.

'Course I did,' said Charlie calmly.

'How?'

'Ah,' said Charlie, 'if I told you, you'd be as wise as me.'

'Those mates of yours been writing to you, I suppose,' said the sergeant. 'A little thing like the censorship wouldn't worry them.' He knew that the Doggy Boys had their own mysterious channels of communication; even now, when the battalion was becoming more and more cut off from the outside world, they were able to place their bets and to collect their winnings, and to live in their accustomed aristocratic ease. The battalion drivers were their loyal couriers; rat-faced little men from the nearby town would come daily to the village to transact their furtive business at the Horse and Hounds with Sergeant Bender, or with Dickie Crawford, or with Rabinowitz. Charlie Venable, hanging about for the last two months in the back rooms of shabby little London cafes, spending his nights at the tracks, could without difficulty have kept in constant touch with them.

'You must be weak in the head,' said the sergeant, 'coming back at a time like this. Any day now the shooting's gonner start.'

'Yes,' said Charlie. 'An' I wanner be there when it starts. Crackers, ain' I?' He felt the need to justify himself. 'D'you think I done a bunk to get out of it? When all me mates was going? Besides,' he added defiantly, 'I'm no onion. Deserting off draft when your battalion's goin' overseas, that's a serious thing. You don't catch Charlie Venable chancin' it like that.'

'Well,' said the sergeant, 'you'd better come down the stores with me and collect your kit and blankets.'

'Comin', my lord,' said Charlie, 'an' don't forget that supper. Prisoner's entitled to his rations.'

Within a half-hour Charlie was comfortably installed in the guard-room, his supper on the table in front of him. The news of his arrival had spread rapidly and the peace of the guard-room was shattered by the stream of visitors that came to greet him.

Charlie sat in the sergeant's chair eating industriously, and holding court like some returned monarch acknowledging a series of welcoming delegations from among his loyal subjects. Baldy sat at his right hand, speechless and radiant.

'Hallo, Fred. Wotcher, Bert, you an'arf looking brown. Bin sunbathin'?'

'Cor, strike a light, Dickie Crawford, ain't you in the moosh yet? I met an ol' china of yours down Clapton last week – Albie Holloway. 'E got 'is ticket with fits last year. Cost 'im twenty nicker, 'e told me.'

''Ave a drop o' char.' Charlie waved his hand royally at the bucket of tea – the property of the guard – standing in the corner. 'There's some mugs on the shelf. 'Ere...' he pushed the guard's evening rations across the table, 'cut yourself some bread an' cheese.'

The guard commander scooped up the rations.

'Here,' he said indignantly, 'what do you think I am? The bleeding butler?'

Charlie took a cigarette from Baldy and leaned luxuriously back in his chair. 'Not yet, my good man,' he said loftily, 'but I'll give you a week's trial if you insist.'

He'll be glad, thought the R.S.M. as he walked crisply up the cinder path towards the colonel's hut, he'll be glad when he knows. He always had a soft spot for Venable. He likes the cheeky type.

He knocked at the door, entered and saluted.

The colonel was sitting at his table, facing the door. He had his hands in his lap; he was looking down at the table. He raised his eyes when the R.S.M. came in, without moving his head. The R.S.M.'s voice came spinning towards him through echoing tunnels of darkness.

The R.S.M. was silent again, and waiting for a reply. The colonel still stared at the table in front of him. He spoke at last, in a flat, remote voice.

'Leave me now, Sergeant-Major. I'll see you in the morning.'

The sergeant-major saw the slip of paper on the table in front of the colonel, and began to understand. 'Yes sir,' he said, a little embarrassed. He turned to leave.

'Oh, Sergeant-Major,' the colonel spoke again, with an effort.

'Sir?'

'We shall have to try and keep Venable out of trouble. He's a good chap. We can keep him under escort till we sail. I'll smooth things out with Brigade in the morning.'

'Yes, sir.' The R.S.M. saluted once more. He looked again at the colonel's bowed head, and hesitated for a moment.

'Sir...?'

'Sergeant-Major?'

'You'll not mind my asking. Is there any...?' the sergeant-major looked at the piece of paper on the table '...Have you had bad news, sir?'

'Yes.' The colonel tapped the piece of paper with his forefinger. 'The boy – he's missing. At sea.'

'Oh. I'm sorry, sir.'

'That's all right, Sergeant-Major.'

'There's hope, sir, if he's missing. Have they sent you any details?'

'Oh, heavens, yes,' the colonel was forcing himself to speak brightly, 'there's hope all right. They say there are still several boats unaccounted for. He'll turn up all right, will my lad. He always does. He's been in many a scrape before now, but he can look after himself.' He thought of a boat bobbing, black and tiny, in the troughs of the great, grey Atlantic waves.

'They'll find him, sir,' said the R.S.M. 'The Navy'll be lookin', an' aeroplanes. They'll find him.' He turned to the door, this time to go, 'You'll please tell your good lady I'm wishin' for the best.'

'You've met her, haven't you?' said the colonel. 'Yes, I'll tell her. Thank you, Sergeant-Major.'

The door closed behind the R.S.M. The colonel put his hands in the pockets of his tunic and rose stiffly to his feet.

'They have supplies in these lifeboats, haven't they, Noel?'

Major Norman was sitting on his bed, in the shadows, smoking.

'Good Lord, yes. They have food and water. Enough to keep them alive for weeks. And brandy. And flares.'

'I know, Noel. Sometimes they pick them up alive after weeks, and they get them well again in no time. Oh,' he said desperately, 'there's no call to worry yet, I know that.'

He fumbled in his pockets for cigarettes.

'It's the wife I'm worried about,' he said. 'I know how she'll be taking it. And the devil of it is, we'll be off into the blue any day now. She'll be on her own, then, with the two of us to worry about. I shan't feel happy, Noel, going off and leaving her like that.'

'Can't you get up to see her? You could do it in twenty-four hours. I'm sure you could get permission from Brigade.'

'Now? Impossible. It's any moment, now, Noel. You know that. I dare not. I shall phone her, though, tonight.'

'Shall I go up to the orderly room and tell them to put a trunk call through for you?'

'Would you, please?'

The colonel lit his cigarette.

'That boy,' he said suddenly, 'he's been in and out of trouble since he was two years old. The frights he's given us...' his voice grew tender and reminiscent, '...and the laughs we've had afterwards. He was two years old, and the wife was out shopping with him; she had him in the pram. She left him to go into a shop and when she came out, there he was choking and blue in the face. The wife started shrieking – she always was like that – "My baby's dead, my baby's dead," she kept on shrieking. Then along comes some big, fat woman and lifts the baby up by his feet and shakes him and thumps him on the back, and guess what comes tumbling out of his mouth? A half-penny and a penny. A penny, Noel – you just try swallowing a penny, sometime. Two years old and he swallows a penny, a penny, if you please. Ah, the laughs we've had about that.'

He puffed his cigarette. He was talking, not to Noel Norman but to the telegram on the green baize tablecloth.

'When he was four he had a little wooden horse on wheels. His playroom was on the top landing. He got the door open, somehow, and came sailing out of the room on his horse, and before we could get to him he went flying down the stairs. A great, long flight of stairs. We thought he'd broken his neck. The wife was fainting with fright. And there he was on the floor at the bottom, howling his head off, not a scratch on him. The little devil, not a scratch.'

The telegram lay on the table, a silent enemy.

'He had concussion when he was twelve, playing football. He got in the way of a lad twice his size. He's like that, my boy. When he was sixteen he was knocked off his bicycle by a lorry. Not a bone broken. He wanted a motorbike after that. The wife begged me not to let him have it. Said she wouldn't sleep at nights if I did. I got him the bike in the end. He smashed it up, all right. But he wasn't touched, himself. Hah!' he laughed unconvincingly, 'that boy of mine!'

'I'll go and put the call through,' said Major Norman.

The colonel blew his nose.

'He's nineteen years old, Noel.' His voice was suddenly that of a sad and frightened man. 'Nineteen years old.'

Lying in the grass on the common was like being drawn down into the silent heart of a whirlpool of noise. Far away, beyond the dark treetops, the voices of the passing crowds could be heard through the dusk, faint, but startlingly distinct; the mumble of traffic, the occasional crash and clatter of a tram. But on the common, amid the gorse and the snowy hawthorn, Alfie and Floss, huddled together in the grass, heard no sound but that of their own breathing.

Alfie was frightened to speak. He did not know what he should say. She had been terrified; she had struggled, whimpering, beneath him for interminable minutes; then she had relaxed, clasped her mouth to his, put her arms tightly about him. Now the sudden, angry courage that had seized upon him was gone. He was empty and apprehensive, trembling a little as he lay with her breath warm against his cheek. The words would not come from his parched throat; he waited for Floss to speak.

She sat up, pulled her coat over her shoulders and squirmed her arms into the sleeves.

'It's getting cold.' She was very quiet and calm. 'Your last bus'll be going soon.'

They clambered to their feet and brushed the bits of grass from their clothes. Alfie was still speechless, in an agony of uncertainty and contrition.

She moved close to him and touched the breast of his tunic lightly with her fingers.

'Alfie?'

'Floss?'

She played with a button on his tunic. 'Do you really care for me?' she whispered. 'Or did you just want...' she hesitated, and indicated the spot where they had been lying, '...you know?'

Alfie struggled to speak; for a moment he only made silly,

embarrassed noises. At last, violently: 'Oh, Floss,' he gripped her arm, 'you hated it, didn't you?' He felt sick with doubt.

She shook her head.

'I don't know. No.'

She was silent, then she laughed suddenly.

'Oh, you big silly. I did – I hated you like anything. I thought you were a beast. It was awful. And then, after, I realised you were more frightened than me. I could feel you trembling. Oh, Alfie, I do like you.' He drew her close to him again. 'I don't mind, really, so long as I know you feel just the same as me.'

The warmth crept back through Alfie.

'Oh, Floss dear, I do, I do.' They kissed. 'I'll walk you home.'

'No, you mustn't. You'll miss your bus and get into trouble. I'll come down to the bus station with you.'

They walked across the common with their arms about each other, leaning heavily, almost drunkenly, on each other. They had no wish to speak; they were deep in each other and the silence was like a warm coverlet. Sometimes as they passed other couples lying like black mounds among the gorse, they laughed together, quietly and knowingly.

They came on to the pavement and the noises of the street closed around them. They walked slowly, listening to the tapping of their shoes on the pavement.

Floss giggled.

'Oh, Alfie. If mum knew. She'd kill me.' They walked on for a few paces. 'The times she's told me!'

Now, in the street, Alfie felt more confident. He was a soldier, strolling with his girl, for all the world to see.

'She won't know. I mean, not about this. She knows about us, though. I told her, Easter, when I was staying round your place. My mum knows too. I wrote to her all about you, sent her a photo. Remember that second one you gave me? I asked you for it, the one with you standing holding the bike. I sent her that one. Next time I get a leave, I'll take you home with me to see her.'

They walked blindly out into the roadway, came to their senses with jeeps and lorries flying past them, dodged frantically across to the opposite pavement and walked on, laughing and breathless.

'Alfie, dear.' Floss was serious again.

'Uh?' Alfie was feeling more happy, more lordly, every minute.

'I might have a baby.'

'Nah,' Alfie, his brain suddenly a whirl, heard his own voice distantly, 'don't be silly. Don't you worry about that.'

'Why not?' She gripped his arm urgently. 'That's how they get babies, isn't it?'

He felt cold again and sick inside.

He heard his own voice again, 'Chance in a million.'

'Why? Why? You don't have to do it a million times before you get one, do you? Look at the girls who have their babies nine months after they're married. That's not one in a million, is it?'

Alfie opened his mouth to reassure her; then the angry heat came surging through him again.

'Look, Floss, I want to marry you. Who cares if we have a kid? Everybody has kids.'

'Oh,' she moaned. In the street, with passers-by bumping into them and the lonely ones turning to look hungrily after them, she sagged against him and put her face against his sleeve. 'Oh, Alfie, dear, I've been waiting to hear you say that.'

Alfie laughed.

'Silly. I thought you knew. We've talked about it often enough. Look, Floss, I'll come into town tomorrow evening after parade – I can do it if I catch the six o'clock bus – I'll come round and ask your mum properly. Then we'll be engaged. I can put in for my credits this week, and we'll go out next Saturday afternoon and buy a ring.'

'Alfie,' the happiness and the laughter made her voice unsteady, 'engaged! Me! Oh, Alfie, wait till I tell the girls at work. I've shown them all your photo already.'

'What they think of me?'

She giggled. 'Don't be conceited.' She grew serious again. 'We mustn't spend too much on the ring. We've got to save up properly now.'

'Don't you worry about that. I'll get you a ring that'll give the girls something to talk about.'

'Oh, who cares about a silly old ring.'

They were at the bus station, a yard with tall buildings around, a din of engines and a crowd crushing them together.

'You will be on the six o'clock bus tomorrow?'

'I'll say. Coming to meet me?'

'Mm. I'll get off work early and come straight down. We'll go back home together.'

Moving with the crowd towards the bus, they kissed.

'Alfie?'

'Floss?'

'Do you love me?'

They kissed again by the platform of the bus, with people trying to shove past them.

'That answer you?'

'Mm. See you tomorrow.'

A grinning red face between them and a beery voice, 'Git on there, mate, it'll wait till termorrer.'

Borne on to the platform and up the stairs Alfie shouted back over the bobbing heads.

'Tomorrow evening.'

As soon as Alfie came into sight of the camp he knew that something was wrong. At midnight the camp should have been dark and silent; but above him, on the hillside, there were lights, there was the sound of movement, voices, hut doors slamming, the engines of lorries warming up.

He walked down the lane and turned into the camp, filled with dread. Men were stumbling past him in the darkness with cases of supplies and ammunition on their shoulders. The transport park was filled with noise and activity, headlamps blinking, tailboards banging, men's steel-shod boots crunching on the cinder surface.

In the hut, at midnight, it should have been dark; two rows of men silent and asleep and the corporal, in the bed by the door, turning over somnolently as he came in and mumbling, 'That you, Alfie? Don't make a noise. Good night, boy.'

But the hut, as he entered it, was lit. The men were sitting on their beds, assembling their equipment, cramming grenades and clips of ammunition into their pouches, stuffing their belongings into their small packs.

Before anyone spoke to him, Alfie knew. Niagara Falls was coming down on top of him and the end of the world was nigh. Lance-Corporal Feather came into the hut with half a dozen full, dripping water-bottles and passed them to their owners.

'Hallo, Alfie boy. You're just in time. Get packed. Battle order. The battalion's confined to camp until further notice as from midnight. We have to be ready to move off tomorrow at a half-hour's notice.'

Alfie sat on his bed, bewildered, unbelieving. His hands fumbled with belts and buckles while he tried to halt the reeling confusion inside his head and to cope with what had happened.

Tomorrow evening. Floss waiting at the bus station, clutching her handbag with both hands; the six o'clock bus coming in, and the six-forty, and the seven-ten, and Floss still waiting, agonised with fear and bewilderment, but still waiting. *I might have a baby. That's how they get babies, isn't it? Who cares if we have a kid? Everybody has kids. I'll come round and ask your mum properly. We'll go out next Saturday afternoon and buy a ring. Tomorrow evening. Where would the Fifth Battalion be tomorrow evening?*

Niagara Falls was coming down on top of him and the end of the world was nigh. Alfie Bradley tested the action of his rifle, slamming the gleaming bolt a dozen times into the breech. He slipped back the safety-catch and loosened the sling. The rifle was ready for use.

CHAPTER TWELVE
Summer holiday

THE SOLDIER LIVES a drama: he never has the time to perceive it. His life, even in battle, is a succession of chores.

The battalion moved off in the morning: to the men, this departure for battle resolved itself into a rush to get out of bed, wash, shave, eat, dump the straw from their palliasses, hand in their blankets at the quartermaster's stores, and finally to sweep and scrub out their empty huts. There was no time for sentimental reflections.

It was not till they were on parade ready to leave, and they saw the advance party of an incoming unit exploring the huts, that they felt a sense of loss and unsettlement. It was disturbing, somehow, to stand in the ranks with rifle and pack, watching these arrogant, inquisitive strangers invading their homes of an hour ago.

Colonel Pothecary came striding on to the parade ground, pulling on his gloves. He answered salutes, spoke briefly to the regimental sergeant-major. Commands were shouted. The Fifth Battalion sloped arms, turned to the right and marched out of camp. Not a man looked round.

It was always like this. They would settle somewhere; make their huts warm and beautiful with life, each a hive of friendships and associations. Then, one day, they would march out, and not a man would look over his shoulder.

The battalion spent most of the day on the dockside, the men squatting on their packs in the heat of the sun, discussing each hour's fresh rumour, reading and exchanging soiled scraps of newspaper, drinking the tea that was brought to them on trolleys. They were mystified and confused, all the more so because the battalion's transport had vanished at dawn, bound for another, unknown destination; but they did not worry deeply. The machine was working again; it had snatched up their battalion in its steel claws and dropped them on to its conveyor belt. Now the belt was moving; whither, they did not know.

It was strange, too, to come into living contact with the machine for the first time, to see it at work. The Movement Control staff, the servants of the machine, hurried self-consciously about amongst the ranks of the battalion. They were irked by a vague, indefinable feeling of inferiority in the face of these fighting men whom it was their occupation to ship across the water like livestock. They were polite; they tried to show respect to the infantrymen. But for weeks they had been working overtime, like checkers in some Chicago stockyard, packing men into trains and ships and moving them on another stage nearer to the furnace. They were tired, losing patience, perhaps annoyed by their own nagging inferiority; and sometimes they became officious, shouted, lost their tempers.

The men of the Fifth Battalion sat on their packs and watched the comings and goings with a placid detachment. They felt no resentment towards these go-betweens of war, and – although they chaffed them, and tripped them up, and shouted after them, 'You lucky people!' – they felt no envy of them. They were the damned, the chosen, the infantry, looking down on the rest of the human race from their own, unapproachable world. The mariner looks with longing at the shore, but will not leave the sea; so these infantrymen lived content in a pride which none of them would ever acknowledge, nor yet betray.

'All right, mate,' said Charlie Venable peaceably to an angry Movement Control sergeant, 'when we're all dead an' buried they'll come an' fetch you blokes. I don' 'arf feel sorry for you.'

But the redcaps and the staff officers – it was their presence which made the infantryman feel that, after all, they were only looked on as brute flesh to be branded and shipped for the slaughter; the menacing cordon of military policemen between the battalion and the dock gates, and the tall, cold officers with red bands round their caps and sheaves of papers in their hands who walked among the squatting soldiers like farmers at a cattle market; they left in the battalion a sense of insult and resentment.

Towards evening they embarked, still lazy and apathetic from the heat of the day, aboard big, flat-decked ferries towed by tugs.

Dumbly and without curiosity they settled themselves on the decks and slept or smoked for an hour while the smooth and sparkling sea slipped past them until, at the unexpected sight of land again, they humped their rifles and packs and crowded, still only half-curious, into the bows.

It was the Isle of Wight. The word spread among them; the officers nodded confirmation. None of the men had expected this; yet none of them, indeed, had known what to expect. The day had given them a sense of climax. Now they were tired, thirsty, sticky with sweat, eager only to drop their packs and slip out of their belts and buckles; and the evening's anti-climax seemed only faintly funny.

They landed on the jetty of a clean little seaside town and marched off by companies, led by guides from Movement Control. They clattered through narrow, cobbled streets, the noise of their boots and their voices echoing among the houses and bringing the townsfolk to their windows. The head of the column moved out of the town, toiled up a steep lane between tall hedges and entered a field that was full of bell tents.

A camp; another bloody camp. Tired, bewildered, vaguely disappointed, the men collected palliasses and blankets and stumbled into their tents.

Before dark the cookhouse was operating, a hot meal was served in the dining tent, a canteen had been opened, Daily Orders were posted and a guard mounted. It seemed as if they were here to stay.

What's happening? Who knows? Why tell us? – we're only the poor sods who have to go and do the job? Hell, who cares? Die in battle, die of boredom – who cares?

The Fifth Battalion went to bed.

The machine remote and inscrutable, had picked them up and put them down. For the next four days they waited, from each day to the next, for the machine to pick them up again; for four fantastic days they lived between two worlds, cut off from both, as if between life and death.

It was a week of sunshine and blue skies. For two days the men of the battalion were allowed to go down into the little seaside town to seek their pleasure. The beaches were crowded with holiday-makers; in the little chalets which lined the sea-wall families sprawled in deck-chairs and cooked meals on Primus stoves. On the day the battalion arrived, the island had been cut off from the outside world. Transport services to the mainland had been stopped. The island was sealed; the holiday-makers, a horde of timid, respectable little middle-class people, resented it; they resented the war which they had come here to forget and which had pursued them, as they might resent a thunderstorm which had come to spoil their holiday. And with unanimity and determination they settled down to ignore, as well as they could, both the unwelcome war and its involuntary representatives in their midst – the men of the Fifth Battalion.

The sturdy, sun-burned, big-booted infantrymen sauntered in pairs along the promenade staring at things they had almost forgotten; the girls, beautiful in their wet bathing-costumes, whisking by with the rainbow drops of water shaking from their hair, leaving behind them the warm, milky smell of flesh and seawater; the children in waders squatting amid their sand-pies and squealing at the water's edge; the laughter and the smell of cooking from the chalets; the crowds round the refreshment huts; and all the confused hubbub, drifting up from the beach in the dizzy sunlight, of surf and shrieking and shouting and gramophones.

No one spoke to them. No one paid any attention to them.

Two soldiers sat on the promenade rails, dangling their legs and talking delightedly to a little boy who stood looking up at them, his head cocked on one side. A pretty little girl appeared; she tugged at the little boy's sleeve and said plaintively, 'Mummy says come away, Rodney; you mustn't speak to the soldiers.'

Dickie Crawford, turned away from an overcrowded tea-room, leaned amicably in at the door of a chalet and said, 'Got a cup o' tea for a thirsty soldier, ma?'

A fierce little woman answered, 'Don't they teach you manners in the Army? Go away.'

A German reconnaissance plane came over and the Bofors guns that crouched on the sea-wall began to bang shells into the blue sky. The infantry-men stood round the sand-bagged emplacements and roared with derisive laughter as the civilians scuttled from the beach.

Every night there were air raids on the town and on the ships that were anchored in hundreds offshore. The soldiers lay in the darkness of their tents, listening with vindictive delight to the bombs falling on the nearby town and muttering reckless encouragement to the raiders.

On the Wednesday evening two riflemen of the Fifth Battalion went into a public house and were refused beer.

'Sorry, lads,' said the publican, mopping the counter, 'sold out.'

The bar was full of civilians drinking.

'What about them?' asked one of the soldiers angrily.

'Regular customers,' said the publican. 'You just clear off quietly, you chaps, and don't make trouble.'

One of the soldiers made a move towards the bar; the other gripped his arm and pulled him back.

'Come on, Bert, let's blow.'

As they turned to go, they heard: a voice from the babble behind them: 'Time they started this Second Front and got this lot out of here. Costing the country a fortune, they are.'

In the tents that night the men of the Fifth Battalion paid no attention to the German bombers droning overhead. The whole battalion knew about the incident in the public house. There was talk of burning down the pub, of wrecking the town. The Fifth Battalion was ready for a fight; by now it was not particular with whom.

There was no fight. The pub was not burned down. The town was not wrecked. On Thursday morning the men awoke to find themselves confined to camp, with orders to stand by in readiness to move off again.

Their fury vanished; they packed and prepared quietly, without excitement, and when their tasks were done, they sprawled luxuriously in the grass and sunned themselves.

During the day a message from the colonel appeared on the notice-board. It did not speak of great events.

The message ran:

An invitation has been received from the management and staff of Messrs. – – (this was an aircraft factory on the other side of town) extending the use of the factory's canteen and bar to all members of this battalion. A dance has been organised for Friday night to which all ranks will be admitted, free of charge, as guests. For obvious reasons it will not be possible for us to take advantage of this kind and hospitable gesture; nor, unfortunately, are we in a position to reveal the reason by refusing or by making any explanation. I have had to accept, in the knowledge that we shall have to let these good people down. I shall write, as soon as it is possible, to offer both apologies and thanks on your behalf. I am sure that the circumstances which will by that time exist will be sufficient explanation – and compensation – for our action.

'Times like these,' said Charlie Venable appreciatively, 'you find out who your friends are, eh?'

Happier now, and confident, the men sat on the grassy heights and tried to count the ships that stretched, tiny as toys in the distance, across the sparkling Solent to the skyline.

The colonel left camp early on Friday morning. He returned a little before midday, and called the battalion on parade.

Standing up in the back of his jeep, he summoned the men to break their ranks and gather round him.

'Sit down, lads, make yourselves comfortable.'

When they were seated and the buzz of conversation had died away he began to speak.

'This morning, my lads, I was taken across to the mainland in a naval pinnace. I went to a commanders' conference. The Army Group Commander was there... Monty to you...'

There was a rumble of laughter.

'...Well lads, I suppose you've guessed it by now – we're off.'

There was silence. The men had waited too long, had been

disappointed too often to be able to absorb the bald announcement quickly. The colonel spoke again.

'I can't tell you where it is yet. You'll know that on board ship. You're embarking tomorrow, by the way. But I can tell you this – it's France.'

They had never expected it to be like this; sitting on the grass, in the sunshine, with the ships spread across the sea below and the calm voice coming to them through the silence; the voice calm and quiet as if this were just another training scheme ahead of them. Stolid and steady men themselves, for the most part, they had nevertheless secretly imagined that this would be a moment of inspiration, of brave words, of stirring, farewell messages from the high and mighty. Still, it felt good to be sitting here on the hot grass, elbow to elbow with your mates, listening, with a first, faint fluttering of excitement starting somewhere inside you.

'Monty gave us all the griff about the forces he's putting across the water. It's terrific lads, really terrific. It would have given you confidence just to hear him reading out those facts and figures.'

The colonel grinned apologetically at his men. 'I'm sorry I haven't got them, lads, but I'm no great hand at writing. They should have let me take Major Norman with me. He's been doing my homework for months.'

Laughter, the warm, responsive laughter now of comrades.

'You should have heard him, lads. Thousands and thousands of aircraft. Battleships and cruisers galore to give covering fire. They're going to have little boats going to and fro picking people up if any landing craft get sunk. Oh...' the colonel grinned at them again, '...and I mustn't forget this. They're even going to have two canteen ships anchored off the coast. In fact, as far as I can see, this is going to be the most luxurious invasion in the history of mankind.'

More laughter.

'Well,' said the colonel, 'almost. There's a lot more, but you'll get that from your platoon officers. There'll be a last collection of mail after lunch. You won't be able to send any letters after that. As soon as you're dismissed I want company commanders in my tent. Junior officers, sergeants and all n.c.o.s leading sections meet for briefing in the dining marquee at fifteen hundred hours. The battalion will parade again at sixteen hundred to draw French money. I think that's about all.'

He paused for a moment.

'Well, my lads. This is it. At last. You know, I'm damned if I know what to say to you. You're well equipped. You're well trained. There isn't a better battalion than this in the British Army – so there certainly won't be in the German Army. Everything that you need to be told you've been told for months past. So I won't tell it to you all over again. Keep cheerful – that goes a long way. Keep your heads down when you can – only take risks when you have to.'

He hesitated again, searching for a peroration, and ended triumphantly: 'Eat when you can, and keep your bowels open. That's all lads. Fall the battalion out, Sergeant-Major.'

For the next hour the men were busy writing their last letters home; brief, guarded and unsentimental letters for the most part, not at all like the last letters of story-book soldiers going into battle.

Dear Mum [wrote Charlie Venable], *You may not hear from me for a week or two, as we shall be busy for a bit. Don't worry, whatever you read in the papers. I'll make up for it as soon as I can with a nice long one. Love and kisses,*
CHARLIE

Most of the letters were like that.

At three o'clock in the afternoon the officers and n.c.o.s went for their briefing and came away looking secretive and important. At four o'clock the battalion filed past the pay table and were handed crisp, new, hundred-franc notes. At five o'clock they had tea – a huge festive meal was served to them to get rid of the battalion's spare rations. After tea they sat in little groups by their tents while their platoon and section leaders passed on the information they had brought from the briefing conference. The Movement Order for the morning was read to them. Get to bed early tonight, lads, their officers told them, there's an early reveille in the morning.

The little groups broke up. Men wandered about inside the wire fence that surrounded the camp, or sat talking softly with their friends. There was singing from some of the tents, not rowdy but wistful and harmonious.

It was a strange, sad, beautiful feeling to know that this was your last evening in Blighty. It was like being very much in love, and very young, the evening before your wedding. Everyone moved about in a subdued kind of way, and all the little everyday things that you continued to do, all the ordinary little communal sights and sounds of the camp, even the clattering of pans from the cookhouse and the noise of the ablution taps running, became strangely poignant.

And it was such a lovely evening, clear and quiet and cool, with the tiny little ships moored in rows on the unruffled sea.

The Fifth Battalion took the advice of its officers and went early to bed.

CHAPTER THIRTEEN
The last night

THE NIGHT WAS STILL, warm, brilliantly moonlit.

Sergeant Ferrissey, commanding the Fifth Battalion's last guard on British soil, moved quietly on his rounds. The moonlight cast shimmering tracks across the dark sea below and bathed the fields in white radiance; but Sergeant Ferrissey had no eyes for the loveliness of the night.

He was burning, aching inside his uniform for the company of a woman. Not for years had Sergeant Ferrissey gone so many days unconsoled; he looked down from the heights towards the town that lay in the shadows around the bay, asleep and silent except for the hum of the nightshift that came ceaselessly from the distant aircraft factory; he thought of the women down there in the darkness, moving softly about in curtained rooms, lying warm and lonely in their beds, smiling insolently across the throbbing machines in the factory; and he raged.

He closed his eyes and stood for a while listening to the distant, hypnotic hum from the factory. He let his fancy carry him away, swooping down through the warm night, to the empty, moonlit streets below. He could see himself running with giant, floating strides through the town, his boots thundering on the pavement; and all along the streets, the doors swinging slowly open and the women stretching out their warm and supple arms in invitation. He opened his eyes, the dream broken, and breathed deeply.

Someone would suffer for this. His strength was leaping and struggling within him. God help the first German I meet, he thought, and the muscles at the back of his hands tightened under the skin.

He continued on his rounds among the silent tents. The sentry on Number One Post was leaning dreamily over the wire fence, his rifle slung at his shoulder, looking down at the sea. The night cook was dozing in a chair by the warmth of his boiler. Outside one of the tents two men were sitting on the ground, talking quietly. Sergeant Ferrissey paused on his way.

'Get to bed, lads.'

'O.K. Sergeant. Good night,' said Charlie Venable.

'Good night.'

Lying in the stifling darkness inside the bell tent, Charlie Venable had been awakened by the sound of whimpering on the other side of the tent pole.

He lay for a moment listening, then raised himself on one elbow. Alfie Bradley was sitting up, his blanket heaped at his feet. His head was bowed, his shoulders were shaking.

Charlie whispered, 'What's up, mate?'

Alfie looked up, then began to sob again.

'Dear, oh dear,' said Charlie, 'this won't do. You'll wake the others up in a minute. Get your head down, boy, an' try to sleep. You'll be all right.'

Alfie whispered weakly, 'I've wet my blanket.'

'Nothing to cry about, boy. Done worse than that in my time.'

Alfie shivered, 'I could die, Charlie. I could die of shame, doing that.'

'Come on outside,' said Charlie, 'get a breath o' fresh air.'

They crept from the tent. Charlie reached back for the blanket and flung it over the wire fence to dry.

'What's frettin' you, Alfie lad? Miss your Floss?'

Alfie shrugged his shoulders.

'Come on, lad, tell your Uncle Charlie. Won't do you no good keepin' it shut up inside you. Talk cures all ills, my ma says. What hurts, Alfie?'

'You don't know what happened that last night before we came here. Me an' Floss. Over the common.'

Charlie pushed Alfie back by the shoulders.

'Did you, boy?' he said delightedly. 'Honest?'

Alfie nodded.

Charlie slapped his thigh. 'Lord love me,' he chuckled, 'our little Alfie. An' you think the end of the world's come because you've 'ad a bit orf your girl. Is that what was worrying you?'

Alfie said, 'She might have a baby.'

'She might not,' said Charlie. 'Anyway, you 'aven't done a murder, boy. They been doin' that all over the world for years an' years. Old Adam was the bloke that started it. Didn't no one ever tell you?'

'I want to marry her,' said Alfie. 'I was going into town last Monday to ask her mum; then we went and moved out of camp in the morning and here we are. What's she thinking of me now?'

'She'll 'ave guessed what's happened. If she 'asn't, she'll know soon enough.'

Alfie answered bitterly: 'That'll cheer her up, I bet. What they want to go and do this to us for? Why can't I live my own life? I don't want to go an' invade somebody else's country.'

'No more do I, boy.'

'Well, what did you come back to the battalion for?'

'Look at it this way,' said Charlie. 'You've 'ad to stop living your own life for a while. Right? You want to get married, an' you can't. Right? Well, you're not the only one, boy. In every tent in this camp there's geezers in the same boat, an' all along the coast tonight there's millions more like them. Geezers who want to get married. Geezers waiting for their wives to 'ave a nipper. Geezers with their ma, or their missus, or their kiddie ill. Geezers with big ideas and ambitions. Geezers with businesses they ought to be keeping an eye on. And all of a sudden, bang, they've 'ad to turn their backs on these things.'

He chewed at a blade of grass for a moment.

'Nothing wrong with that,' he went on. 'It's like this. You're sitting at home by the fire reading the paper. Your ma calls down the stairs, "Alfie, go up the corner for a tin loaf." Nothing else for it. You put the paper down an' you go up the road for the loaf. Then you sit down by the fire again and carry on reading the paper. Same with this now. Just like goin' up the road for a loaf. It's got to be done, Alfie boy, before we can live right again. What's the use of marrying your Floss, an' buying a home, an' raising nippers if this lot's gonna go on for ever? Wouldn' like that, would you?'

'No.'

'Well, then, that's what we're goin' over there for, to finish it all off an' pay out the ones that started it. You're doin' it for Floss. I'm doin' it for the old lady. All of them others I spoke about are doin' it for someone.'

'Won't be much use to Floss if I don't come back,' said Alfie.

'If,' jeered Charlie, 'if ifs an' ands was pots an' pans... You're not a bad boy, Alfie. All them millions of others, you don't mind taking your chance with them, do you?'

'I'm not frightened,' said Alfie, 'if that's what you mean. It was just thinking about Floss, an' worrying, an' doing that in my blanket. I felt so ashamed, Charlie. I see it different now, though.'

'That's the boy. Lord love me, worryin' about that. You won' 'arf laugh about that one day, you an' Floss, after you been wed.'

A voice interrupted them from the other side of the wire fence. 'Get to bed, lads.' It was the guard commander on his rounds.

'O.K. Sergeant,' said Charlie Venable, 'good night.'

'Good night.' The sergeant went on his way.

'That git,' said Charlie, 'he oughter a known what you was worryin' about. He'd a killed hisself laughing. Come on, boy, into kip.'

Alfie looked doubtfully at the blanket on the fence.

'That's all right, cocker,' said Charlie, 'you oughter know me by now. Charlie Venable the wide boy from Bow. Never wants for nothing, an' no more do 'is friends. Got three blankets in there, I 'ave, an' just for tonight I'm gonna be Santa Claus an' tuck you up in two of 'em. In you go.'

He settled down on his palliasse and lay for a while, until he was satisfied that Alfie was asleep. As he slid down at last under his own blanket, a voice came softly from the darkness.

'Charlie.' It was Lance-Corporal Feather.

'You awake, Corp?'

'Been awake all the time, Charlie. Charlie, you know what you are? You're a gentleman.'

'Dear, oh dear,' sighed Charlie, 'I do get called some names. Good night, Corp.'

'Good night, Charlie.'

Lieutenant Paterson was a sturdy young man with fair hair that lay gleaming like a golden cap across his brow, and smooth, ruddy cheeks. He was twenty-two years old but did not look more than nineteen; when he was alone with his mother he still called her 'Mummy'.

At four o'clock in the morning Lieutenant Paterson had still not yet gone to bed. He had lived a long time for this night, and it seemed stupid and pointless to sleep through it. Instead, he strolled slowly round the camp perimeter, chewing the stem of his unlit pipe and trying to summon up thoughts appropriate to the occasion.

He had thought of all the poems he knew, dreamed a dozen battle scenes in which he had won a dozen decorations, drifted into a sentimental vision of his mother hearing the news of his death, written in imagination his first letter home from the front, conjured up a picture of himself lying bandaged in a hospital bed with his family tiptoeing respectfully to his side; and it was still not yet dawn. The night had become terribly long and terribly quiet; to Paterson the distant hum of the factory had already become a torment.

Towards the morning the moon was obscured by cloud and the sea grew dark; the air became chill. Lieutenant Paterson, as he breathed, felt the air in his throat and his lungs like ice. It was hard for him to breathe, harder still to dream. He was beset by thoughts more dismal than he had yet known; thoughts of himself being delivered home to his mother like a helpless package, handless or armless or legless; thoughts of his mother weeping over his smashed and frightful face; thoughts of himself sprawling dead, face downwards by the roadside, with the battalion plodding by as if he had never existed and his mother waiting in anguish far away for news of him.

It had not been difficult to soldier these last three years, at OCTU, at battle school, with the battalion; there were leaves, and weekend visits, letters from Mummy and parcels from Mummy. Mummy sent his laundry to him every week, wrapped daintily in sheets of tissue paper and sprinkled with lavender which reminded him of her each time he opened the parcel.

He could see his Mummy now, tall and slender, with hair more golden than his own, sitting at table in the white-frilled blouse with the cameo brooch at her throat, smiling at him across the spotless tablecloth and the glittering cutlery and the gleaming cut glass and the flowers.

For the first time it seeped into his understanding that he was going now far beyond her reach, where it would not be in her power to help or comfort him.

In Lieutenant Paterson's mind there was no place for fear; but for the first time he discovered the strange terror that afflicts the soldier's body regardless of his will, a twitching in his calves, a fluttering of the muscles in his cheeks, the breath like a block of expanding ice in his lungs, his stomach contracting, the sickness rising in his throat.

Far below him the sea was shrouded in the last darkness before the sunrise. He began to plod down the slopes towards the sea, to drive the weakness from his legs, to rout the palsy from his body. From the horde of memories which assailed him he seized on one, of himself as a small boy at the seaside, in a little family hotel, lying all night in the darkness of his room consumed with impatience for the morning; and in the morning, dressing, and kissing Mummy, and scrambling down the steps and down the street towards the sea, and on to the promenade, to make sure that the sea was still there; and every morning it was still there, whispering and serene.

And he was suddenly a little boy again, running down to the sea through the long grass, heedless of the brambles and of the dew that soaked his trousers, vaulting over fences and squirming through barbed-wire barriers in his haste, with the warmth of movement bringing eagerness and confidence flowing back into his body. Through the dark woods now that barred his line of vision; and here he was, leaning against the rail at the sea's edge, with the salt breeze playing in his hair.

The sea lay before him in the chill dawn light, grey and smooth and silent, the orderly rows of ships at anchor as peacefully as if they were waiting for the start of a regatta.

The longing for his mother melted into pride and exultation. The little boy was going to show his mother how brave he was; there was a fine, new game for him to play.

Lieutenant Paterson turned from the sea and ran joyously up the hill towards the camp. He wanted to laugh aloud, to shout up at the pale sky. He was ready for the fine, new game.

He checked himself as he came into the camp; the guard commander was standing by the fence, looking at him curiously.

'Good morning, Sergeant,' he said self-consciously. 'Grand morning, isn't it?'

'Mornin', sir. Goin' to be a lovely day.'

Sergeant Ferrissey looked at his watch and stretched his body. Ten minutes to reveille. He turned out his off-duty men to awaken the battalion.

He stood watching as they went from tent to tent, stumbling over the guy-lines, drumming with their fists at the taut canvas, shouting, 'Wakey, wakey.'

He heard the first sounds of movement inside the tents, the muffled voices; the first dishevelled men appeared, stumbling across to the ablution benches. As the white light crept across the sky the camp came to life with noise and movement. The Fifth Battalion was awake.

At eight o'clock in the morning, while the holiday-makers in the town below were crawling from their beds and looking gratefully out of their windows at the radiant sunshine and blue sky of a perfect summer's day, the men of the Fifth Battalion marched quietly down to the sea and went aboard ship.

CHAPTER FOURTEEN
Between the shores

FOR THREE DAYS the ships lay at anchor in the Solent while the men of the Fifth Battalion, who by now had left excitement far behind them, settled down to make themselves comfortable in yet another home.

They lounged at the rails and sprawled in groups on the decks, sleeping, eating, playing cards and talking. They slept soundly and ate heartily, as if eating were a pastime in itself. Men were haunting the ship's galley all day long, cadging extras, and sneaking back into the meal queues for second helpings. The talk was of everything but the war – much of it, indeed, consisted of grumbling at the food – except when, two or three times a day, a rumour would sweep through the troop decks that the time had come to up anchor. The card players took up most of the deck space. They squatted in little groups, their upturned berets lying on the deck between their knees to hold their money; for once neither n.c.o.s nor officers interfered with their gambling. For the most part, they played the soldiers' games, Brag and Nap. Here and there was a little party of men playing Blind Brag; Brag is a game of bluff, Blind Brag a game of reckless chance, and these men were playing it recklessly, grinning as they heaped all the money they possessed on their cards. The Doggy Boys, who had monopolised a snug corner protected from the Channel breezes, played solo for hours on end, as absorbed over their cards as at this moment the generals were – somewhere back on the mainland – over their maps.

There was no sentimental talk, no soft singing or playing of harmonicas, no writing of farewell letters, no men sadly gazing at the distant shore. Three days with nothing to do but eat, sleep and gamble was an event in the lives of the men of the Fifth Battalion. They made the most of it, and thought of nothing else.

In the late afternoon of Monday, June 5th, the officers and n.c.o.s aboard ship were called to another briefing. They were firstly given an outline of the whole operation, with the British and American sectors being shown to them on a huge map, the areas of airborne attack on the flanks, and the exact position of their own beach; then they were given maps – large-scale topographical maps of the area into which they were going to attack, and special, wonderfully-detailed, mauve-shaded maps of the German defences in the same area. Business-like, a little self-important, and more confident than ever, they dispersed to talk to their men.

By evening the convoy was on the move, the endless lines of ships passing slowly down the Solent while Spitfires from airstrips which were plainly visible on the shore swooped and snarled overhead.

The men felt the ship vibrating and saw the coast moving past them, looked at each other meaningly, and bent again to their cards.

A couple of hours later they were out in the open Channel. A few of the men stood listlessly at the rails, watching the Needles slowly drop back and become indiscernible in the dusk. There was a strange, flat feeling, a sensation as of living suspended between two planets, as the ship crawled with maddening slowness across the grey, bleak sea, against the grey, bleak, evening sky. There was no shore to be seen, only the walls of purple dusk creeping in from the farthest limits of the sea; no sound to be heard but the thudding of the engines below decks and the snarling of Spitfires in the clouds that thickened overhead.

CHAPTER FIFTEEN
Shannon ain't so tough

THE DAVITS ON THE BOAT deck groaned and the men lining the railings on the deck below saw the landing craft come jerkily down to their level. It hung motionless for a moment, then descended slowly until it was bobbing on the grey swell below, with the scummy white foam swirling round it.

Charlie Venable shivered. 'Bleed'n cold,' he complained. 'Lousy mornin' for a battle. We oughta complain to the union.'

'You should ha' worked in t'mills,' said Sergeant Shannon. 'Fourteen year old, up at five on a raw mornin' an' off to work.'

'We're too wide for that in London, Sarge,' grinned Charlie Venable.

Mister Paterson, the platoon officer, came up and began to talk quietly to the sergeant. They checked their watches. It was growing lighter; the strip of white light across the eastern horizon had spread like a sliding roof across the sky, and now it was daylight.

The sergeant turned to Charlie Venable. He asked: 'Sorry you come back to the battalion, Charlie?'

'Nah,' said Charlie. 'Wouldn'a missed this for a million quid.' He looked out across the grey waters to the mist that hid the shore. 'Ever been down the East End, Sarge?'

'Not since the war.'

'They done it up proper in the blitz,' he said, 'the —ers.' He hawked, and spat down into the water. 'Ev'ry night down under the stairs, my ol' lady was. Fifty-six the ol' gal is. Never done 'er no good. They want showin' a lesson, them —ers.'

'Think a lot of yer ma, don't yer Charlie?' said the sergeant.

'The only gal in the world for me,' said Charlie. 'Your mum's dead, ain't she?'

'Aye,' said Sergeant Shannon, 'me dad were killed in t'last war. 'E were Irish. Mum died when I were a kid. I lived wi' relations till I were sixteen, workin' in t'mills. Then I left 'ome an' come down t' London.'

'Where'd yer live in London?'

'Battersea, in lodgin's. I worked in a fact'ry, in a pickle fact'ry. Lab'rer. It were all right in London, but I were always pretty lonely. It's not a good place for a stranger. Anyway, I lost me Lancashire accent there.'

'Well,' grinned Charlie, 'you don' exactly talk like a Cockney now.'

'You're a lucky lad,' said Sergeant Shannon, ''avin' a mother like yours.'

'Tellin' me!' Charlie answered him. 'It musta' been a dog's life for you.'

'Aye,' said the sergeant, 'I were pretty sick of it. This is t' best life I've known, in t' Army.'

'Strewth!' said Charlie Venable. 'Never mind. I'll take yer to see the ol' lady when we get back. She won' arf go to town. She'll cook yer a meal you'll never forget.'

The sergeant laughed. 'That's a date.'

'Talkin' a meals,' said Charlie, 'that was a lousy —in' breakfast they gave us. Three biscuits an' a mug a char. A sparrer couldn' fight on it, never mind a swaddy.'

'Never mind,' said Sergeant Shannon, 'they've got champagne where we're going,' and moved away.

'— me drunk,' exclaimed Baldy, who had been listening quietly all the time. 'Never 'eard 'im talk so much since 'e joined the battalion. 'E ain't so tough, is 'e?'

'Shut your jaw,' said Charlie Venable.

Sailors pulled at cords and the wet scramble nets thumped over the sides.

Mister Paterson pulled himself up on to the bulwarks and looked at his watch again.

'Off you go, laddie,' said the bearded naval officer who was in charge.

Paterson disappeared over the side. The men swarmed over after him and down the scramble nets.

The landing craft was wallowing on a wicked swell, riding high and falling away again. As it came up, Mister Paterson and two of the men leaped clear of the net and crashed on to the steel deck. 'Wait for her to come up,' Paterson shouted up at the men on the net. Each time the landing craft rose, three or four men dropped clear of the nets, while above more came clambering down like spiders hurrying across a great web.

Now they were all in place, crouching along the steel sides of the craft, settling their weapons across their knees and fumbling with cigarette tins. They had a long trip ahead, four miles to the shore.

The sailors were shouting.

'All gone forrard.'

'All gone aft.'

The engines throbbed more loudly and they could feel the tug of power beneath them. The landing craft began to sidle away from the troopship; the waste foam and heaving water between the two vessels widened. The engine note became deeper and more powerful and the squat craft began to move forward, butting into the waves, painfully climbing them and slithering down into the troughs to attack the next hillock of grey-green water. Paterson stood up and looked around him. As far as he could see other little craft were bobbing towards the shore. Somewhere ahead of them the first flights of assault craft must be piling in now.

'Make yourselves comfortable, lads,' he told the men. 'There's plenty of time yet.'

Some of the men were talking, some smoking, some vomiting quietly into brown bags of greaseproof paper. The wind was bringing to them now the sound of shells bursting ashore. Each man could feel each thudding detonation somewhere inside him. The talking stopped. Men took up their rifles and machine carbines; there was the clack of bolts being drawn and rammed home. The slow, wallowing motion of the craft eased; they were coming into shallower water. Orders were being shouted in the stern and a marine heaved himself up over the side and began to take soundings. There was smoke sprawling across the beach ahead, and the black plumes of explosions, each with a cherry-red flicker of flame at its heart, were leaping up in front of the high bows.

The landing craft nosed inshore through a mass of floating rubbish. A dead sailor came floating out to sea, face and legs under water, rump poking upwards; then a dead soldier, his waxen face turned up to the sky, his hands floating palm upwards on the water; he was kept afloat by his inflated lifebelt. Ahead of them lay beached landing craft, some wrecked, scattered untidily along the waterline.

There was a jarring explosion beneath the bows and the whole craft lurched forward. Men toppled forward in a heap, clambered to their feet as the ramps crashed down, and ran splashing down into the water. They had no time to stop for the two men who had been caught by the mine exploding beneath the bows and whose blood stained the dirty seawater as the boat began to submerge. They were all away now, and wading with weapons held above their heads towards the wet sand ahead.

A dirty tape wriggled across the beach and the riflemen came stumbling along it, shedding water from their sodden trousers. Mister Paterson flopped beneath a wrecked landing craft that lay broadside on and waited for his platoon to come up. One by one they dropped to the sand behind him. There were German shells falling a little inland, where the first assault troops had already passed, and somewhere among the yellowed, battered houses scattered along the waterfront and the smashed rubble of wrecked pillboxes a machine gun was rapping remotely.

'All right, my lads,' said Paterson breathlessly. He ducked under the bows of the beached craft and ran heavily along the tape. There was a tangle of wire ahead, with German mine warnings poking up everywhere and a few British dead lying with their faces in the sand. They followed the tape along a path torn through the wire and came on to a narrow track running laterally. In front of them now were gentle, dreary dunes rising from pools and runnels of water, with grass growing scantily on their upper flanks. On each side of them sappers were rooting up mines as hastily as potatoes, and a little away to the right a beach dressing station had just been established, with a row of loaded stretchers waiting on one side and a row of corpses laid out on the other, each a still mound under a grey blanket, with big boots protruding at the end. Some pioneers were trying to dig in along the far side of the road, in the wet sand.

They moved on. There was the sudden wheep-wheep of bullets. Paterson could not see where they were coming from; then the grating, shrieking descent of their first shell. They flopped, pressing themselves frantically into the sand, then staggered to their feet and went lumbering after Paterson.

Someone was whimpering loudly; it was like the crying of a spoilt child. Sergeant Shannon stopped and looked round. Little Alfie Bradley was lurching about in a wide circle, well away from the tape, pressing his hands to his face. The sergeant raced after him and pulled him down to the ground.

As the boy felt the pressure of the sergeant's hands on his shoulders he tried to stifle his crying; he kept on sniffling jerkily. There was a red pit where one of his eyes had been. Blood welled darkly from the other.

'I can't see,' he whispered, 'I can't see.'

The sergeant comforted him.

'All right lad, there's nowt t' worry about. Yer eyes are full of blood. You'll be all right when they've washed them.' He whipped out the boy's field dressing, his hands already bright with fresh blood. He knew the boy would never see again. He bound the dressing tightly over the boy's face. It began to stain red at once.

'There, lad,' he said soothingly, 'that'll do just t'keep dirt out.' He steered the blind boy back to the tape, forced him down to his knees and put the tape between his fingers.

'Foller this back, lad,' he said gently. 'When yer get on t' that road again you'll be by the dressing station. They'll take you in.'

He stood for a moment watching Little Alfie crawling back towards the beach on all fours, the tape between his fingers. Then he stooped, wiped his bloody hands in the sand and doubled after the platoon.

Most of the Fifth Battalion were across the beach. As the last of them clambered up a steep bank of sand, sticking close to the tape for fear of mines, they moved aside cautiously to pass Corporal Shuttleworth.

He was sitting, dazed, on his pack by the tape. Where his right boot had been there was a raw red stump. 'Mind the mines,' he muttered dreamily to the men passing him, 'or you'll get what I got.'

No one had time to stop for him. One after another the riflemen looked curiously at him, as if they had never known him, and hurried on. The blood was draining away from him fast. There was no pain and he was becoming sleepy. Some of the men trudging past him were his friends; sometimes one of them would stoop over him and tell him apologetically that the stretcher-bearers would be along in a moment to look after him. He would shake his head drunkenly, and once he giggled. One of his old comrades from the Green Howards, bending over him, heard him snigger, 'Half a man, half a bloody man. The cow, she'll get my pension.' The blood was running away from him into the thirsty sand. He shook, as if enjoying some great secret joke. He mumbled something and toppled forward across the tape. The last rifleman of the Fifth Wessex stepped over the body and plodded on.

Lieutenant Paterson walked lightly at the head of his platoon. The first numb, obsessed rush was over. He was beginning to enjoy himself. For months he had wondered what his first day in battle would be like. There would be fear to conquer, he had thought; there would be sickness and disgust at the sight of death and mutilation. But the time had come and there were none of these things. Instead he felt free, triumphant, detached somehow from all that was happening around him; as if he were seeing it on a cinema screen, as if all the noises were on a soundtrack and there were no fleet bullets or whanging steel splinters to harm him. And everything – he puzzled about it – everything was so familiar. He had seen it all before, on newsreels, in war films, in the war books on which he had grown up. There was nothing new here, nothing to shock. He had grown up in the aftermath of one war, with the shadow of another already over him.

The first corpses and the first wounded aroused only curiosity in him, and a strange craving to look more closely and note every detail. Only once was he shaken. He was marching with Sergeant Shannon close behind him when he heard a shell coming. He shouted, 'Get down, there!' and flopped. As he lay with his head between his arms, quailing under the explosion, he heard something thump into the ground in front of him. He looked up and saw, lying only a yard ahead of him, a human trunk with a head but no limbs. He spewed over his tunic as he rose to his feet and lurched forward, white-faced and overcome with sudden nausea. He looked over his shoulder. Sergeant Shannon was quite unmoved.

The platoon moved in open file along a sunken road running inland, weapons ready. There were broad ploughlands on both sides, with *Achtung, Minen* boards every few yards. Far away on the left there was a wood. A machine gun opened fire from the wood and they dropped into the shelter of the road's steep bank. 'Keep moving, chaps,' called Mister Paterson, and they moved forward on hands and knees with the bullets squealing overhead.

Charlie Venable swore bitterly; he was finding it hard going and his hands and knees were raw already. There were the first houses of a village ahead of them now, and shelter; behind them the German machine gun stopped its fruitless probing; then they heard it firing again at another party coming up behind them. The village was captured and the cottages were swarming with British infantrymen searching for German stragglers. There was some looting. A mob of German prisoners squatted at the foot of a long wall, listless, furtive, uninterested in the army that was streaming past them. Paterson and his platoon trudged past the prisoners. Charlie Venable swore again, this time at the top of his voice. 'You —ers,' he shouted at the prisoners, 'you're lucky I never got 'ere first.'

D-Night. The Fifth Battalion were dug in beyond the village, waiting to be counter-attacked. The men lay in their holes listening to the German bombers which had been prowling about the sky since the coming of darkness. The night was lurid with flares and tracers. Guns were booming. The Germans were shelling the beach. Colonel Pothecary, standing at the foot of the steps leading down to the cellar which was his headquarters, brooded over the casualty return he had just signed; the first. He watched the gun-flashes over the dark silhouettes of the treetops, and wondered where his boy was, whether he was alive or floating in some grey waste of water like the corpses of the morning's assault. There was a party of his men still out doing an ammunition fatigue. He worried for them. Colonel Pothecary could not forget his boy, or the parents of the men he led; his burden was heavy upon him.

As they heard the shell rushing down at them through the night the file of men who were moving across the dunes dropped the boxes they were carrying and flung themselves to the ground.

They pressed their bodies into the wet sand, cowering from the blast which buffeted them. They heard the clang of splinters striking the sides of wrecked landing craft and felt the upflung sand raining on to their clothes.

'On your feet,' called Mister Challis, the platoon officer. 'Everyone all right?'

'The Swedebasher's stopped one,' somebody answered in the darkness.

The lieutenant recognised the voice. 'That you, Martin?' he asked, moving towards the speaker. Martin was kneeling beside a dark bundle on the sand.

'All right...' this time it was the strong, dark voice of Sergeant Ferrissey, '...Hit the trail. Golly, you an' Martin look after the Swedebasher.'

The men heaved the boxes on to their shoulders and moved off towards the anti-aircraft guns whose intermittent flashes were stabbing the night.

'He's all right,' said Corporal Gonigle, 'it's a head wound. He's breathing.' The wounded man was breathing hard; each time he expelled his breath he made a little snoring noise. Martin had already pulled a field dressing from the wounded man's thigh pocket, and he applied the bandage with quick and expert movements.

The corporal straightened up after his scrutiny of the wound. 'Looks like a splinter. Opened up the side of his head; messed his face up a bit, too. It's knocked him cold for a bit. I reckon he won't take long to come round, though.'

They lifted the Swedebasher carefully between them and bore him to the beach dressing station.

When they handed him over to the orderlies and were walking back to rejoin the platoon, Martin spoke again. 'That'll just suit that bastard,' he said, 'the miserable sod. He's got a Blighty one there.'

The corporal laughed. 'The Swede's all right,' he replied. 'He just can't keep his troubles to himself.'

'I'd've given 'im trouble if 'e'd kept on much longer,' said Martin savagely, 'moanin' all the time. Give me the sick, that bastard did.'

Martin was right, and the corporal did not answer. Two months ago the sergeant had brought a new man into the platoon's Nissen hut. 'Golly,' he had said, 'here's Private Gotham. He's fresh from the farm. Find him a bed.' They found him a bed and humped his kitbag up from the gate for him, had poured him a mug of tea from the can that was boiling on the stove and had squeezed together on the benches on which they were sitting round the stove to make room for him. They were offering him a place in their community. But Gotham – after ten minutes of his Gloucestershire accent they named him Swedebasher – had refused their kindnesses, without thanks, and had crawled into bed with his face to the wall. The next day he had started grumbling: about his farm, about the money he was losing, about the injustice of dragging him away into the Army, about his wife, about his three children, about the food and the beds. The rest of the platoon were preparing for an invasion; they were trained to the limit and impatient to go. They had no time for Gotham and his grumbling. At any other time he would have been accepted as a character and tolerated; but now they turned their backs on him and let him sulk in solitude. His loneliness, his bitterness against this strange and hostile world, his longing for his farm and family had grown every day. He had gone aboard the troopship like a convict to the hulks.

'You know,' said the corporal, as they fell in again with the platoon, 'he was pretty quiet all through the day.'

'Know why?' growled Martin. 'Before we went down the nets I told him I'd put a bullet in him if I heard him moan once, just once.'

They were back at the dump now, each lifting one of the boxes of ammunition that were stacked there. 'He said his wife and kids came first,' said Martin. 'I've got a wife and kids, too. The bastard.'

They delivered their loads and plodded back towards the dump. There was no time for rest.

Somewhere in the darkness they could hear the throb of aero-engines. Red, dotted lines of tracer were sailing slowly up into the sky; more and more of them until they criss-crossed in pyrotechnic patterns. Bombs were falling in the distance, and the men watched with fascination as they exploded, first seeing the second's incandescent glare of white flame, then hearing the noise, as if all about them giant furnace doors were swinging open and slamming shut again.

The ground shook with the thudding reply of distant batteries. Guns on a nearby beach joined in, the heavies with a dull booming, the Bofors with their insistent banging, the little quick-firing Oerlikons, noisiest of all, with their incessant crack-crack-crack. The ships out in the anchorage were firing now with all their armament, and the noise rose to a hysterical crescendo.

The droning of engines grew louder, challenging the din of the barrage. The ammunition carriers heard the battery ahead of them open fire and each man, as he walked, looked about him for cover.

There was the sudden drumming roar of an engine, low over their heads. The corporal, leaping into an abandoned slit trench, thought he saw the shadow of wings flitting past. He landed heavily on top of someone else who was already crouching in the narrow pit and gasped instinctively, 'Sorry.'

They did not even hear the explosion; the sides of the trench closed in on them like clapping hands; the weight of sand and splintering timbers pressed the corporal down into suffocating darkness. He heaved and struggled, and felt the man beneath him fighting to move. He forced one hand up through the wet, scratching sand and felt it moving free. There was movement above him, and voices strangely muffled; the timbers were being lifted from his back and he was out, gasping, into the sweet, fresh air.

He gulped and raised himself on all fours. Everyone was safe. The platoon trailed off again for more ammunition, the corporal, breathing painfully, in the rear. Mister Challis watched his men plod by, and counted them. One, two three – the fourth man's head was a strange and shapeless blob of white against the box on his shoulder.

'Gotham?' exclaimed the lieutenant. 'What the hell are you doing here?'

The Swedebasher looked sheepish in the gloom.

Corporal Gonigle came up to him. 'Look,' he said, coming close to the Swedebasher, 'he's still got an evacuation label tied to him.'

He took the Swedebasher by the shoulders. 'Swede,' he shouted, 'Swede, did you walk out on them? Did you come back here on your own?'

The Swede nodded his bandaged head violently in the darkness. He managed to speak at last. 'I felt a fool in there,' he said. 'There were some terrible bad cases there, Corp.'

'You silly old bastard,' the corporal chuckled, and punched the Swede affectionately in the ribs.

'Here, Corp,' said Private Gotham suddenly, taking his handkerchief from his pocket and unfolding it, 'the doctor gave me this. It's what he took out of my head.'

'Wait till I show the missus,' he said with gloomy pride. He wrapped the splinter of steel carefully in his handkerchief, replaced it in his pocket, shouldered his box again and stumbled away in pursuit of his comrades.

In the sweet, summer orchards the men of the Fifth Battalion crouched in their slit trenches listening to the guns and watching the gun-flashes tearing the darkness apart. Sometimes men dozed off, no longer kept awake by the ceaseless rumbling of artillery; but the faintest rapping of machine carbines in the distant woods brought them trembling to their feet.

Sergeant Shannon peered into the darkness, consumed with terror. His day in battle was catching up on him, and living in retrospect the hours through which he had shown no sign of fear, he huddled shivering against the earth wall of the trench, feeling his stomach muscles contract and his lungs freeze with the physical sensation of fear until the pain became unbearable. He had known this in Africa and Sicily, in the secret moments of the night; there was no escaping it. He looked at the rifleman who was slumped sleeping in the bottom of the trench, and wondered that the mad shattering of his teeth did not awaken the man. The darkness was alive with shadows and strange shapes. He saw again, against the flares and the gay rockets that were dancing over the treetops, little Bradley crawling on all fours back along the tape, his own hands bright with blood, the limbless trunk in the roadway in front of him. He heaved himself up on to the parapet and leaned forward, supporting himself with one hand on the ground while he vomited loudly and violently.

Charlie Venable and Baldy, who were on duty behind a Bren in a heap of rubble that commanded the roadway nearby, lay silently watching the sergeant retching. They were close enough to see his dreadful shivering, the shivering of his whole body – limbs and trunk and flaccid cheeks.

'See,' whispered Baldy, 'what did I tell yer? Shannon ain't so tough.'

'Quiet, you cowson,' hissed Charlie Venable. 'Keep your eyes on the road.'

CHAPTER SIXTEEN
Wild roses

THE INFANTRYMEN PLODDED along at the roadside while the tanks, each enveloped in its own clattering roar, hurried past them. The men were dusty and sodden with sweat, marching in straggling single files, each man keeping his own uneven step.

For miles across the meadows and ploughlands that sloped down to the Channel thousands of little files of men were moving inland; from the air it must have looked less like a battle than the advance of a multitude of little worms across the face of the land. Every little file was the same: six, eight or ten tired men, more aware of the weight of their packs than of the enemy who awaited them; looking idly across the silent fields on either side with the lethargic unconcern of the early workman's bus: not talking, not singing, unstirred by the thudding artillery but waiting, always waiting and alert, for the crack of small arms fire and the quick squeal of bullets. There was no drama, no earthquaking bombardment, no masses in conflict; only the ten men plodding along a lane in single file, tired and out of step, the ten men multiplied ten thousand times.

A shell would burst in the fields a hundred yards away and the earth come pattering down on the helmets of the men sprawled in the dust, and on the backs of their necks. Then they would be up on their feet again and raggedly marching. A shell would explode across the roadway, obliterating half a dozen men; but the files, dispersed, would coalesce again and plod onwards past the shallow crater and through the vanishing brown smoke.

A wood echoed with the nervous clamour of machine guns; a farmhouse burned. Desperate little fights flared up and ended suddenly, for a barn, for a hedgerow honeycombed with weapon pits, for a roadside cottage, section against section, platoon against platoon; ten, perhaps twenty men on each side, rarely more. Wary riflemen hunted snipers in the cool gloom of vaulted cellars among the great cobwebbed cider barrels. Men died on the warm dungheaps with hens fluttering a panic about them. An old French peasant woman lugged a dead German on to her cabbage patch and began to dig his grave there, 'to enrich the earth, m'sieu'. This was the battle on D-Day Plus One.

The Fifth Battalion was moving up through a village. The unpaved road climbed steeply between the splinter-pitted grey walls of the cottages and turned sharply into a tangled, five-forked junction. Here there was chaos, with platoons of riflemen in file threading in and out of each other and of the slow-moving columns of tanks and guns that filtered across the road junction.

A tank accelerated to climb the hill into the village, with a foot or two to spare on each side between its racing tracks and the cottage walls. Infantrymen scattered, cursing, or flattened themselves against the walls; re-formed their files and scattered again for the next tank; ducked into doorways and emerged with silly little pilfered trinkets which they threw away five minutes later; drew back to let the next tank go by, and formed their ranks again.

Sergeant-Major McBean stood at the crossroads and watched the battalion marching by. He was worried. These men were not like the Highlanders with whom he had fought before. With the exception of the men from the Green Howards, scattered here and there along the battalion's ranks, they were new to battle, and by God, he thought, they couldn't look less like soldiers. Big, awkward country boys with flat fair hair poking raggedly from under their helmets; red, round faces that were frightened faces, empty faces now; bewildered as lost children, looking around them for the sleek Wessex valleys, the dairy herds and the great shire horses that they knew, finding instead the clamour and confusion of a multitude of men, hearing the sickening reverberations of the guns, wandering in a wilderness they could not recognise. They wore long fighting knives sheathed in leather at their belts but they did not look warlike. They had bandoliers of spare ammunition slung over their shoulders and anti-tank grenades tied to their equipment with untidy bits of string; they carried machine carbines and bayoneted rifles; but they only looked like overburdened errand boys.

There was a quick, cut-off shriek from along one of the lanes. A tank swerving too close to a cottage wall had caught one of the riflemen, some slow-moving country boy day-dreaming perhaps of trout in a clear, cold stream, and nudged him against the wall. The thirty tons of steel lumbered on. The boy slid down the wall leaving a long smear of blood and filth; he huddled in a mound at its foot, a bundle burst in its rags. The tank was out of the lane and across the road junction: its crew would never even know what had happened. The riflemen, too, moved on. No one had more than a curious glance for the huddled body. Like a bug, thought the sergeant-major. Killed in action; what a joke. The last rifle company was coming up, and he fell in with its commander.

There was a group of houses where two roads came together. The leading section of riflemen, moving cautiously up towards them, drew fire from the houses on the left and hit the ground, huddling behind the low stone wall that surrounded the war memorial which stood in the fork of the road.

They lay there for a few moments, listening as the bullets shrieked off the granite of the memorial. One machine gun, noted Corporal Meadows, in one house on the left; with a couple of riflemen covering it. He eased himself round the end of the wall and fixed a short burst with his machine carbine. The quick *wheep-wheep* of bullets close by answered him and he drew back. He lay, crouching uncomfortably, with his men waiting behind him. He felt trapped, irresolute, foolish. The passing seconds and his men behind him seemed to accuse him of indecision.

'Bugger this for a lark.'

It was Scannock the Scouse. Scannock the lousy, the drunken, the shiftless. Scannock heaved himself to his feet and stepped quite deliberately over the wall. He walked across in front of the war memorial and stepped over the wall into the roadway on the other side. A light machine gun and two rifles were firing at him across the width of a country lane. Nothing hit him. He walked unhurriedly across the lane, pulling the pin from a grenade. He put the grenade in at the window as if he were posting a letter, and flattened himself against the wall of the house.

'What youse all waitin' for?' he jeered as the grenade exploded. 'Openin' time?'

There were roses growing in the Norman hedges, pink, wild roses; and roses straggling round the cottage doorways.

A rifleman stopped to pick a rose, and fixed it in the netting of his helmet. All down the ranks men stooped to pluck flowers. They passed through another village. There were people here, peasants, old men and old women who stood impassively and watched the soldiers march by. Inside a cottage children squealed and came tumbling suddenly into the roadway between the legs of their grandparents.

'Maman! Les soldats! Les Anglais, les Anglais!'

A pallid little girl in a black smock ran alongside the ranks and gave a soldier, a sturdy English soldier, a pink Normandy rose. Now the children, hidden for days in the cellars during the shelling, came swarming into the road, laughing and shrieking, pursuing the soldiers with flowers and running back to their parents crazy with delight and clutching fistfuls of chocolate.

The soldiers marched on, with the pink roses twined in the netting of their helmets.

Corporal Gonigle sat on a grassy bank reading Voltaire. He was excited; he had no desire to read; the print would not take shape before his eyes. But he had always dreamed of sprawling languidly on a grassy bank and reading Voltaire during a battle: and here he was doing it.

'Hallo, Corporal.' It was Mister Challis, his platoon officer, stocky and aggressive. 'Having fun?'

'Yes, sir.'

'What's the book?'

'*Candide*.'

'Ah,' Challis was pleased with himself. 'All is for the best in the best of all possible worlds, eh?'

'Yes, sir.' Gonigle's bubble of affectation was pricked. He felt intensely disgusted with himself.

'There's a spot of bother up the road, Corporal. A couple of Boche in a house. They're very obstinate. Care to come along?'

'By all means.' Gonigle felt relieved. 'Have you got any grenades?'

'Oh, heaps.'

The corporal put his book away carefully, and rose to his feet. The sun was shining and a pleasant breeze was stirring the hedgerows. It was all very rural. The two men sauntered away down the lane.

'Right!' shouted Sergeant Ferrissey, and crashed in through the doorway of the house.

In the blink of a second he saw the silhouette of a man up on the landing, against the blinding daylight of a shattered window. His machine carbine came up to his waist – the movement was a reflex, quicker than thought – and leaped in his hands. He heard the rapid-fire thunder in the hallway as if from someone else's gun. The body came crashing down the stairs, and he went bounding past it, up to the first landing and beyond, with his men behind him.

'Raus!' he roared, and fired another burst through the door that faced him on the top floor. There was a confusion of movement and frightened voices behind the door, and he crouched on the stairs with his carbine ready as the door opened. A German artilleryman emerged, with his hands above his head, and two more men behind him.

'Come on,' snarled the sergeant. 'Schnell!'

The Germans tumbled down the stairs. He followed them, and as he reached the foot of the stairs, turned the dead German over with his boot. There was no weapon in the man's hands: only a white handkerchief in one clenched fist.

Sergeant Ferrissey was not a sentimental man; he wasted no pity on the German who need not have died. But he rebuked himself as he stepped out into the sunlit street. Michael Ferrissey, he thought, Michael Ferrissey, you're slipping. One round would have done there, not half a bloody magazine.

'All right, my lads,' he roared. 'Keep moving, my lucky lads, keep moving.'

A week after D-Day the Fifth Battalion was dug in along the gentle hillsides towards Caen. The frightened country boys crouched in their slit trenches listening to the blasting crack of mortars and watching the black plumes of smoke leap up all around them. The ground rocked and quaked with the explosions of eighty-eight millimetre shells as the German artillery searched the folds in the ground in which they were entrenched and blotted out their shallow weapon pits one by one. At night snipers crept in through their positions, to open fire in the morning with rifle and machine gun on parties coming up from the rear. Dozens of bloody little battles were fought behind the forward positions. The snipers were everywhere. Officers, their chosen prey, learned to conceal all distinguishing marks, to carry rifles like their men instead of their accustomed pistols, not to carry maps or field glasses, to wear their pips on their sleeves instead of conspicuously on their shoulders.

The counter-attacks came in one after another. Panzer grenadiers came creeping like cats through the corn and swarming in from the surrounding woods. A forward platoon was overrun. A field was lost. A company was forced out of a village, went stumbling forward to win it again, huddled in the ruins under ceaseless mortar fire, was driven out and won it back once more. The frightened country boys were facing troops who, man for man, were craftier and better trained, who had been reared as warriors; they were outfought at every turn; but they managed, somehow they managed, heaven only knew how they managed, to stay where they were.

A straw-haired boy lay in a crater watching the green-clad giants moving crouched among the apple trees towards him. He was livid, twitching, trembling, dribbling with fear. Inside him thought had ceased and there was only the great yearning of a child for a mother a million miles away. But he stayed where he was; and each time his rifle leaped against his shoulder another of the giants stealing up among the trees clawed air and crashed to the ground. They were coming up closer now, all round him. His eyes watched them like the eyes of a trapped kitten; but every few seconds his rifle jerked again in his shoulder and another of them toppled. A stick grenade sailed up in a lazy arc against the white daylight, turned over and came spinning down towards him. He did not move. His eyes were fixed on the grenade as it came down, turning over and over, hurtling down bigger and bigger until its explosion blotted out the daylight for ever.

Twenty yards to the rear another boy from the shires licked his gummy lips and drew up to his Bren. The wispy smoke of the explosion cleared and the grey-green giants disappeared as his machine gun rapped briefly and severely. They were grey-green humps in the uneven ground now, crawling forward flattened against the turf. A half a dozen of them rose and came in with a rush; the machine gun drove them to ground. Another group were up and moving forward. Now they were stumbling up on to their feet all about him, looming again to the stature of giants, more and more of them. The boy from the shires struggled more closely up to the butt of his Bren. He waited for a second as the grey-green giants came crowding into his sights. Gently he squeezed the trigger.

'My bumpkins. My poor bumpkins,' said Lieutenant-Colonel Pothecary. He was standing on a hillside with the R.S.M. The pale blue sky was radiant with sunlight, the larks were singing, the countryside below was a lovely summer panorama, and in the cornfield at the foot of the hill a platoon of the Fifth Battalion was moving forward in open order to clear a village.

The men moved forward through the tall corn, breasting it with their rifles held high across their chests. They must feel at home in the corn, thought the colonel; these boys ought to be harvesting, not fighting, these bewildered, red-faced boys and their tired schoolmasterly officer.

The sound of small arms fire came to him through the dizzy

summer heat, less near and less real than the song of the larks. Men were hit and disappeared in the corn, drowned in a golden sea. The others moved on, tiny, scattered little figures bobbing up and down in the billowing corn. The officer, the tired man with fear in the corners of his eyes who had stood before the colonel ten minutes ago and who was now moving out there in front of them, toppled to one side; the corn parted for a second, then closed in, rustling, where he had been. The platoon sergeant went down. Now, thought the colonel, with a strange dread which was half full of longing, now they're without leaders, now they'll come streaming back, now they're finished; but the little black figures went bobbing forward through the corn, through the dizzy sunlight, towards the distant, woodpecking machine guns.

The counter-attacks grew less frequent, the mortaring less murderous. One morning the men of the Fifth Battalion, stirring sleep-sodden in their shallow slit trenches, heard the birds shrilling in the pale, vast sky, listened to their own aircraft droning in the cloudless infinity above and, wondering, puffed their cigarettes in peace. Their ears were ringing with the quietness.

They were relieved that day, and as they sprawled along the roadsides, too tired to feel or to remember, waiting for transport to take them to the rear, they watched the newly-landed support troops who were moving up the line and jeered at their freshness and their frightened, vacant faces.

'Garn,' yelled Charlie Venable, as the men of another county battalion trudged by, 'you ain't arf bleedin' late. We been 'ere since D-Day.'

'You haven't got very far then!' flung back one of the relieving infantrymen.

'No,' Charlie Venable shouted back to him. 'An' there's a lot of bloody good lads never got this far.'

There was a placid meadow, rich with clover and tall, wet grass. The Fifth Battalion had gone but its dead remained, littered about the field, staring up at the sky with the flies buzzing over them and their big boots poking up in the long grass.

They were silent and still. All the field was dreadfully still. Nothing stirred in the field but the petals of the pink hedge roses which fluttered in the helmets of the dead.

CHAPTER SEVENTEEN
No bloody fags

THERE WAS A CLUTTER of signboards where the two roads met; rough box-tops with the emblems daubed on them of battalions and brigades blazing a trail across the countryside for their rear echelons to follow; neatly-painted diagrams put up by the military police to guide the thundering convoys to their destinations; arrows, figures, initials, hieroglyphics indicating the distance and direction to dumps, headquarters, assembly areas, transport parks; and above them all, the warning: TO THE FORWARD AREA.

In the ditch by the road junction, four men of the Fifth Battalion crouched in a tangle of weeds and bracken. They watched the great supply trucks come lumbering up to the fork, slow down, swing on to the main road to the front and gather speed again.

A convoy went by. The men in the ditch waited, keeping down out of sight, until a lorry came towards them, three hundred yards after the others and with none behind it – a straggler, probably, trying to regain its place in the column.

As the lorry passed them, slowing down, one of the men leaped up from his hiding-place, hurled himself at the tailboard and swung nimbly up into the lorry. He put his arms round one of the stacked packing-cases in the lorry, tipped it over the side, and – as his companions reached forward to pull the box down out of sight – slipped over the tailboard and dropped back on to the roadway. The lorry accelerated and raced away down the road.

The men looked about them; there was no one in sight. They rolled the box through a gap in the hedge and crawled after it.

'Gold Flakes,' grunted Sergeant Bender, as he inspected the box. 'No bloody fags, eh? – we'll show 'em.'

The others joined him: Dickie Crawford, Scannock, MacGuinness. Two of them lifted the box and they trudged across the fields to the orchard in which the Fifth Battalion was resting.

They put the box down by a tree. Bender smashed the lid in with a spade.

'Look nippy,' he said. 'Let's split these up and get 'em out of sight.'

'Just a minute, Sergeant.'

Scannock pushed him aside and stood over the box.

'These is for the lads.'

Bender swore derisively.

'These is for the lads,' said Scannock stubbornly. 'The lads is goin' mad for a smoke.'

The battalion had been short of cigarettes since D-Day. Its rear transport echelon, which should have joined it by now, but which was still somewhere in England, held up by the bad weather, contained a truck loaded with the month's free ration of cigarettes which the NAAFI had given to every man in the invading army. Meanwhile, although the battalion was resting, although mail and newspapers were reaching the men regularly from home, although they each received seven cigarettes a day in their composite ration packs, they were bitterly dissatisfied.

'Get off that box,' said Bender, 'before I crown you with this shovel. What you think I done this for? Charity?'

Scannock did not move. 'You never done it. I jumped that wagon an' slung the box off, not you.'

'Don't argue. You're wasting time. Gettin' soft in your old age, aren't you? Never used to be no love lost between you an' the lads.'

What had happened to Scannock during his first week in action was something for which he could not find words, something his foggy brain was not even able to define.

'These is for the lads,' he said.

Dickie Crawford spoke, after a moment's silence, 'The boy's right. Got brains, 'e 'as. We'll never smoke all these fags ourselves, nor sell 'em while we're 'ere. If we 'ave to move orf we won't be able to carry 'em, an' Gawd 'elp us if there's a search. Me, I'll settle for five 'undred, an' share the rest out.'

Each of them stowed a carton of five hundred cigarettes inside his battle blouse. Then Dickie Crawford called to the men who, all around them, had been watching in silence from the dug-outs and bivouacs under the apple trees.

'Fags up, my lads. Come an' get 'em.'

In five minutes the cigarettes were gone, the crate and the litter of cartons burned.

'Scannock,' said Corporal Meadows later, carefully packing cigarettes into a little tin box, 'you're a bloody great thievin' old bastard – bless your little cotton socks.'

Scannock sat on an upturned ration box and glowed with inarticulate delight. For the first time in his life the world – gone mad to his comrades – was coming right for him. In battle other men were close to you; they admired you; they talked to you; they passed a mug of steaming tea to you; they crawled under a blanket with you; you marched with them, you felt safe and strong with them, you were one of them.

'Aw, Corporal,' he said gruffly, 'I done nothing there to shout about. I'll get yer a chicken tonight, I will.'

'Lovely dairy country, this is,' said Private Smith.

Private Barnicoat, a fellow-member of his platoon, with whom he was taking an evening walk, answered, 'Aye, I've never seen so much cheese an' yeller farm butter in my life. Our lass'd go crazy wi' delight if she were 'ere. An' they call this starvin' Europe.'

'I dunno,' said Private Smith, 'they say it's only in these parts as there's plenty. There's none worth talkin' of in the rest of France. There's millions o' kiddies in this country never tasted milk since they finished wi' their mothers'.'

'Who's been gettin' it all, then?'

'Bloody Germans 'as been gettin' it. An' the rich people. Why, even in this village the lab'rers never get a taste of the meat or the butter they raise. You've seen the kiddies here – white faces, sores all over, poor, thin little legs.'

'Aye,' said Private Barnicoat, 'I reckon it's the same everywhere. Them wi' the money gets it an' poor people gets nowt.'

He took an apple from his pocket, rubbed it on his sleeve and bit noisily. 'Bloody war,' he said. 'Roll on the peace.'

They walked on in silence for a while. It was pleasant, in the warmth and peace of the evening, to listen to the noises of war in the distance – the thudding of the guns now seeming so remote, the mutter of aircraft, the roar of the convoys on the main road beyond the woods.

They passed a group of village women laughing and singing as they knelt over their washing around a trough. There was a shrill twitter of talk among the women as the soldiers went by.

Munching their apples, they came to the Mairie, its buff walls gilded by the evening sunlight to the pleasant colour of ripe peaches. There was a casualty clearing station in the Mairie. Bloody stretchers stood against the wall to dry; beyond the wall they glimpsed, through the tall gates, a row of dead awaiting burial, with blankets flung over them.

A jeep ambulance drew up at the gates of the Mairie.

'How's it goin' up there?' Private Smith called to a wounded infantryman who sat by the driver.

'All right, mate,' the man replied weakly. He held up one hand, a great mitt of bandages. 'Got a nice Blighty one 'ere,' he said.

On the stretchers above his head two men were lying, very flat and still. They did not answer, nor even turn their heads, when Bill Barnicoat spoke to them. There was an unpleasant, medical smell about the jeep.

Barnicoat threw an apple core over the wall of the Mairie. 'Come on, Smithy,' he said uneasily.

'I'd rather get killed than crippled,' he said suddenly, when they were a little way along the road.

Private Smith laughed. 'You silly great big donkey,' he said, 'I've no intention of gettin' killed or crippled. That's not the way to talk, lad.'

'It's 'appened to a few, any road.'

'It won't happen to you, Bill, if you don't think about it.'

'Oh aye, mister clever, an' what do you think of when them mortars is comin' down? Zeez-zeez-zeez-CRACK! Zeez-zeez-zeez-CRACK! What do you think of then?'

'Me?' Smithy furrowed his brows. 'I dunno. Better times after the war, I suppose. That's what I think on most o' the time.'

'Better times?' jeered Barnicoat. 'I can see myself now, wi' a wooden leg an' a medal, queuein' up for dole.'

'I dunno about queueing up for dole,' answered Private Smith. 'It looks as though we'll have to queue up for cider.'

They were approaching the village's only cafe. Its sunlit, dusty *terrasse* was thronged with soldiers. Others were crowding into the dark interior of the shop. Others stood in the roadway clustering in excited groups round villagers who had come to barter eggs and potatoes for chocolate, and to exchange gossip and war news in a flutter of gesticulation and pidgin-talk.

'An I'll tell you this much,' said Private Smith fiercely, as they pushed their way into the cafe, 'it's only them without ambition as talks about the dole. I've had a new job offered me when I get back. Scientific farming. Learning, Bill, that's what you want these days – learning.'

'Learnin'!' exclaimed Private Barnicoat. He reached through the crush towards the counter. 'You'll start learnin' when you get back. You'll learn all right.'

'Well, Padre,' said Colonel Pothecary, 'what do you think of 'em?'

The padre laughed: 'Silly question. Look at them.'

They were standing, with Major Norman, on the touchline of a football field. The final round of an inter-company tournament was being played out.

'Look at them,' said the padre. 'Every time that ball soars up into the blue, their spirits soar with it. They're boys again; fresh, eager boys. A week ago they were plunged for the first time in their lives into the most dreadful ordeal that men can devise. They saw their dearest friends killed or mutilated. They – oh, heavens, just look at them. I wish I could forget as easily as they forget.'

'Are you so sure that they've forgotten, Padre?' asked Major Norman.

The padre stared. He was an honest and devoted chaplain, well loved by the men for his courage under fire, and for his zeal in providing comforts for them; he was young, however, and his experience had not been such as to endow him greatly with understanding.

Colonel Pothecary chuckled. 'Wonderful what a couple of days out of the line'll do, isn't it? Good as new again. Oh, good man!' – one of the footballers was racing down the wing; the whole game was surging down the field with him; and the battalion was roaring encouragement from the touchline – 'Oh, come on, Charlton. Try it from there!'

The ball sped between the drunken goalposts. A whistle shrilled.

The spectators swarmed noisily across the field.

Colonel Pothecary watched them contentedly. 'Yes,' he said, 'we've quite a battalion now, quite a battalion.'

Mister Paterson listened to the referee's whistle and the clamour of cheering. Boots thudded on the grass and the shadows of the men running past him flitted across the pages of his book. He returned to his reading.

'What's the book, sir?'

He looked up, annoyed at the interruption. Shannon, his platoon sergeant, was standing over him.

He held up the book. Shannon took it and read the title aloud.

'*Pickwick Papers*. Oh aye,' he said. He seated himself on the grass beside his officer, 'I've 'ad some rare good times wi' that book.'

Mister Paterson answered delightedly, 'Oh, I think it's wonderful. I never get tired of it. Whenever I'm cheesed off I just open it and start reading – it doesn't matter where – and the world begins to seem sane again.'

'Good thing to have by you,' said Sergeant Shannon, 'in times like these. P'r'aps I could borrow it from you now an' then?'

'Of course.' Mister Paterson was mildly surprised. He was not a snob; nor did he keep himself apart from his men. Yet he had never really come to understand them. They were mostly of his own age, or little older, yet he always felt so adolescent beside them.

'You like books, do you?'

'Oh aye. I always were a great reader. Specially when I were out o' work. Used to spend 'alf my time at Corporation Library, I did. Four books a week was nothin' to me in those days. Only I never see a book now. I've got no one to send 'em to me.'

'I have,' said Mister Paterson. 'You're always welcome to anything I get.'

'Thanks. You know,' said Sergeant Shannon, 'it's queer, sir, isn't it? – but them old writers is still the best to read. Myself, I like Dickens best. He's so rich, like, an' ripe. I reckon *David Copperfield* is the most beautiful book I've ever read in my life.'

He was silent for a moment. 'All that first part of it, where the little boy lives with his young mother. The games they play, an' all that. Till Mr Murdstone comes along like a big black raven. He writes it so tender, like. My own mum died, y'know, when I were a nipper. Aye, he were a great man, were Charles Dickens.'

'Aye,' he went on, 'the old writers is the best. Take Thack'ray, now. Right sarcastic he is, sometimes. An' Jane Austen. Have you read any of her stories?'

'My mother loves Jane Austen,' said Mister Paterson.

'Did you know,' asked Sergeant Shannon eagerly, 'she were only the daughter of a country parson? She used to sit in't parlour pourin' out tea for visitors, an' bein' polite to neighbours an' family, like. An' all the time she was writin' these books, an' hidin' it under the blotter if anyone came near.'

He sighed. 'It's a wonderful thing to have that gift, to write stories people will love for a hundred years an' more.'

He fell silent. Mister Paterson searched for words. He knew that another five seconds of silence would break this rare moment of communion, that the sergeant would retire again inside his armour of reserve. He opened his mouth to speak; he was too late.

'It's quiet this evening,' said the sergeant. 'Too quiet. I reckon we'll be movin' up again soon. Don't you?'

'We're sure to,' said Mister Paterson. 'This is too good to last.'

Shannon brushed grass from his trousers. He was the tough and uncommunicative sergeant again.

'We'll inspect the Brens in't morning,' he said. 'Good night, sir.'

The battalion was marching back towards the line. As the grumbling of the guns grew louder, the jesting and singing in the ranks died away and the men felt the sickness of fear deep within them; for they had not forgotten.

But the padre, standing at the road junction as they trudged dustily by, saw only the firm brown faces, the cigarettes perked up at the corners of their mouths, the tousled hair under their steel helmets; and he marvelled that men could be so strong.

CHAPTER EIGHTEEN
We've had a loverly day today

IN THE MISTY DAWN, with the rain battering upon them and the ground trembling beneath the artillery, the men of the Fifth Battalion slithered up the muddy, sodden banks behind which they had been crouching and lurched forward, heads down against the rain, into the attack.

Tanks rumbled across the fields, the infantry moving behind them in scattered groups. As the daylight crept across the countryside the enemy artillery and mortars came into action. Exploding shells flung their pillars of smoke up towards the black, low-bellied rainclouds. Tanks were hit, heeling into the soft ground on their broken tracks, burning fiercely, so that the fog of smoke ahead of the infantrymen thickened into a dense wall out of which, as some burning tank exploded, would come sailing ribbons of white smoke and bright coloured lights that vanished in the driving rain. The riflemen, plodding across the broad ploughlands, seemed to ignore the din, the explosions that leaped about them, the rising crackle of small arms fire. These things were only incidental – the real burdens that oppressed them were the rain that trickled on to their collars from the rims of their helmets, the slippery ground on which they tried to keep their balance, the muck that clung in great, clotted masses to their boots, making them as heavy to lift from the furrows as if they were soled with lead.

The leading platoons were moving towards the gentle, wooded slopes on which waited the first German outposts, little groups of men dug cunningly in among the trees and bushes, crouching unseen in narrow pits under the hedges behind the thin barrels of their machine guns. The British infantrymen came trudging in among the trees, miserable and sodden; bewildered at first as the mines with which the ground was sown exploded beneath their comrades' feet and the bullets came whining among them; then spreading out rapidly and moving from tree-trunk to splintered tree-trunk, crouching, alert, angry; angry with the rain, with the mud, with boredom and fatigue, and closing in to vent their anger on the enemy. To many of the Germans who tried to surrender at the last possible moment they gave short shrift; others were fortunate enough to escape with a kick in the stomach or a blow in the teeth with a rifle butt before they were sent stumbling to the rear, while the rest of the Fifth Battalion came streaming past.

It took an hour for them to clear the slopes and the rest of the morning before they had moved down the narrow lanes beyond the crest to take the village which nestled in the next hollow; an eternity of weary marching and of lying in the ditches, under the dripping hedgerows, in strange, sudden lulls when each man was assailed by an unutterable loneliness, a feeling of timeless unreality, a sense of muddy, sodden desolation, when the patter of rain sounded louder than the thudding guns; until the obstacle ahead had been battered into the ground by tanks or artillery and the infantrymen were able to heave themselves up out of the mire and trudge onward.

From the timbered loopholes of a dugout amid the under-growth that clothed the steep sides of a winding lane, a German machine gun rapped. The British riflemen tried to rush the slope to get in close with machine carbines and grenades. Twice they tried; their dead littered the rain-dappled puddles in the narrow roadway. The rest crouched back behind the bend; they watched the sappers crawling along the bank with the fat, coiled flamethrower on their backs; they watched the liquid leap from the flamethrower's nozzle and spread in two great breaths of fire across the dugout; then they marched on, past the trees that burned in the rain, past the serpents of flaming liquid that still blazed on the timbers of the dugout, past the stench of burned flesh that hung heavily, for a few seconds, in the sweet, rain-washed air.

Aircraft muttered in the sky above them; the first they had heard during the day. They did not even look up; so great was the confidence they had acquired in their own air support; until the mumble of engines swelled suddenly to a rising thunder, and they heard the stutter of machine guns.

The Messerschmitts swept over their heads like great shadows. The infantrymen grovelled in ditches. Major Norman stood, feet astride, in the middle of the roadway shouting, 'Get down, there! Get down!' His high-pitched voice, clearly audible amid the roar of engines as the aircraft streaked past him, was as hard and compelling as the whistle of a lashing whip. 'Get down, there! Get down!' But Major Norman did not get down. When the enemy aircraft finally dwindled away up into the grey haze, and the first anti-aircraft guns began vainly to bang shells after them, he was still standing in the middle of the roadway, feet astride, looking up into the dismal sky.

Throughout the day they trudged on, soaked and tired, sickened and stunned by the smoke and the din, until in the evening, with the German defences broken behind them, they halted. Numbed with fatigue, they pulled the spades from beneath their packs and began to dig. Later, while a relieving battalion passed forward through them to continue the attack, they sat in their shallow pits at the roadsides, huddled in their waterproof gas-capes, while on the little tommy-cookers that they sheltered between their feet they brewed boiling, life-preserving tea in their mess tins.

They had been on their feet for ten hours, marching and fighting. On the map, their advance measured precisely three miles.

They rested for four hours; then, in the late evening, they clambered up out of their holes and stood in groups in the roadway, exercising numbed arms and legs, and exchanging rumours, as they waited to move off again. The enemy were pulling out; a million airborne troops had landed in his rear; an invasion of Holland was taking place simultaneously with this offensive; Caen had fallen to an attack from the other side of the Orne; Hitler had been seen at the front; Hitler was wounded; Hitler was dead; the battalion was waiting for requisitioned motor buses to come up and carry it deep into the territory from which the enemy was fleeing; a chateau full of cognac had been captured and the divisional commander had ordered the issue of one bottle per man to the infantry; and leave to Blighty was going to start in ten days' time. At this stage of an attack the rumours always reached their height. The men, standing in the gathering darkness, not knowing where they were, where they were going or when, wondering how many miles of marching lay ahead of them, and how many hours would pass before the next assault, nourished their hopes on every fantasy that reached their ears.

Darkness had fallen by the time the battalion was on the move again. They marched through the night, following the narrow lanes up and down hill. It was a strange, maddening thing, this marching through the darkness for hour after hour, with nothing visible but the dark mass of another man's back bobbing in front of you, lurching and stumbling in the deep, soft ruts, sloshing through puddles you could not see, feeling the road slope sickeningly away beneath you into the black pit of another valley and feeling the burden of your weapons, equipment and ammunition dragging at your shoulders as you slogged up the far slope. This was so different from the route marches at home, when you could set your teeth and tick off the miles one by one; here there was no end to the road, no way out of the tunnel of darkness; you just had to go on, for hour after hour, pulling your leaden boots up out of the mud and setting them down again.

Hour after hour crept by in the darkness; until each man, marching with as little consciousness as a machine, had lost all touch with everything outside himself and trudged on, wrapped in his thoughts, or his dreams, or the strange, waking sleep of the soldier.

* * *

Charlie Venable was thirsty. Sticky and sodden with rain, marching in four inches of water, he was frantic with thirst. Deep in a foggy, swirling reverie he had lost for hours all consciousness of the needs and discomforts of his body; until he had become aware, remotely at first, then more and more unpleasantly, of his parched throat and gummy lips, of the sickening metallic taste in his mouth. There was a half-filled water-bottle strapped to his belt. Feeble with sleep, he fumbled at straps in the darkness. Marching, marching, not daring to stop for a moment in the darkness, he stumbled and cursed and groped at straps, without result. Maddened by failure yet too weary to persist, he leaned forward again to the weight of his rifle and pack, hooked his thumbs once more into the webbing straps on his chest to ease the strain on his shoulders and marched on, trying to ignore the itch of impatience that now tantalised him and made the night crawl by more slowly than before. He dreamed of a whirling spray on the sleek lawns of a park, flinging a cool mist of water against his face, hurling its glittering droplets high into the sunlight. He listened to his own feet sloshing in the waterlogged ruts. A sound battered vaguely at his consciousness; he shut it out; then another; there was a faint echo of recognition inside him; then another, this time deafening and jolting him into awareness like a blow in the face – the ear-splitting banging of a battery of field guns firing in rapid succession close by.

He was awake now, and he felt a stir of awareness running down the column of men in front of him. Away in the fields to their left British twenty-five pounders were coming into action. The night was riven by the white lightning of their muzzle flashes. Guns were firing away to the right now. Charlie saw the flashes spreading away into the darkness as if a trail of powder had been touched off.

Someone asked what time it was. Charlie lifted the face of his wristwatch; he was surprised to see that it was after four in the morning already.

Along the whole front the field batteries were firing, with a noise like hundreds of great steel doors banging in a vast, high-roofed corridor. From the rear came the thud and rumble of the mediums and heavies joining in.

'Barrage,' shouted Charlie above the uproar to the man in front of him. 'Must be the Third Battalion getting ready to go in.'

Somewhere ahead of them the battalion that had passed through them the evening before was waiting along its start line to launch a fresh assault; this was the preliminary barrage.

The roar of the guns increased in fury. From the muzzles of the nearest guns on both sides leaped great golden tongues of flame which seemed to meet in a dazzling blur of light about the battalion. The men staggered on with their heads down, terrified as children at each nearby stab of fire, pummelled by the blasting explosions, with the earth quivering beneath them like living flesh that was being beaten.

From the top of a hill they could see in the distance a sea of fire in the plain below where the British shells were falling. In the flickering white gun-flashes they glimpsed the silhouettes of tanks lumbering forward and the shadowy files of marching men moving into position.

Towards daylight the barrage slackened in intensity. As the rumble of the guns diminished they heard through it the childish, distant tapping of small arms fire. The attack was going in.

'Our turn next,' grunted Charlie Venable as the order came to halt and once again the men of the Fifth Battalion pulled the spades from out of their webbing and began to dig.

They were still digging when the white light of morning had filled the sky. The plain below them was a wilderness of grey mist and dark, smudgy smoke, through which explosions winked like will-o'-the-wisps and the sounds of battle filtered.

Mister Paterson came hurrying up from headquarters towards his platoon. His cherub's cheeks were pink with delight; he was whistling.

'Well, my lads,' he said, as he came among his men, 'you all want to know, don't you?'

The men straightened up from their digging.

He went on, 'Here's this morning's situation report from Division. Yesterday's attack – that was us – went right through the top crust. This morning's attack is aimed at getting a bridgehead across the river. It's going fine so far. I expect we'll move across into the bridgehead this evening or tomorrow, and carry on from there. That's all there is so far. Everyone all right, Sergeant Shannon?'

'They could do wi' a drop o' rum, in them wet clothes,' said the Sergeant.

'It'll be up,' said Mister Paterson, 'and there's your compo rations to be picked up from Company H. Q. That's about three hundred yards down the road – you'll see a gap in the hedge on the right-hand side. You can send Lance Corporal Feather with three men.' He turned to the men again. 'Don't dawdle now, my lads. Get yourselves dug in. It's for your own good, you know.'

The men bent over their spades again. They knew now how they were faring and what was happening around them; that was fine, that was all they needed. They began to talk and laugh; they threw off their weariness and dug with a will.

The sun struggled with the mist, triumphed as the morning advanced and by midday was shining again from a clear sky. The men, rested and fed, were in better spirits when the battalion moved off again in the afternoon. They squelched cheerfully forward along the muddy lanes, through country that bore the marks of the night-long barrage and the morning's battle. The cottages at the roadside were smashed and gaping, sometimes burning. The fields were pitted with shell craters; there were dead cattle and eviscerated horses sprawling everywhere. The roads were littered with the rubbish of war – the blackened, twisted skeletons of burned-out vehicles, spades, packs, tunics, blankets, weapons; food tins and cartons, letters and coloured documents fluttering from a wrecked lorry or an abandoned command post; and British and German dead lying where they had been pushed to the roadsides.

The leading troops ahead were driving on fast, covering ground without troubling to mop up the enemy whom they scattered. Sometimes the most determined of the Germans would come together in little groups which filtered back into the villages behind the British spearheads; so that, more than once during the day, the Fifth Battalion was halted in the narrow lanes listening to the sound of machine guns and grenades as a village was cleared ahead; more than once the leading platoon, coming round a bend, would find a file of British riflemen crouching against the grey stone wall exchanging fire with a sniper in the farmhouse ahead; more than once the battalion heard the sounds of battle in its own rear. But the men were marching, fast and free, into enemy territory, and they were too confident to care.

It was in Mister Paterson's platoon that the singing began; and Charlie Venable's was the first voice raised.

155

Oh, we've 'ad a loverly day today, today,
We've 'ad a loverly day today.
We don't know where we are,
We don't know where we been,
We don't know whether we've 'ad it out
Or whether we've 'ad it in –

The song was interminable. Raggedly, the whole platoon joined in, and the song spread along the files plodding at the roadsides.

Oh, we've 'ad a loverly day today, today,
We've 'ad a loverly day today –

'There it is,' said Colonel Pothecary, pointing downhill with his cane, 'the river. The sappers have got a bridge across it already.'

Major Norman looked about him at the ravaged, smoke-hung countryside. Behind him he could hear the riflemen singing:

Oh, we've 'ad a loverly day today –

'Such a lot of fuss,' he said sadly, 'about such a little river.'

The crossing was under mortar fire. There were troops ahead of them blocking the roadway, while small groups rushed at intervals across the bridge.

Colonel Pothecary cursed. 'Bloody fools,' he grumbled. 'Who the hell do they think they are, blocking the road while they scuttle across like mice? This is a fine time to be afraid of getting hurt.'

A tall, black-moustached officer in a British warm strode across the bridge from the other side. He lifted a megaphone to his lips. 'Come on, you officers,' he shouted, 'up on your feet and get your men moving.'

He stood on the bridge unflinching while the mortar bombs exploded on the banks and in the water downstream.

'Come on,' he roared through the megaphone. 'Who's in command there? Get them moving. Get them moving.'

The unit in front began to clatter across the bridge in a continuous stream.

'Thank God for that,' grunted Colonel Pothecary as the road ahead of them cleared. 'Let's go.'

The battalion crossed the stream under fire and marched under fire for another mile into the bridgehead. For the third time they deployed off the roads and dug in. The men were punch-drunk with fatigue by now, pausing to rest after each shovelful of earth, toppling in sleep into half dug trenches.

As they lay in their shallow holes there was a fresh outburst of artillery fire. A mile ahead of them the Germans were counter-attacking, their tanks milling in the midst of the forward British infantry. The ground shook as the artillery on both sides exchanged furious cannonades. Earth sifted and pattered down from the sides of the slit trenches on to the faces of the men of the Fifth Battalion, but they were utterly weary and they did not even stir.

They crouched in their holes all night while the sky flickered with action and the German rockets soared and burst in a gaily-coloured firework display. Sometimes bullets came squealing out of the darkness as German patrols crept through on the flanks, and the Brens would hammer their darting lines of tracer into the darkness in reply.

Major Maddison was inspecting his company's positions. He made his way cautiously along a gully in which a section of his riflemen were entrenched.

'What's this?' he asked as he stumbled over something soft and bulky. He bent forward and felt with his hands; it was a corpse, with a blanket flung over it.

'One of ours?' he asked.

'Not one of our own,' answered the corporal. 'He must be from the Third Battalion.'

'Get the bloody thing out of here,' said Maddison curtly, 'before it stinks.'

'Yes, sir,' said the corporal, not moving. The darkness shielded

Maddison from the hatred in the men's eyes.

Maddison clambered up out of the trench. 'Don't forget,' he said again, 'get the stiff out of the way before it's daylight.' He walked away.

'Whoreson,' said the corporal. He knelt by the corpse and gently replaced the blanket over the waxen face.

'Some poor mother'll be weeping for this lad,' he said tenderly.

Early the next morning, the battalion moved up again and took over the forward positions. The day was cold and cloudy.

The first counter-attack came in during the morning, a dozen tanks lumbering across the broad heath with infantry creeping behind; there was no artillery preparation.

The forward platoons of the Fifth Battalion opened fire but the attack came on. When the tanks were half a mile away there was a sudden rumble of aero-engines in the clouds. The men of the Fifth Battalion listened joyfully as the noise of engines swelled – they had not expected air support on a day like this.

There was a rush and roar of bombs and rockets in front of the battalion. The noise in the clouds grew as more aircraft took off from their advanced airstrips in the battle-scorched cornfields. Tanks burned under black canopies of smoke. The attack was stopped.

The enemy tried again during the day, and again, each time with fewer tanks. Each time they were stopped by British aircraft or by a leaping, murderous wall of artillery fire. During the night they tried to infiltrate towards the river but the men of the Fifth Battalion, fighting off sleep, stopped them and wiped out in the first light of dawn a few small groups that had got back to the river.

By the next morning – the fourth – the offensive, it seemed, had petered out. So had the enemy's counter-attacks. The men were roused by a fine drizzle of rain against their faces. They lay in their pits listening to the rumble of gunfire far away to the left. It sounded as if a fresh British attack was going in on another sector, giving the enemy no time for rest.

Everything seemed delicious to the men this morning; the cold, sweet air, the drizzle against their skins, even the ache of fatigue in their limbs; everything that reminded them of their survival was delicious.

They breakfasted on tinned, fatty bacon, thickly-buttered biscuits and tea laced with rum. They stripped to the waist and washed, resting their tired arms luxuriously in the clean, cold water.

And they shaved; every man shaved by order of Colonel Pothecary; for the British soldier is no black-bearded warrior. Whenever there is a lull in the battle he shaves, and with his beard he seems to get rid of all the misery and filth and degradation of battle.

Glowing and clean-shaven, with their self-respect restored, the men of the Fifth Battalion passed the morning away, some sleeping huddled in their pits under blankets, greatcoats and gas-capes; some sitting in the dry corners of shattered barns and cottages talking, smoking, scribbling letters. The Doggy Boys emptied the cargo from a wrecked lorry and played cards in comfort under its canvas hood.

Mister Paterson eased the boots from his swollen feet and pulled his socks off. He showed the tattered, filthy socks to Sergeant Shannon, then rolled them carefully and pushed them into his pack.

'I shall send them home for my mother to wash and darn,' he said, 'as soon as I get a chance.'

'There's not much left of 'em to darn,' said Shannon.

Paterson laughed tenderly. He could see his mother inspecting the socks in shocked surprise, and writing to him in blessed innocence: whatever have you been doing with your socks?

'She'll probably tell me not to walk so much,' he said.

Beneath the hedge which marched across the slopes of a Norman hillside lay a slit trench, a deep and narrow slot of darkness hidden by the riotous grass and overhung by the green tangle of hawthorn.

A man, standing in the trench this summer evening, would look out across a quiet valley to the gentle hills that rose opposite, their flanks clothed with orchards and cornfields and clumps of dark woodland.

It was something for a soldier to wonder at, the calm and beauty of this unscarred battlefield, in which there stirred no sign of human life, and in whose peace the thudding of guns and the roar of traffic on rearward roads had faded to a scarce-heeded background, drowned by the clamour of birds.

The pale sky, in which wisps of cloud lost themselves subtly, was still lustrous with the last dazzling shafts of sunlight.

Nowhere could a sign of war be seen; no charred patches in the corn that billowed like a golden sea in the valley; no columns of black smoke. The rifles, the mortars and the machine guns were silent.

The only occupant of the trench was sitting on its floor with his back to the earthen end wall, his knees drawn up to his chin. His blanket was draped over his back like a poncho and he was smoking a cigarette.

It was true that in this position Corporal Meadows could not enjoy the view. But, although he was not a man without feeling, he took greater joy in the luxury of relaxed muscles than in the sight of a picture which by now was only too familiar to him. He was, too, a sufficiently experienced soldier (as the Africa ribbon on his soiled tunic bore witness) never to show himself unnecessarily above ground. Besides, he liked the view from where he sat – the patch of sky with a pattern of overhanging leaves fretted against it.

For the last few hours Corporal Meadows had been mainly concerned with trying to keep himself from feeling lonely. He had glanced twice through a newspaper which he had already finished, he had written a letter to his wife that filled eight pages instead of the usual two and he had smoked even more cigarettes than was his custom. Now he was content to watch the leaves stirring against the sky.

It is not usual for a soldier to occupy a slit trench on his own. For Corporal Meadows, a sociable man, it was especially rare.

During such quiet spells as this he was used to enjoying the company of his friend. He and Corporal Warne had survived two years of front-line service together. In Africa and Sicily their platoon commander had always known where to find them when they were free from their duties as leaders of rifle-sections; together, always together, sitting facing each other knee-to-knee in a slit trench or sprawling side by side under a tree; perhaps brewing up some tea, perhaps smoking, perhaps sharing a newspaper, but talking little.

Two nights ago, however, Warne had gone quietly down into the valley at the head of a patrol. He and his men had not returned; and now Corporal Meadows was spending his leisure time alone.

It was not that he grieved. The men of the Fifth Battalion had already learned – and Corporal Meadows had learned long ago – that it did not pay to grieve for absent friends. There were too many of them; a man who let their passing hurt him would carry more unhealed wounds than he could bear; and so the riflemen of the Fifth Battalion had grown, as all soldiers grow, into a state of mind in which a friend killed yesterday became as remote in the memory as some half-forgotten schoolmate, to be talked of with the same detachment.

For instance, the platoon sergeant, talking to him earlier in the day about ammunition requirements, had remarked quite suddenly, 'Pity about Warne. Nice bloke.'

Corporal Meadows had answered, 'Yes, he was.'

They had gone on talking about ammunition.

There was another occasion, too, when Meadows was sitting with his men against the bank of a sunken lane, eating stew from his mess tin.

Someone had begun to talk about Warne, recalling some episode in which he had made himself ridiculous, talking as soldiers often talk of their dead, not out of heartlessness, but because the telling of these stories and the brief merriment they evoked helped to forget the fact of the man's death.

There was a gust of noisy laughter; then someone looked quickly at Meadows, apprehensively. He, too, was laughing.

But now, in the evening, he was not laughing. He was listening to the shrilling of the birds and watching the smoke from his cigarette climb the brown wall of the trench, writhe among the hawthorn branches and lose itself in the blue of the sky.

Noises of life came from other trenches hidden along the hedge;

laughter from one, the clatter of mess tins from another, the soft whistling of a tune from another. These sounds he hardly heard.

Nor did he hear the rustle of boots in the grass, so that he was startled when the light was blotted out from above him by the shape of a man, and unready for the voice of the man speaking to him.

'So there you are.'

He knew whose voice it was before he looked up. He felt as if someone had thumped him on the chest, breathless and a little sick.

'Hallo, you old rogue,' said Corporal Meadows at last. 'Where've you been these last two days? In some bloody farmhouse wenching I suppose?'

Corporal Warne clambered down into the trench and grinned at his friend. 'Too true,' he replied. 'Anyway, I see you've succeeded in keeping out of trouble. I bet you haven't poked your nose out of this hole since I've been away.'

'You're damn right I haven't,' said Meadows, throwing a cigarette across to him. For a few seconds they smoked in silence; then Meadows spoke again, 'What happened?'

'Nothing much. There was a lot of movement down there. We had to lie up for a while. It was a bit dodgy at times.'

'Lose anyone?'

'Grant. On the way back. Got mortared.' Warne tapped the ash from his cigarette. 'Any mail in?'

'Nothing for you. But I kept a newspaper for you.'

'You kept it? For me?'

Meadows grinned. 'Well, you can always look at the pictures.'

Warne settled down with the newspaper. Meadows lit another cigarette. They sat propped against the ends of the trench, facing each other, knee-to-knee. The birds still shrilled; the leaves in the hedgerow still stirred in the evening breeze. Somewhere in the rear the twenty-five pounders were firing, making a noise like the slamming of doors. Warne read. Meadows smoked. Neither talked.

As far as both of them were concerned, the incident was closed.

CHAPTER NINETEEN
Always...

MISTER CHALLIS was speaking to his platoon:

'Tomorrow is July 14th, the French national holiday. It means a lot to the people here this year, as you can understand; it's the first time in five years they've been able to celebrate it in freedom.'

'Now, what the padre is proposing amounts to this. They haven't had a real holiday in five years. Their kids haven't had anything worth speaking of to eat in that time – some of the younger ones have never tasted sweets since they were born. We get a bloody big ration of sweets and chocolates in our compo rations every day. More than we can eat; you all know that. Well, there you are. The padre wants you to put two and two together – he wants the whole battalion to club together and give one day's sweets and chocolate ration to the children of this village. He wants us to give these kids the holiday of their lives. The colonel says it's up to you. You talk about it. You vote on it. And whatever the majority of platoons says, goes. Right, my lads. It's all yours. Who wants to speak first?'

There was a mutter of conversation for a few moments. Then one of the men put his hand up.

The lieutenant said, 'All right, don't let's be formal. Just get up on your hind legs and speak when you want to. Martin? – You want to say something?'

'A question,' said Private Martin. 'Why the French kids and not our own? There's been an order out ever since we came over here forbidding us to send parcels of sweets or chocolate home to our own families. Why?'

'Blowed if I know,' confessed Mister Challis cheerfully. He was not a very profound young man. 'Anyone else know?'

Someone said, 'To keep the prices up.'

Mister Challis said, 'There you are. To keep the prices up. O.K.?'

'I'll be —ed if it's O.K.' said Private Martin. 'I've got a wife and three kids. I never went to war to keep the prices up. Why can't I put a piece of chocolate in their mouths if I want to?'

Corporal Gonigle spoke, 'I think the reason's much more simple than that. It's just that they've got so much essential stuff to carry across the Channel that they can't handle a parcel post home. Probably when things get easier they'll lift the ban.'

'When things get easier,' jeered one of the men. 'We've been bottled up in this bloody beachhead for five weeks. We'll still be here a year come Christmas, by the look of things.'

'Don't you be so sure,' said Gonigle. 'You never said that last Friday night when you sat up on the hill, there, watching all those bombers going in over Caen, nor the next day when we heard our chaps had got into the town. You were cheering your bloody head off last Friday night.'

'Children, children,' said Mister Challis, 'let's get back to business. Sweets or no sweets?'

'Well,' said Sergeant Ferrissey, 'I've got no bloody chocolate to spare, for one.'

One of the men shouted, 'He wants it for the women.'

Someone else said, 'Do 'im good to give some up, before 'e shags 'isself to death.'

There was laughter, then an uneasy silence.

'Too much rabbit,' said Private Martin. 'Take the bloody vote.'

The platoon voted.

'It's a lovely idea,' said Private Smith (037). 'He's a fine man, the padre.'

'Aye,' said Private Barnicoat, 'it's a lovely idea. People 'ere 'aven't a good word to say for us. We come an' liberate 'em an' they charge us the bloody moon for a glass o' cognac.'

'It's not the people,' said Private Smith, 'it's the profiteers. Same as at home. How much d'you have to pay for a glass o' brandy in Blighty?'

'Brandy?' Barnicoat laughed bitterly. 'Don't ask me! I've ne'er bought a glass o' bloody brandy in me life. I'm a workin'-class lad I am, not a bloody Piccadilly swell. What would the likes of me be doin' buyin' brandy?'

'There you are,' said Private Smith, 'an' the poor people in this village don't drink cognac, neither. Can't afford it, they can't. It's not them you're dealin' with when you go up that cafe. Can't run 'em all down, you can't, not because of one or two.'

'Aye,' said Barnicoat doubtfully, 'there's that to it. Lab'rers is all right. They 'aven't got nowt, 'ardly, but they'll give you 'alf on it. That old fella up by the orchard, there, 'e filled me tin 'at with new potatoes, an' 'e never asked for nowt in return. I gave 'im some fags. But 'e never asked for nowt.'

'Shall we vote?' asked Private Smith.

'Oh, aye,' said Private Barnicoat.

'Vote?' said Charlie Venable. 'Don't make me laugh. Ever seen one of our chaps say no to a nipper?...

'Vote?' he said. 'I see them poor bloody kids when I shut my eyes at night. Legs like bloody matchsticks. Bloody great big eyes...

'Run along,' he said to Lance-Corporal Feather. 'You don't want to waste time countin' votes. You run along an' tell 'em.'

'Orders for tomorrow,' the colonel said to the R.S.M. 'French flags to be displayed in the windows of all requisitioned cottages. Men to be inspected for shaves. Boots to be cleaned. One platoon only to parade for the ceremony. See that they're well turned-out.'

'What about a little spontaneous enthusiasm?' asked Major Norman.

'Ah,' said the colonel, 'that's a point, Noel. Get a party of men out tonight chalking on the walls. And tell all the drivers to chalk messages of greeting on the sides of their wagons.'

'Yes, sir,' said the R.S.M. 'In English or in French?'

'In French of course,' said the colonel. 'Now let's get organised. Noel, I want you to write out a lot of little clips of paper with slogans on them. In capitals, so that the men can copy them; and not too long. Sar'major, get a party detailed for the wall-chalking, and have the drivers parade at the quartermaster's store to draw chalk for their wagons. Anything else we can do, Noel?'

'The French let off fireworks on July 14th, usually,' said Noel Norman.

'Hmmph,' said the colonel, '"fraid not. Half the artillery in Normandy will open up if we send up a few flares.'

'They have dancing in the streets.'

'No streets here,' said the colonel. 'Only the main road, and that's jammed with traffic.'

'A concert?'

'The padre's got that laid on. And a film show in the afternoon. All we want is decent weather.'

'Sar'major,' said Noel Norman, 'see about the weather.'

'Yes, sir,' said the R.S.M. woodenly.

At eight o'clock that evening the padre stood by the door of his billet, behind a trestle table that was piled high with tins of confectionery.

The delegates from the platoons arrived in a steady stream with their contributions.

'Thank you, my lads,' he beamed. 'Thank you. Thank you.' He bobbed his head delightedly as each of the representatives came up to him. 'Thank you, Corporal. Thank you, Bailey. Sweets on the left, chocolate on the right. Thank you. Thank you.'

He was a very happy man.

* * *

The sun shone brilliantly on the morning of July 14th; the birds shrilled in the trees; the children squealed with excitement in the cottage doorways; and the back lanes leading into the village were full of soldiers and plump, ruddy-cheeked peasant girls making their way to the parade.

The village war memorial, at which the parade was being held, stood at the junction of a main road and two side lanes, both of which ran into it at the same point. The side lanes were crowded; military police were on duty to keep the main road clear, for a few miles away the front was still active; the area was seething with ceaseless toil; troops, guns, tanks, supplies were pouring forward day and night.

A streamer, prepared during the night by the battalion's pioneer platoon, hung across the roadway from roof to roof above the memorial, flaunting the inscription: VIVE LA FRANCE. The windows were full of flags and faces.

There was a clamour of excitement as the battalion's guard of honour marched into position. The men had spent the whole of the previous day pressing their uniforms and scrubbing out the stains; they had bleached their webbing equipment with builder's lime. Their boots shone; they marched with precision. The battalion gloated.

'A tonic!' said Charlie Venable ecstatically, watching them.

There was a crash of rifles as the platoon halted and stood at ease.

Again the babble of excitement and the blur of white faces all turned in the same direction. A procession was winding its way from the village church to the war memorial. At its head stumped the war veterans, a group of fat, black-clad little men with fierce moustaches; men with wooden legs, with empty sleeves, with faces seamed with scars; comical little men who remembered Verdun. Behind them trooped a rabble of children, dressed in their stiff, white, best clothes, shepherded by the village schoolmaster, a thin and upright man with an unexpectedly gentle face and an ancient trilby hat. In the rear came the women, clustered round the curé, anxiously watching over their children.

The guard of honour presented arms as the ex-servicemen came by. The fat little men thrust their chins up proudly and came to a halt in front of the memorial. One of them walked up the steps to the memorial and turned to face the crowd; the mayor, small and fat and sleek as a pigeon. For ten minutes he spoke. The battalion listened uncomprehendingly as his voice rose and fell, now trembling with emotion, now thundering with indignation, now rising to a peak of patriotic fervour. The mayor concluded, scarlet and sweating; and mopped his face amid a rattle of applause. The colonel came forward and laid a bunch of flowers at the foot of the memorial. He straightened up and saluted rigidly; then he relaxed and shook hands with the mayor.

The village schoolmaster raised his hand and the street fell silent. He brought his hand down and the children began to sing, shrilly and discordantly.

It was some moments before the men of the battalion realised what the children were singing.

Gawsavahgreeshuskeenk,
Lawngleevahnobelkeenk,
Gawsabahkeenk –

The children plunged frantically through the song, straining to remember phonetically the unfamiliar words, racing each other to finish.

Sendeemveectorious,
Hahpeeanglorious,

The mothers rocked in an agony of pride and suspense. The schoolmaster beat time faster and faster.

Longtoreenawvrus,
Gawsavahkeenk.

They finished triumphantly amid a hubbub of shrill congratulations from their mothers and the delighted cheers of the Fifth Battalion.

Arm-in-arm, soldiers and girls strolled quietly through the orchard in the cool, blue dusk. On the four rows of chairs round the improvised platform the villagers perched in their stiff, best clothes. Behind them, sprawling on the grass under the apple trees, were the men of the Fifth Battalion, their bronzed, resolute young faces lit in the shadows by cigarette glow. As the concert progressed and the darkness gathered about them, it became more and more difficult for the entertainers on the platform to discern them, until the audience was only a roar of song or laughter sweeping in on the platform from the gloom.

Private Rabinowitz was playing the piano. He battered tirelessly at the keys, bouncing madly on the upturned ration box that served as his stool, drumming with his boots at the front panel of the piano, turning every few minutes to roll his eyes at the villagers in the front row and hurl a frenzied, 'Ha-chah-chah!' at them.

Corporal Gonigle came up on to the platform. The solemn little corporal, who only took his horn-rimmed spectacles off when he was going into action, was the battalion's poet laureate. After the first week of action he had published a poem in his company's wall newspaper which began: 'At Tilly, at Tilly, A little town in France, I didn't half look silly, I had to change my pants.' For tonight he had prepared a ballad set to the tune of 'Casey Jones', entitled 'Craphouse Dan'. He pranced and clowned about the platform, glowing with delight at the laughter that surged from the half-darkness, chanting the adventures of 'Craphouse Dan, an infantry battalion's finest sanitary man, he took his ripest bucket into battle one day, the panzers took one sniff and then they ran away.' He capered along the front row of the audience between verses, scattering sheets of toilet paper among them as if from a horn of plenty, and goading them to join in the chorus:

Craphouse Dan, always on the fiddle,
Craphouse Dan, a wily lad is he,
Craphouse Dan, he deserves a medal
The finest crap house wallah in the infantry.

He ducked from the platform amid frantic applause, hurried away into the trees, tripped over an outstretched leg and, amid laughter and shouts of welcome, seated himself happily among his comrades.

One after another the entertainers climbed on to the platform, boys from the rifle platoons, from the Signals, from the Mortars, shy or swaggering, to sing, to play the fiddle or the mouthorgan. The padre led community singing. The battalion was having a wonderful time.

The concert was drawing to a close, and the orchard was cloaked with warm darkness, when the back rows of the audience began a four-syllabled chant, 'Di-ckie Craw-ford, Di-ckie Craw-ford, Di-ckie Craw-ford.' The whole battalion took up the cry, roaring, 'Di-ckie Craw-ford, Di-ckie Craw-ford.'

Rabinowitz left his piano and came to the edge of the platform. 'They want you, Dickie boy,' he shouted. 'Come on up and keep me company.'

A group of men appeared, lurching towards the platform with Dickie Crawford kicking and struggling in their midst. He heaved himself out of their grasp and vaulted up on to the platform.

There was a roar of applause which continued as he consulted with Rabinowitz. The clapping and shouting died away as he announced his first song. 'Oh,' he sang, doing a double-shuffle round the edge of the platform, 'we all got blue-blind paralytic drunk when the Old Dun Cow caught fire.' More applause. He began to sing again. This time it was, 'Cherry Ripe'. His voice was strong and sweet and pure. There was not another sound to be heard in the velvet night.

Applause; then the hush again. The battalion waited, listening to the distant rumble of the convoys and the thud of the guns from the forward area; then the noises of war swam away out of their consciousness and there was only the sweet, tenor voice in the darkness, singing 'Sweet Lass of Richmond Hill'.

When Dickie Crawford tried to leave the platform, the men in the front ranks rose to bar his way, and the whole battalion began to chant again, this time the one word: 'More. More. More. More.'

He sang, 'When the Lights go on Again'. The men sat in the darkness rocking to the sad, sweet, silly words. Then one more song; this time, he told them, the last one.

I'll be loving you,
Always,
With a love that's true,
Always –

All over the orchard men were joining in, humming softly with him, or singing tenderly.

When the things you've planned
Need a helping hand
I shall understand,
Always –

A fragile tune, soft and nostalgic and heartbreaking; and the darkness, the warm, summer breeze and the sweet scent of apples.

Days may not be fair,
Always,
That's when I'll be there,
Always,
Not for just an hour, not for just a day,
Not for just a year,
But always.

Next morning the villagers stood in silence and watched the men climbing into the lorries that waited to take them forward again. The men in each lorry sat facing each other in two rows, their packs piled along the middle at their feet, their rifles propped between their knees, their cheeks resting against the muzzles of their rifles.

One by one the lorries shuddered and jerked into movement; from each of them, as they moved into line, could be heard the same nostalgic chorus:

Not for just an hour, not for just a day,
Not for just a year,
But always.

CHAPTER TWENTY
There was some activity

UNDER THE SUMMER mists the front lay silent. As the last days of July slipped by, the men of the Fifth Battalion looked out over the parapets of their trenches, watchful as cats, and wondered at the breathless quiet that was only broken from time to time by the crack of a sniper's rifle, the flutter of a shell passing overhead or – back at headquarters – the rattle of farmhouse windows as the guns on some distant sector opened fire.

Each day the weather changed; one day it was hot and close, heavy with storm; the next, cold and cloudy; the next, rainy; the next brilliant. The roads lay under swirling, white dust clouds one day and were rutted with deep troughs of water the next.

From the slopes on which the battalion was entrenched the Norman landscape seemed peaceful and asleep, the summer harvest flourishing richly on the flanks of its hills, its valleys dotted with grey old farmhouses and lovely spires. Even the scarred and pitted trees around the battalion were growing fresh foliage. Only the overpowering, sweet stench of the dead cattle that lay, bloated or decomposing, in every field, dispelled the pastoral dream.

Yet the front was not asleep. Every night the fields were aflicker with the ghostly movement of patrols creeping out from both sides to probe for information or to play at hit and run in the darkness, with a sudden panic of flares and rockets and small arms fire. Men and material were pouring into the forward area, day and night, disappearing into the shadowy shelter of the woods. The daily situation reports brought news of attacks on other sectors of the front; the men, crowding round the maps which the Intelligence Officer pinned up for them, saw the British line bulging gradually forward. Rumours flourished again, hopes and disappointments crowding on each other's heels.

Each day the tension grew; to the men of the Fifth Battalion the faint rumbling of the guns each morning, as far away on the flanks yet another attack went on, sounded like the muttering thunder of an approaching storm.

'Barney,' said the patrol leader. 'You and Smith search the house.'

Smith and Barnicoat moved cautiously in through the cottage doorway. The ground-floor room was empty. They climbed the creaking staircase, Barnicoat leading.

There was a door facing them on the top landing. Barnicoat kicked the door open, lunged forward and fired his rifle from the waist with the butt held under his elbow.

Smith followed him into the room, sniffing cordite fumes, and looked down at the wounded German groaning on the floor.

'He went for his gun,' said Barnicoat. He stood over the German and lowered the point of his bayonet to thrust.

'Let him be,' said Smith, laying a hand on his arm. 'He'll not hurt us any more. Poor devil's not got many moments to live, by the looks of it.'

Barnicoat raised his rifle again. They turned to go out of the room.

Private Smith, in the doorway already, was deafened by the sudden thunder of a second shot. He turned, to see Barnicoat topple to the floor. The German, lying by the wall, had raised himself on one elbow and was glowering over his pistol.

Smith fired twice, then stepped forward and struck with his rifle butt. Three times he drove the butt downwards, with all his weight behind it. He stepped back, breathing heavily, and went across to Barnicoat. Barnicoat was dead.

Private Smith stood for a few moments, looking down at the two bodies with a puzzled frown. Then he tore a strip of peeling wallpaper down, wiped the mess from the butt-plate of his rifle, and went downstairs.

* * *

Cook-Corporal Southcott put down the dixie of hot tea he had been carrying and rested for a moment. His face was scarlet, shining with sweat and smarting in the sunshine. His rough, khaki shirt chafed against his body.

'All right, lads,' he said, 'let's get this grub up. The lads likes it hot.' He picked up the dixie. The two fatigue men with him picked up the big haybox they were carrying. They moved on.

There was another mile to go to the forward positions, uphill, on a road deeply rutted by the rain and baked hard by the sun. But the men liked their food hot – even in the most torrid weather they grumbled if their stew was not piping hot or their tea not quite at boiling point; and the cooks, hardworking and devoted men, did not begrudge their labour.

A couple of hundred yards ahead of them, on the left-hand side of the road, stood the three jagged walls which were all that was left of a cottage. 'Come on, lads,' he urged, 'we'll have another blow when we reach the cottage.'

They toiled on, too breathless to talk.

Wheep.

Southcott heard the first bullet, dropped his dixie and flung himself to the left-hand side of the road. The two fatigue men stood bewildered for a moment.

Wheep. Wheep.

The two men dived for cover as Southcott shouted angrily at them.

'Sniper,' he said, over his shoulder, unslinging his rifle. It was not uncommon for enemy snipers, alone or in small groups, to come creeping through the forward positions at night and to open fire during the day on troops coming up from the rear.

Wheep. Wheep.

Two bullets kicked up dust in the roadway near the dixie.

'Bastard!' roared Cook-Corporal Southcott. He plunged out into the middle of the road and picked up the dixie. *Wheep. Wheep.* He was back in safety, panting, with the precious tea at his side.

'Come on,' he said, 'we won't do ourselves any good cringing down here.' Cook-Corporal Southcott did not mind being shot at. But for a sniper to take pot-shots at a can of tea on a hot summer day; that was uncivilised. He was an angry man.

They wriggled forward, hidden from the view of the sniper in the cottage by the steep bank.

'When I go in,' said Southcott, 'keep your eyes open and start shooting.'

'Now!' he shouted. He rose to his feet and rushed forward. A rifle cracked again from the rubble. There was the glimpse of a human shape behind the wall. He heard his two fatiguemen firing over his shoulder and saw brickdust spurt from the cottage wall. Something moved again behind the wall. The grim silhouette of a German helmet was plainly visible. Southcott plunged on, his flesh shrinking, waiting for the red-hot impact of a bullet.

They were almost at the cottage now; still no shot from the ruins, Southcott crashed through a litter of bricks and stood, breathing harshly, within the three walls.

By the wall, his helmet just visible above it, knelt a German soldier. He did not look up. There was another, cowering in the far corner.

'Up!' growled Southcott. The German in the far corner rose to his feet, white-faced and trembling violently. He was very young and lanky. He clasped his hands behind his neck and waited for orders. Southcott shoved with his rifle butt, and the other German toppled backwards on his knees. There was a small, red hole in his forehead.

'One of you two can shoot better than you think,' he said. The fatigue men were delighted. They inspected the corpse closely and argued fiercely as to who had fired the shot.

'Well,' said Cook-Corporal Southcott, 'we can't hang about all day. Tea'll be getting cold.'

'What'll we do with this?' asked one of the fatigue men. He raised his rifle to his shoulder and looked appealingly at Southcott. The lanky German huddled against the wall, palsied from head to foot.

'Not likely,' said Southcott. 'Giddyap, there.'

A few moments later they were on their way again to the forward positions. The two fatigue men panted uphill with their haybox. Cook-Corporal Southcott, rifle slung, hands in pockets, strolled at ease in front of them; and ahead of him stumbled the lanky German, bowed under the weight of the dixie.

At a signal from the men crouched by the roadsides the Bren carrier clanked to a stop.

A corporal rose from the ditch and came alongside. 'Don't go past that bend, sir,' he said. 'The road's under observation from there. They start dropping eighty-eights on it as soon as they see anything move.'

'Thank you, Corporal,' said Major Maddison acidly, 'I've come up here to take a look at the enemy. That's what I'm going to do. No objection, I trust?'

'No, sir,' said the corporal, lying, for he and his men dreaded anything that might bring the enemy's fire down on the road.

'Good,' snapped Major Maddison. 'Carry on, Sergeant Bender.'

Sergeant Bender swore quietly at the controls; the two riflemen in the back of the carrier looked at each other; the carrier lurched forward again.

The carrier rattled along, swaying on its tracks, as it drew close to the bend. Bender pulled in close to the hedge and brought it to a standstill.

'What's the matter, Sergeant?' asked Major Maddison icily. 'Did I say anything?' He felt fine; contemptuous of these creatures with him who cowered from death; flushed with his own manhood.

'There's someone coming,' said the sergeant.

One of the riflemen was running towards them, bending low, keeping close to the hedge, obviously terrified at being above ground. He came up to the carrier, stood swallowing for a moment to get his breath, and gasped, 'From our platoon officer, sir.' He passed a slip of paper to Major Maddison.

Major Maddison read the note, screwed it up and threw it away. 'Tell your officer,' he said, 'that I'm not in the habit of taking orders from my juniors.'

'Yes, sir.' The man disappeared again.

'Carry on, Sergeant,' Major Maddison said stonily.

The carrier moved off again. Sergeant Bender's cheeks were twitching with fear and fury. Maddison's behaviour was no surprise. A couple of days previously Maddison had made another reconnaissance. He had driven past the British outposts into a

German-occupied village, turned the jeep round under a hail of fire and come speeding back with his bodyguard sprawled, dead, in the back seat. On reaching headquarters Maddison had jumped out of the riddled jeep, said to the sergeant-major, 'Get me another jeep and a fresh bodyguard,' and gone to make his report to the colonel.

The carrier rounded the bend and scuttled forward along the white, peaceful road. Bender kept his eyes on the road; the two riflemen sat with their heads pulled down inside their collars as if they were sheltering from the rain. Maddison stood up in the swaying jeep, legs braced, the war photographer's perfect fighting man.

The shell dropped within five yards of the carrier.

Bender did not hear the explosion. He felt himself lifted up, borne as in a nightmare on a scorching gale; then a frightful jolt jarred through his whole body and he was lost in darkness. He came swimming up into consciousness to feel the sunlight burning his face as if the flesh were skinned and cooking. He could see with his left eye, although it streamed with blurring tears in the bright sunlight. His right eye was open, but it felt as if it were full of sand, and with it he could only see the sky and the hedge and the road through a red film. There was a stabbing, prickling feeling all down the left side of his face. His mouth was full of blood, and as the blood ran back down his throat he felt very sick. Apart from the sickness and dizziness he felt no pain in his body. He was very tired.

For a while – he could not tell how long – he lay sprawled on his back, relaxed, looking up at the sky in a strange, disembodied apathy. Then he began to move his head slightly from one side to the other, and to move his limbs about. As he did so, pain stabbed at his spine, downward from the back of his neck, and his legs began to hurt abominably; but he was able to move them; and when he drew his arms up and fought to raise himself on his elbow, his muscles and his body responded.

Slowly he forced himself up into a sitting position. Something tugged at his neck. He became aware that his machine carbine was still slung across his chest. Understanding of what had happened began to seep back into him. Dazedly he looked about him, seeing with his one good eye through a blur of tears.

The carrier was a dozen yards away, upside down, burning. Red flame crackled round it and a column of black smoke rose from it and spread into the sky. A pair of human legs protruded from under the carrier; the body was pinned down from the waist. Hawking blood up from his throat, Bender turned painfully the other way. The body of one of the riflemen was in the hedge, stuffed into the thick bush well above the ground, head downward and doubled up, like a doll.

Something moved in the smoke. Maddison came crawling towards him on all fours. The major's face was blackened, his clothes were torn and burned. He seemed weak and dazed; otherwise, Sergeant Bender could see no sign of wounds.

Sergeant Bender became aware again of the fury rising against the blood in his throat and of the machine carbine thumping against his chest. He grasped the carbine and turned the muzzle towards Major Maddison.

The officer stopped crawling; He stared, for a moment, without comprehending; then he fumbled at his revolver holster.

Sergeant Bender spat more blood from his throat. He squeezed the trigger and felt the carbine quivering in his hands. Maddison slid forward and lay on his face in the roadway, his blood spreading darkly in the dust.

'All right, Sergeant.'

Bender jerked with fear at the voice in his ears.

'Take it easy, Sergeant.' The voice was coming from the ditch. 'We'll get you out of this all right.'

Strong hands reached under his armpits, closed round his chest and dragged him down into the ditch. A hundred knives of pain stabbed at him as he was moved. He became aware of two faces over him; of the firm, pitiless pressure of hands pulling away cloth and skin, dabbing away dirt; of the cool dressing laid against his face; of the bandage winding, winding, winding, until his face was smothered, bound, immovable, with only his lips, his nostrils and his left eye free.

More pain; again the jolting agony of movement; and he was back round the bend and swaying dizzily, dreamily, on a stretcher.

At last he was back at the regimental aid post. He lay on the stretcher, trapped, helpless, trying to follow the two stretcher-bearers with his one good eye, waiting in terror for them to speak.

They were behind him now. He could not see them, but he could hear their firm, friendly voices distinctly. They were talking and joking about some private affair; to the sergeant, lying helpless on the stretcher, it was disconcerting, almost infuriating, that they should talk as if he were not there.

A face appeared over his again. He recognised the medical officer.

The M. O. smiled. 'They've made a bit of a mess of your face, Sergeant,' he said, 'but they haven't hurt you too badly. You'll be in a plane to Blighty in twenty-four hours.'

Bender tried to speak; he only succeeded in making a croaking noise.

He heard one of the stretcher-bearers speaking, into his right ear, 'Tha'rt a lucky fellow, Sergeant. Ah wish ah were in thy place.'

The other bearer spoke, 'Want a fag, Sergeant?' Bender nodded. 'Can I give him one, sir?'

'Of course,' the doctor said 'till he's on the jeep. So Major Maddison is not among us any more?'

Bender stiffened on the stretcher.

'No, sir.' It was one of the stretcher-bearers again. 'Shell splinter got him.'

Bender relaxed. He felt himself borne aloft, floating in space again as they lifted the stretcher and moved towards the waiting jeep ambulance.

'That Maddison,' he heard one of the stretcher-bearers say, 'he was always after a decoration.'

'Aye,' the other bearer replied, 'he got decorated all right. Right in the kisser.'

Gently they eased the laden stretcher on to the jeep.

CHAPTER TWENTY-ONE
Roll on, the peace

THE LOFTY BARN smelt of rats and rotten straw. The uncertain light of a hurricane lamp, on a wooden table in one corner, warred with the cavernous gloom. Draughts pried at the documents which littered the table and attacked the struggling lamplight through the aperture above the protecting glass.

Colonel Pothecary signed a casualty return, put the pen down and sat staring at his signature while his right hand groped for the mug of tea which stood on the table.

'A bad day for the butchering business,' he said, 'only eight killed.' He sipped, and shivered with disgust; the tea was cold, curdled and too sweet.

'There's some hot tea coming up,' Major Norman said softly, 'Higgs has gone for it.'

Colonel Pothecary looked up. The colour of his face was ghastly in the lamplight.

'I had a row with the Brigadier today,' he said.

'I know.'

They listened to the rats squeaking and scampering in the enveloping darkness.

'I think he's going to get me shifted. He thinks I'm a washout.'

'Why?' Norman spoke without conviction. 'The battalion's done every job he's given it. You're a good commander. The men like you.'

'I like the men,' said Colonel Pothecary, 'that's the trouble.'

In his heart Norman agreed with the Brigadier. For weeks past he had watched the colonel, racked by his responsibilities and by his private griefs, ageing and tiring under the strain.

There were two worlds in which men lived, Norman had come to realise; the world which was summed up in the word 'home'; and the world of the soldier, to enter which a man had to cast out from himself the luxury of feeling, the world in which death had become a trivial incident, a tedious matter of report forms and burial fatigues.

A shell kills half a dozen men. In the soldier's world the men are forgotten. They leave nothing behind them. A truck-load of rations lost causes more stir. But away in the other world half a dozen families, perhaps a hundred human beings, are rocked with grief. To each of them the one dead man is their whole horizon. For each of them the world is plunged into blackness.

Colonel Pothecary lived in both worlds at once. Outwardly stolid and resolute, moving cheerfully among his men, he ached behind the mask for his missing son; he waited for every delivery of mail in terror and suspense; and at the same time he could not banish from his imagination the fathers, the families of the men whose lives were in his hands. Each time he sent a platoon to clear a farmhouse or comb a wood, each time the report came to him of three or six or ten men killed, he felt as if the news of his own son's death had come to him three or six or ten times over.

It was more than sympathy that he felt for the families of his men; it was a complete and terrible identity with them. Marching through the night or lying wrapped in his greatcoat he imagined them waiting in their silent kitchens, and as he thought of their hearts turning over at the postman's knock so his heart turned over, too.

The conflict was becoming too much for him, the burden more than he could bear. To the men he showed nothing of this, but to his superiors, when they came day after day with fresh orders, fresh demands, he became short-tempered and dispirited. His work had given them nothing to complain of; but they were expert drivers of men, old hands at calculating the last straw; and they knew his breaking-point was near.

'Jerry's beginning to crack,' said Norman. 'In a week or two we'll have finished the job. And then...'

'And then another battle.'

'And then,' Norman went on, 'we'll get some rest and we'll all feel better.'

It was strange, he thought, this feeling of anti-climax, of weary flatness that had descended on them now that the battle was at its height.

They had fought since the landing, through the rain and the mud, with hope and savage confidence. They had looked ahead and spoken of 'the big push', 'the breakthrough', of a time of joy when they would reap in victory the harvest of battle. Now the time had come. In the warm, golden days of this first week of August the great Allied offensive had at last got under way. Far to the west the Americans had broken through and for days past their armour had been rumbling south, leaving the ruined battlegrounds of June and July behind them, thundering away into the blue – fast-moving columns of tanks, lorry-borne infantry, huge ammunition and petrol trucks travelling at top speed across the enemy's flanks in great clouds of blinding, choking dust. In the centre the British had concentrated secretly at Caumont, had struck southwards with terrific force and now, after battering forward day and night through the hills, were on the move and gathering speed. As the great wheeling move developed, the British left flank began to move forward too. The troops of this flank – the Fifth Wessex among them – had seen more and harder fighting than any others in the entire campaign. For two months they had pinned down most of the enemy's crack divisions. When the offensive began they were already weary with the endless routine of marching and fighting, they were already punch-drunk with battle; so that for them there was no elation, no feeling of the great and wonderful days that had come at last; only the determination to stick it out a little longer, to conquer the numbing weariness, the fear that grew suddenly a hundredfold at the prospect of dying at the moment of victory. Tired, deafened men in filthy uniforms forced themselves each day to march once more, to attack once more the succession of tiny, stupid objectives into which the battle resolved itself, went forward in night attacks that were truly like nightmares to them, with the darkness torn apart by the thunder and the flashes and the earthquaking vibrations of artillery, with the searchlights flooding the clouds with ghostly grey light and the rockets and tracers drawing mad patterns of colour across the sky.

'I wonder,' said Colonel Pothecary, 'if we'll get a full night's rest?' The battalion had been lying up in a wood for five hours, since seven o'clock in the evening, ready to move again at a half-hour's notice. 'There's nothing from Brigade.'

'Here's the tea,' said Norman.

Higgs came padding in with a bucket of tea. He filled their mugs and one for himself.

'Mister Cutbush come in with the rations, sir,' he said to the colonel. 'Sack of mail in as well.'

'Anything for me?' asked the colonel. 'Have they sorted it yet?'

'Yes, sir.' Higgs sipped his tea noisily and stared down into the mug, avoiding the colonel's look. 'I waited. That's why I took so long with the tea. There was nothing for you. Or for you, sir,' he added, turning to Norman.

'Thank you, Higgs,' said the colonel dully. 'Don't wait. You'd better get some sleep in case we have to move off again.'

'I'll leave the bucket, sir,' said Higgs, 'in case you want some more tea. It'll stay warm for a bit.' There was a clatter as he put the bucket on the table.

'It wasn't much of a mail, sir,' he said. 'Only a few letters and newspapers. There's sure to be another one up in a day or two.'

Higgs went. They sat in silence, listening again to the busy rats.

'Get your head down for a couple of hours,' said Norman. 'I'll wake you at two o'clock and you can relieve me.'

'You sleep,' answered the colonel.

'No. That's all right.'

'God Almighty!' exploded the colonel. 'Do as I tell you. It's bad enough to have my batman feeling sorry for me without you behaving like a wet nurse.'

'All right.' Norman rose, and draped his greatcoat over his shoulders.

'You know where to find me.'

The colonel smiled apologetically. 'I'm sorry, Noel,' he said. 'Good night.'

It was pleasant to lie among the trees, in the cool of the night, not heeding the flicker and rumble of battle in the distance, feeling the blood throb again in aching legs; talking quietly or sinking into the dizziness of a half-sleep.

Charlie Venable eased his boots on over a fresh pair of socks and sighed luxuriously.

'You should 'a seen my feet,' he said. 'I got blisters so big I could walk across the Channel on 'em.'

'Why don't you?' asked Baldy, lying flat on his back.

'What,' said Charlie, 'after we've come this bloody far? Be quicker to push old Jerry right back and get a train home from bloody Berlin in comfort.'

'Roll on, the peace.' Baldy muttered the soldier's incantation piously.

'It's quiet,' said one of the men, 'isn't it? Reckon we're out for good?'

'Oh, sure,' mocked Charlie, 'sure. We're all getting our tickets. Special order from Montgomery.'

'For a rest, I mean.'

'We're on a half-hour,' interjected Lance-Corporal Feather. 'You know what that means.' Whenever the battalion was resting the men were given a period of notice – twelve hours, or three hours, or an hour perhaps; each period indicated a certain state of readiness which had to be maintained. A half-hour's notice meant that the men had to keep together in platoons, forbidden to wander away, with their weapons and equipment at their sides ready to be donned immediately. It was the most advanced state of readiness.

'Ah,' said one of the men, 'that's all hooey. You can't go by that. They're always changing their minds. When I went down for the rations they were saying we were all going back to the corps rest camp.'

Everybody began to talk at once.

'Mail up, lads.' Mister Paterson had appeared. He gave out two or three letters. There was a tearing of envelopes and quiet again for a few moments.

Charlie Venable had a letter, in a bulky packet. He opened it and sat frowning over it for a while. Then he climbed to his feet and moved among the men of his section. He bent over as he came to each of them and put something down in the grass.

The men watched him, puzzled.

'Fags?' said Baldy. 'What's up, Charlie?'

'Four fags each,' said Charlie, 'and five left for me. Guess who they're from?'

'Your ma,' said Baldy. Someone said the Red Cross. Someone else said the Overseas League.

'Alfie Bradley,' announced Charlie.

There was silence again. It was a long way back to remember.

'Listen to this,' said Charlie. His voice was tight and hard.

Dear Charlie [he read]: *I expect you'll be surprised to hear from me after all this time. I would have written earlier but I haven't been well enough. Well, Charlie, I've had it. I lost one eye on the beach and they've been trying ever since to save the other one. They thought they could do it, but the doctor has just told me straight out that it's no go, and I've got to settle down to the idea of being totally blind. He says they're going to get me into Saint Dunstan's, and that it's not so bad really. They teach you all sorts of things there. The worst thing is telling Floss. She still thinks it's going to be all right and I haven't had the nerve to write to her yet. What does feel rotten, Charlie, is lying here in the dark and listening to the news on the wireless. I'm wondering all the time what's happened to you chaps and whether you're all right, and I feel so rotten and helpless not being with you. Well, Charlie, the nurse is writing this for me and I can't go on for ever. Give my regards to all the boys and write as soon as you can. Enclosed are fifty fags. Sorry I can't send more, but it's the best I can do on hospital pay. Look after yourself. Keep well. Ever yours, ALFIE*

'He's worried about us,' said Charlie. 'The poor little bugger's lying there with his eyes out an' he's worried about us. Bastards,' he said savagely, 'whoreson bastards. Wait till I get up there again.'

When they heard the throb of a motor-cycle among the trees they sat up, their hearts quickening with excitement and foreboding.

'Dispatch rider,' said someone. They knew what that meant.

They did not have long to wait. A few minutes later the company sergeant-major came stumbling through the darkness calling for platoon officers. The junior officers and sergeants went off towards headquarters, talking together in self-conscious little groups. They came back very soon and dispersed among the platoons, some quiet and preoccupied, some nervously boisterous.

Voices were raised and mingled in the darkness. There was the noise of movement, the clatter of weapons and equipment.

'On your feet, Number Seven Platoon.'

'Fall in here, Number Ten Platoon.'

Hurry and confusion, eagerness and disappointment, fear and excitement, all mounting together in the darkness.

'All right, my lads.' Here was Mister Paterson. 'Get dressed. Eat what you can. No, you can't brew up.' Cold sausage-meat, bully-beef, cold pork-and-vegetable stew scooped from the tin; fluffy fragments of biscuits salvaged from pockets and pouches. Swallow it, wash it down with stale, metallic water from your bottles. Hurry, hurry, hurry. Eat while you can; it may be your last chance. 'Thirty minutes, chaps, ready in thirty minutes.'

No news. No briefing. Surmise; wild rumour.

'All right, my lucky lads. On your feet. Come on, come on. Move, MOVE. Over here, Nine Platoon. Fall in here, Number Nine. Put that fag out, you bloody fool. I won't tell you again. Over here, Number Nine Platoon, under this tree. Everyone here, Sergeant Shannon?'

The men talking rapidly among themselves, leaning on their rifles.

Us again. Always us.

Some dirty job, I suppose.

It's the breakthrough. We'll go right through this time. All that stuff that's been going up the line these last few days. Tanks. Guns. Carriers. Jeeps. Halftracks. This is it, boys. This is it.

B— to you. Every time we go up it's the breakthrough to you. Where's the preparation? Where's the artillery? Breakthrough my foot.

They don't do that barrage business no more. This is it, Albert. I tell you this is it.

And the band played believe it if you like.

With a clatter of equipment Number Nine Platoon moved off, in single file, into the darkness, singing defiantly:

And the band played believe it if you like, if you like,
And the band played believe it if you like.

The Fifth Battalion of the Wessex Regiment had been ordered to deploy along its start line before daylight. Throughout the night the files of riflemen, plodding up and down hill along the narrow, tall-hedged lanes, had looked over their shoulders at the barrage flaring on the horizon, fretting the edges of the night with fire, and had felt its thudding rumble against their eardrums.

Now, towards dawn, the barrage was slackening. The men moved over the last hilltop that faced their objective and walked quietly downhill, their rifles at the trail or slung, hidden from view by the milky, white mist that clung to the hillsides.

Their start line lay along the valley between the two hills, and as they filed down to it, the mist that shrouded their objective began slowly to recede, heaving and billowing, like a glacier in a dream. As the mist crept down towards the valley it revealed the meadows and woods that clothed the hillside, still sombre in the dawn.

The infantrymen filed silently into their positions along the valley, sinking down out of sight against the banks of sunken lanes. The icy dew soaked through their trousers; the chill of the dawn lay like cold steel against their cheeks.

The first light, stealing over the ridge, touched the black fringe of treetops up on the hillside, and a multitude of birds awoke to shrill song.

There was no other sound in the morning.

CHAPTER TWENTY-TWO
The hill

ON THE MAP THE RIDGE was easy to distinguish; a little bar of chocolate brown set in a nimbus of lighter shades. Many times in the preceding weeks it had attracted the attention of the commanders of the brigades and battalions moving south towards it.

Now that they faced it, it looked less distinctive, less dangerous, a ridge of woodland and meadow looking less than its actual twelve hundred feet, a false horizon beyond the lines of gentler hills.

It lay athwart several roads vital to the British advance. With the hilltop in their hands the Germans were in a position to paralyse any movement by the British for several miles in almost any direction. Possession of this feature was the key to the communications of a wide area on this sector of the front.

The hill rose rather more steeply from the west than from the east, where the approach was across fairly open ground. On the western side the ground was close, covered with orchards and woods, and with streams cutting irregular gullies across the main approach roads.

The Germans, with every advantage of ground, could drench with fire any force that tried to establish a footing on the lower slopes. The wooded banks on either side of the road from the west offered ideal machine-gun positions from which a withering cross-fire could be poured across the bridge bottlenecks. With whatever superiority in numbers an assault might be made, this country called for the greatest staunchness and courage by the infantry, since the difficult slopes would extend to the full their staying power.

So it turned out.

The assault was launched at brigade strength, with the Fifth Battalion of the Wessex Regiment in reserve during the first phase.

The first infantry attack went in from the south-west, with a group of tanks in support. Close orchards and woods, and irregular ground, made the going terribly heavy. The narrow tracks imprisoned the tanks. The area had been widely mined and there was a river in their path, meandering across the lower slopes, over which the bridge had already been blown up. Pioneers, working under enemy fire, rooted up mines like potatoes and strove to build a tank crossing across the river bed with the rubble of the demolished bridge. In a half-hour they had nearly all been killed and the tanks, grinding desperately forward, were hit one by one and burned fiercely. Meanwhile the Germans shelled and mortared the British infantry. Hidden observation posts reported every movement to the enemy artillery. Each time the infantry surged up out of the folds in the ground in which they crouched they were met by intense shelling. Only here and there were men able to get forward, moving in twos and threes, sprinting forward in short bounds separated by long periods during which they were pinned tight to the ground. In vain the tanks tried to get across the river. Only the first few outposts of the enemy had yet been encountered, but already the assaulting battalion had suffered heavy casualties.

Late on the first evening the Brigadier switched his plan of attack. Two other battalions – one of them the Fifth Wessex – moved forward during the night to take up their position for an assault across the river from due west.

The men lying along the sunken lanes felt the morning breezes die away, and as the sun rose in the sky the daylight grew radiant and the summer's heat became intense. The chill and the fatigue fell away from them and they felt a momentary surge of confidence as their own artillery opened fire on the ridge with high explosive and smoke-shells that wrapped the enemy positions in a blinding white screen.

Then they moved forward.

They advanced across the meadows, unchallenged for the first few yards and filled suddenly, as they always were at such moments, with the wild, unreasoning hope that this time it was going to be easy; until the first shell quavered down on them and they were out there, soft, human flesh clad only in khaki serge, with the angry splinters of steel whining among them, searching the ground, seeking them out, cutting them down, widening the gaps in their scattered ranks, and each man found himself suddenly alone amid the noise and the smoke, lurching blindly forward to gamble with blind death; doubly bewildered because the enemy machine guns were firing not only from the front but from the flanks.

A hundred yards in front of them was the stream and across the stream a narrow, stone-walled bridge, too small for tanks but treacherously inviting for infantry. There was no room in their minds for the enemy waiting on the upper slopes; now there was only one objective – to cross the bridge, to put the stream behind them. Men goad themselves on with strange illusions, with mad freaks of fancy, and their illusion was that somehow this field they were now crossing was the source of all their peril, that the bridge was a bridge to safety, that life lay on the far bank of the stream They stumbled forward against the machine guns and toppled forward, faces upturned in agony, hands clawing at the sunlight; more men came sprinting on, without even a downward glance at the littered dead, and fell writhing among them.

A half a dozen men reached the bridge; none of them got across. There were no more men moving across the open ground now. Only the dead and wounded sprawled in the open; the rest of the battalion was scattered in little groups, cowering in ditches, in gullies, against the backs of sunken sun-baked lanes, in shallow folds in the ground, under the probing machine-gun fire.

Colonel Pothecary crouched among his men. He had gone forward with the leading platoons, a prey to changing moods. On the start line he had felt at first only the awful responsibility of this moment; he alone, of all these men, knew exactly what they were facing. Then the very weight of the burden had aroused in him, as they moved off, a feeling of complete, almost light-hearted abandon, a determination to absolve himself by being the first to dare, the first to gamble. Now, as he tried to steady the whirling confusion of his thoughts, to clear his mind so that he could work out the next step, he felt drained of resolution. He longed for someone to tell him what to do; he envied the riflemen who lay, passive but expectant, waiting for the next order.

He wondered what was happening to the other battalion. If only, he thought, they would get forward across the stream and open the way for his battalion. If only someone else would take the initiative. If only someone else would lift the burden from his back.

The other battalion, in fact, had suffered even more heavily. It had reached the stream, after losing most of its officers; and the survivors had abandoned the attempt to get across and were fighting their way upstream, not going forward against the crest but pushing out towards the left flank in order to try to reduce the murderous fire that came from this quarter.

Colonel Pothecary lay wondering what was happening to the other battalion. If only, he thought, if only. He watched the second hand of his watch crawling round; an object of attention, an alternative to thought.

My poor Biddy, he thought. How will you bear it, Biddy?

The watch ticked on. But I am a battalion commander, he thought. Men are watching me. Men are waiting for me. We have to cross a bridge. To cross a bridge. A bridge.

Colonel Pothecary rose to his feet. He could see the upturned faces all about him, he could feel the suspense of the men waiting in folds and crannies in the ground.

He walked, easily and unhurriedly, along the uphill track, his cane tucked under his right arm. Men saw him smiling at them, a confident, beckoning smile. They saw him stoop, pick a white flower from a hedgerow and fasten it, without haste, in his lapel. Everywhere in the meadow men rose and moved forward with him.

The colonel strode calmly along the road as if he were walking on to a parade ground, looking back sometimes to call encouragement to his men, ignoring the bullets that squealed about him and kicked up little devils of earth at his feet.

He was crossing the bridge now, with men streaming after him. It was as if he had, by his own physical strength, lifted the battalion up out of the ground and borne them with him.

The bridge was behind him and he felt turf underfoot. Ahead of him was a sudden dip; dead ground, safe ground. Into the exultant dream there intruded the consciousness of safety, of survival. Colonel

Pothecary began to run.

The men behind him saw the cane drop from his right hand. He ran on, heavily, for a couple of paces, and pitched to the ground. The men who had crossed the bridge with him plunged blindly past him to safety. A couple stopped in shame, seized his arms and dragged him with them.

There were no more men crossing the bridge. The machine guns were masters again. What was left of the battalion had gone to ground.

A handful of men cowered in the hollow on the far side of the bridge. Colonel Pothecary lay among them, breathing heavily, his eyes closed.

A sergeant knelt over him. The colonel began to snore loudly and mumble unintelligibly. The sergeant bent lower, his ear close to the colonel's mouth. The colonel opened his eyes and looked up without recognition. He tried to raise himself; he put one arm up about the sergeant's neck and pulled himself up.

'My poor Biddy,' he said, very clearly, and fell back dead.

Radiotelephone message, Fifth Battalion to Brigade Headquarters, thirteen-forty hours:

> *Attack held up on start point. Leading troops under very heavy machine-gun, mortar and artillery fire. Battalion commander killed. Not possible for leading troops to advance.*

Brigade Headquarters to Fifth Battalion, thirteen-forty-six hours:

> *Advance to crossroads two hundred yards beyond river.*

Fifth Battalion to Brigade Headquarters; fourteen-ten hours:

> *Forward troops under heavy fire and still on this side (behind) river. Fired on from woods to south-west.*

Brigade Headquarters to Fifth Battalion, fourteen-fifteen hours:

Advance to crossroads two hundred yards beyond river.

Fifth Battalion to Brigade; fifteen-oh-five hours:

Not possible for leading troops to move.

Brigade to Battalion, fifteen-ten hours:

Advance to crossroads.

Battalion headquarters was a pit about six feet square and five feet deep, partially covered by a sheet of tarpaulin. Major Norman sat in the pit with a private of the signals platoon who huddled over the radiotelephone set.

Norman scribbled desperately and passed a message to the operator. The man spoke softly into the microphone. They waited, while the ground shook to the German cannonade. The radiotelephone began to quack.

'Reserves,' said Norman bitterly as he studied the reply, 'we've got no reserves. Our cooks and clerks are out there fighting now. Tell them we want more men. We want tanks. We want more artillery.'

Quack. Quack. *Quack.*

'God Almighty,' said Norman, 'what do they want? We're men, not walking miracles.'

Quack. Quack. *Quack.*

'The Brigadier,' said the operator, 'for you.'

Norman took the earphones and listened. His face flushed darkly as the earphones quacked at him. He straightened up suddenly, cursing, tipped his steel helmet forward a little, picked up a machine carbine that lay at his side, and clambered up into the open.

He hurried uphill, among the crouching groups of men.

'Up,' he shouted in his thin, lashing voice as he came among them, 'up on your feet.'

He moved among the men, careless of the enemy's fire, ordering them forward. Bitter and despairing, he lashed at them with words, threatened with his gun, used his boots sometimes on men clinging to the ground. The most resolute of the men, who had been held back only by the fear of going forward alone, rose to their feet again. Officers and n.c.o.s, seeing him approach, led or drove their men forward. Tired, bitter and despairing, the remnants of the Fifth Battalion streamed towards the river.

Battle has its own strange chemistry. The courage and endurance of a group of men is greater than the sum total of the courage and endurance of the individuals in the group; for, when most of the group have reached the limits of human endeavour, there is always one among them who can surpass those limits, who will hold the others together and drive them on. It is not the romantic picture of war; but it is the truth of war.

And broken men, thus driven forward, can become – at the last pitch of exhaustion – whole and strong again; for movement generates its own strange inspiration.

The Fifth Battalion swept across the stream. As the men stumbled up the slopes beyond they came within sight at last of the dark, German helmets moving in the folds in the ground, the thin black barrels of the machine guns quivering against the grass. All the pent-up fury and bitterness they had felt towards their own commander was transferred to the enemy. In twos and threes they rushed forward, up and down, moving and firing, a dozen yards at a time, up the bare hillside. Now they were closing in; their anger swept them up and they went forward, all together, at a run.

Radiotelephone message, Fifth Battalion to Brigade Headquarters, sixteen-forty-five hours:

Have crossed river and reached crossroads two hundred yards beyond. Consolidating.

CHAPTER TWENTY-THREE
Ahoy there, Wessex!

GUNS THUDDED AND SMALL ARMS fire crackled in the distance but at the crossroads it was quiet. From a distance there was even a faint, fantastic flavour of Box Hill on a Bank Holiday about the scene, with groups of men sprawling on the hot grass and others toiling up the brown, rutted tracks. The position was newly taken; the enemy artillery was not yet ready to fire on it; for a little while there was respite for the Fifth Battalion.

The men scattered along the tracks and across the slopes and began to dig. This was the worst of battle – not the fire, nor the marching, but having to dig, dig, dig, to refuse yourself rest and to stand – in the uneasy quiet of a brief lull or under a rain of steel – hacking a hole in the ground, tired and heartbroken, with your hands like raw beef, your muscles aching, the straps of your equipment burning into your shoulder-blades; and knowing all the time that when you have sunk into the hole you will be hustled up again to stumble forward for another few miles, with another hole to dig at the end of it.

Major Norman sat at the roadside watching the men digging. In thirty minutes, he reckoned, the shells would begin to fall. After that there would probably be counter-attacks. The sun was already going down; soon the light would fade and the dusk and the evening mists would crawl across the hillsides; then he would have to watch his right flank where the enemy waited, over the shoulder of the hill, ready to filter into his battalion's rear.

Somebody spoke to him and pointed down the hillside. The Brigadier was coming up towards him, a great bear of a man, conspicuous in a swashbuckling, light raincoat, with a pipe in his mouth and a thick, black moustache. Unhurrying and preoccupied, he came across the open ground; as he saw Norman he took the pipe from his mouth and waved it in greeting.

Norman waited, drained of energy. He remained sitting until the last moment, then climbed indecisively to his feet and nodded to the Brigadier.

'It took you a long time,' said the Brigadier gruffly.

Norman shivered with resentment. Careless himself of praise he waited now for a word, for just one word of praise, of recognition, for his battalion.

'It wasn't easy,' he said.

The Brigadier shrugged his shoulders: 'Pretty thin on the ground, aren't you?'

'We've lost a lot of men.'

The Brigadier frowned, and poked at the turf with his cane.

'I don't think there's enough of your battalion left to assault up to the crest. You'd better consolidate here and keep this crossroads clear. I'm going to send a battalion in up the hill from the south-west. You'll be able to protect their left flank. With you here the Hun won't be able to infiltrate down this road into their rear.'

Norman nodded. Just one word, he thought, one word of praise for my battalion.

'Another thing,' said the Brigadier. He blew harshly through his empty pipe. 'The Hun mustn't know that the main assault isn't coming in from this side any more. You'll have to keep your crowd active.'

'What's left of them,' said Major Norman.

'Don't let them go to sleep,' said the Brigadier. 'Keep the Huns up on the crest busy.'

'We're terribly exposed here.'

'Well,' said the Brigadier irritably, 'it's not going to rain, if that's what you're worrying about.'

'We've no cover at all. They can see every move we make.'

'All the better. I want them to keep an eye on you. It'll help my attack from the south-west. Do all you can to keep him engaged. Push a platoon up the hillside as often as you can, just to keep him guessing.'

What a job, thought Norman. After all this we shan't even take the hill. We'll just stay here and take punishment. Human bait.

The Brigadier fidgeted. He had dreaded this interview and had hardened himself for it all the way from his headquarters. 'Don't stand there mooning, man,' he said angrily, 'this hillside's too damn quiet already. Get yourself organised. Let's hear something from your Brens. And push a platoon up there as soon as you can.'

'Right,' said Major Norman curtly.

The shells were falling again; the evening mists were gathering on the slopes. Norman hurried from group to group, and the Brens and rifles began to crack and clatter once more.

Mister Paterson and the dozen survivors of his platoon were lying in the shelter of a grassy mound.

Norman paused at Paterson's side and studied the ground ahead.

'There's another bit of dead ground about thirty yards on, Pat,' he said. 'See it?'

Paterson looked up at him broodingly. 'I see it,' he said.

'You'd better get on up there,' said Norman. 'You can use your Brens better from there.'

Paterson searched his impassive face, in vain, for a hint of feeling. 'Now?' he asked.

'Now.'

Paterson looked at him for a moment with smouldering eyes; then he signalled to his men and began to move forward.

One or two of them rose. The others looked up, hesitant.

'Come on, my pretty pets,' called Mister Paterson. His voice was hard, high, desperate. 'Come to daddy.'

The platoon straggled forward and topped the slight rise ahead.

From the mist the Spandaus began to rap. One of the men toppled headlong backward, his legs astride, his body braced rigidly. His helmet rolled away and he lay staring up at the sky, his mottled, bald head gleaming downhill towards the major.

Norman stood looking into the mist for a few moments, then stumbled down the hill to the crossroads.

All the evening the remnants of the battalion clung to the hillside, while a pitiless fire, like waves sweeping away the clusters of men clinging to the mainmast of a sinking ship, obliterated one group after another.

All through the evening little parties of men went stumbling up the hill, to be beaten down into the ground again.

And each time there came a few moments of quiet and the men rested their heads in their arms in blessed relief, Major Norman, half-mad with despair, his eyes burning, lurched in among them, goading them to open fire again and draw down upon themselves the nightmare fire from the crest.

A man under fire, sickened by the unending din, shaken by the detonations that come jolting one after another through the ground, with great domes of smoke and flame blossoming around him, his eyes seared by the leaping, white flashes, the explosions flinging great fistfuls of earth into the air all about, does one of two things.

Either he surrenders to fear and becomes useless; not fear of death – fear at such a time is not a process of the brain, but a frightful, physical seizure. The frightened man wants only to escape from his ordeal, but he is robbed of his will, he is unable to go forward or back, he is death's easiest prey; and he welcomes death. In his fear he does not shrink from death, but sees it as a deliverance, as an end to the pain and the terror.

Either this, then, or he cultivates the ability to withdraw himself from his surroundings; to crouch in his trench or lie pressing himself against the turf like a child against its mother, with his soldier's faculties alive and alert but with all the rest of his being sealed off in a private world of dream or memory.

Private Rabinowitz, crouching in his hole, was stubbornly whistling to himself a Jewish lullaby, 'Almonds and Raisins'. His head was cradled in his arms, his eyes were closed. Immured in an anguish of memories he could only half-hear the uproar of battle.

Someone thumped his back and he raised his head like a sleeper awakened. Men were streaming past him to the right, hurrying, bowed low. Above the noise of the bombardment he could hear a whistle shrilling, voices raised, the cackle of a machine gun.

It was so hard to rise from the consoling earth, to cast off the protecting dream. He felt so lazy and remote. He could not understand what was happening, or where his comrades were hurrying; but they were moving, and his instinct compelled him to stumble after them.

He plodded forward, frowning at the ground like a day-dreamer in a crowded street. He did not hurry, for his steps were measured by the tender lullaby he was still whistling to himself within the bombardment.

At eight o'clock in the evening the Brigadier's attack went in from the southwest. Protected by dusk, mist and an artillery smokescreen, the assaulting troops were able to work their way steadily up the hill.

They were already desperately tired, having been fighting for days before, and having marched several miles in full kit to take up their positions for this attack. They met heavy opposition at first, in spite of the fact that the Germans were unprepared and were already weakened by the tenacious attacks of the Fifth Battalion.

It was dark already when a troop of British tanks gained the crest; and within an hour the infantry, heartened by the sight of the tanks, had overrun the summit.

The moon had risen when an officer of the victorious battalion went forward over the hilltop in search of the Fifth Wessex.

His own men were trying to dig in, and as he passed through them he saw that they were so exhausted that they were falling asleep over their spades.

He moved cautiously down the opposite slope. He could see no sign of life.

He halted and raised his hand to his mouth.

'Hallo, Wessex!' he called. His voice echoed in the green moonlight, among the broken trees.

'Hallo-o-o!'

He picked his way forward another few yards, fearful of the mines with which the ground was still thickly sown.

'Ahoy there, Wessex!' he shouted.

'Wessex – ahoy!' There was no reply.

Two hundred yards in front of him a man rose from a fold in the ground, slowly and silently, like a corpse from the grave. Another man rose, and another. As more and more men rose to face him the officer felt as if a legion of ghosts was springing from the earth.

None of them spoke.

They began to move towards him. Silently, like sleepwalkers, they began to make their way up the desolate, moonlit slopes, towards the summit.

CHAPTER TWENTY-FOUR
The beginning of a story

THEY WERE SCATTERED along the sides of a country lane resting. To the south the ridge peeped above the hedgerows as pastoral and innocent in the serene sunlight as when they had first seen it. There were other troops up on the ridge now, and they were being shelled; but the remote thudding and the little puffs of smoke that blossomed against the blue seemed from this distance to possess no menace. Down here the birds were singing.

There were not many of them sprawling at the roadsides. Most of them lay flat on their backs, staring up at the sky with eyes as void and cavernous, as the windows of empty houses. Some squatted cross-legged, rummaging nervelessly in their packs. They were unshaven, their shirts and tunics unbuttoned to the waist, their boots unlaced. There was little talk. They were deafened, numbed still to the fact of their survival. The summer's beauty hurt them, as returning consciousness brings hurt to the wounded. The song of the birds was heartbreaking.

A column of prisoners shambled by; a line of men bobbing past with the slow and melancholy rhythm of captivity; dazed and sagging, stumbling over their own broken boots, their eyes intent upon the dusty ground. Their skins and their tattered, hanging clothes were smothered in the same dark grime and powdered, over that, with the same grey covering of dust; so that it was hard to tell the men from their rags, moving bundles of misery.

The men of the Fifth Battalion looked up at them dully, without interest. There was little to distinguish the victors from the vanquished; all were bowed under the same burden of shock and exhaustion, all were masked alike in filth and clad in indistinguishable rags; all might have belonged to the one, defeated army.

* * *

Major Norman envied the men their apathy. As exhausted as any of them, he found himself unable to rest. He was seized by a terrible, trembling impatience. His body seemed to be out of control, waiting for something in a physical agony of suspense; for what he did not know. His gums itched; the muscles of his cheeks ached with the strain. He smoked hurriedly at a cigarette, unreasoningly impatient to throw it away, as he had thrown away a dozen already, and to light another.

He stretched his arms; not in fatigue, but because the muscles were contracted unbearably. He felt as if cotton wool were being packed into his head, stopping his ears, pressing at his eyeballs from behind, threatening to burst his skull.

A jeep came wallowing down the uneven lane. It jolted to a stop and the Brigadier walked across to him.

'Hallo, Noel.' The Brigadier's eyes were anxious under their thick black brows. He studied Norman's face, trying to find behind the mask of sweat and dust a clue as to how he should talk to this man.

The mask cracked. Norman was smiling. It was a stupid smile. It revealed nothing.

'I'm very grateful,' the Brigadier said quietly.

The eyes glittered from their depths behind the mask. The lips tightened. The corners of the mouth turned up more. The smile broadened.

'The whole division's on the move,' said the Brigadier. 'Your battalion has done a big job.'

The bowed shoulders began to shake. Norman looked up, quaking with a scarcely-audible laughter. 'No?' he gasped. 'Really? That's too good of you.'

The Brigadier took his pipe from his pocket and blew through it. He looked into the empty bowl.

'What's your strength?'

Norman sobered. 'Ninety-two accounted for. There may be a few more wandering around.'

'Officers?'

'Three. And myself.'

'What sort of state are the men in?'

'Dead to the world.'

'Can they march?'

'They couldn't march to a meal. You'll have to take us out on transport.'

The Brigadier was silent for a moment. He worked his fingers inside his tobacco pouch, filling the bowl of his pipe. 'All my transport's going forward,' he said at last.

Norman's eyes flickered. The lids narrowed intently.

'What are you going to do with us?' he asked. 'Putting us into one of the other battalions? Or sending us out for a rest?'

'A rest,' said the Brigadier, 'a long one.'

Norman relaxed. He made a little gesture with his head and shrugged his shoulders. 'They've earned it,' he said.

The Brigadier bit at the stem of his pipe and lit up. He looked at Norman over his cupped hands. 'I've got a job for you. One more job.'

Norman brushed the hair from his brow, and began to tighten the waist buckle of his blouse. 'What is it?'

The Brigadier opened his map-case.

'In the village here,' he pointed with a nicotine-stained finger.

'An anti-tank ambush. A troop of eighty-eights. We want to get our armour on the move, on to the main road, here – ' his finger-nail scratched across the mica – 'but they're held up until we can find infantry to winkle the guns out.'

'And so naturally – ' Norman's voice was high-pitched, ' – you thought of us?'

'You were the nearest disengaged infantry.' The Brigadier knew he dared not go on in this apologetic way much longer. A few more moments of this and he would have to talk brutally.

'I've hardly enough men left to make up one rifle company.'

'It's a job for one company.'

'Well,' Norman's voice suddenly became light-hearted. 'It's an honour, I'm sure. The men will be delighted.' He spoke with the unnatural relish of the slightly tipsy.

'I'm sorry, Noel.'

'Oh,' Norman waved a deprecating hand, 'don't worry. Don't let it worry you one – ' he paused between each word, ' – little – bit. It happens every day.'

The Brigadier puffed at his pipe. 'I'll see you later today,' he said harshly. 'I'll have transport waiting to take you out.'

Norman smiled wearily. 'Poor man,' he said gently, 'you mean well, don't you?'

The Brigadier looked at him unflinchingly.

Major Norman laughed. 'Those men of mine,' he said loudly, 'I'll have to pick them up one by one and prop them up like skittles.'

'Good luck,' said the Brigadier.

'Well,' said Major Norman, 'this won't buy the frock a new baby.' He threw his cigarette away. 'You can tell those tanks of yours to start their engines up.'

He picked up his helmet and machine carbine.

'Bye-bye,' he said.

The Brigadier watched him go.

'God forgive me,' said the Brigadier aloud, and walked back to his jeep.

An hour later the tanks began to move. The Shermans came lumbering out of the woods and lurched up, one by one, on to the metalled surface of the main road. The earth shook to their weight and their clattering roar as they gathered speed and passed majestically through the silent village.

One after another the great steel monsters rumbled between the broken walls, their commanders standing like conquerors in their open turrets, the long snouts of their guns questing angrily to left and right; each tank with a name, ribald, challenging or nostalgic, white-painted on its dark green flanks.

WINNIE FROM WIGAN
EL ALAMEIN
THE ALDGATE BOYS

The last splinters of glass fell tinkling from shattered windowpanes;

fragments of plaster rained from gaping ceilings.

FRANKLIN D. ROOSEVELT
CLAN MACDONALD
HORACE HORSECOLLAR

Among the rubble, beneath the smoking ruins, the dead of the Fifth Battalion sprawled around the guns which they had silenced; dusty, crumpled and utterly without dignity; a pair of boots protruding from a roadside ditch; a body blackened and bent like a chicken burnt in the stove; a face pressed into the dirt; a hand reaching up out of a mass of brick and timbers; a rump thrust ludicrously towards the sky. The living lay among them, speechless, exhausted, beyond grief or triumph, drawing at broken cigarettes and watching with sunken eyes the tanks go by.

OUR LASS
GEORDIE HINNIE
JOE STALIN'S CHICKABIDDIES

The earth and the air shook with their passing. The upflung dust rolled away, to right and left, in two white screens, and settled, in fine, grey veils, upon the upturned faces of the dead.

The humped, crouching silhouettes of the tanks covered the white road for miles. Still gathering speed they rumbled on, a black, dotted line reaching out across the map, towards Germany.

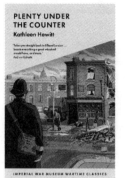

ISBN 9781912423095
£8.99

'Takes you straight back to Blitzed London... boasts everything a great whodunit should have, and more.'
ANDREW ROBERTS

ISBN 9781912423088
£8.99

'A tremendous rediscovery of a brilliant novel. Extremely well-written, its effects are both sophisticated and visceral. Remarkable.'

WILLIAM BOYD

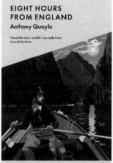

ISBN 9781912423101
£8.99

'Much more than a novel'

RODERICK BAILEY

'I loved this book, and felt I was really there'
LOUIS de BERNIÈRES

'One of the greatest adventure stories of the Second World War'
ANDREW ROBERTS